Scorched Earth

The Halo Trilogy
Book Two

Kathleen McFall

Clark Hays

ISBN: 978-1-7345197-2-3
Copyright © 2021 Kathleen McFall and Clark Hays
All rights reserved.
Library of Congress Control Number: 2020924007
Pumpjack Press
Portland, Oregon
www.pumpjackpress.com

Tired of wasting your credits on sonic laundry? Try our regenerative undersuits. They never stop growing so they never need washing.

Essential is bridging through a hollowed-out ad that's lingering on my scroll. I can always count on my kid sister's talent for piggybacking on the most irritating ads and hitting me with them at the worst possible moment.

"Now is not the greatest time," I say as a slug hits the wall I'm hiding behind.

It's a small wall and a big slug, fired from a shoulder-mounted rail gun and moving at just south of two kilometers per second. At that speed, you could bring down a quantum rocket with a slug no bigger than a rat raisin. These slugs are much bigger than a rat raisin.

The wall explodes in a spray of myco-dust and the force of the impact sends me and two other cops sprawling, along with leveling the broken-down building next to us.

I'm tired of getting shot at. This is the third time in as many weeks and I'm starting to take it personally.

Shooting at cops is a terminal offense. Possessing a rail gun, or any gun, is a life-plus-one family member labor sentence. Even researching some weapons on the tangle can earn you a crime debt. But this shooter doesn't seem to care.

I struggle up, coughing and choking and swearing, and regroup with a few others behind a burned-out jitney rocket.

"Crucial, quit mucking around and listen to me," Essential says through the ad. "This is serious."

Everyone is shouting orders, calling for backup, running perp profiles and trying to get a lock on the shooter. And here I am taking a covert ving from my sister, who also happens to be a member of the resistance. "Member" doesn't quite capture it—more like second in command—but since the Variance operates on a strictly non-hierarchal basis, she'd argue until the sun went down, twice, that I was wrong.

"I'm trying not get my head blown off here," I say. "That seems fairly serious to me."

Normally our conversation would be monitored by Halo—all conversations are—and analyzed a hundred different ways. The fact that I'm talking to a resister who is supposed to be locked inside a terrorium blasted into the bedrock of Mars should set off alarms in 200 separate facilities on Earth, Mars and every orbiting facility in between. In less than two minutes, I'd be on my way to a labor camp and she'd be vaporized in the radioactive cloud left behind by a dozen organic nukes, and our debt would be passed along to someone unlucky enough to share even a single Larsen gene in their bio-map.

Halo is the AI system the Five Families use to run everything. And watch everything. And track everything. Everything and everyone. It predicts what you'll be thinking before you even think it, and that's when it's not telling you what to think. It probably somehow smells us too, too bad for it. But Essential and I have a little secret that even the mighty Halo doesn't know about. Not yet anyway.

Nanites. Surveillance disrupting, digital information-rearranging nanites. An army of nano-robots swirling around in our veins, spending every restive second shielding us from Halo, letting us monitor and deflect and reorder the digital world around us as we see fit.

It's been a little more than six months since the resistance infected me with the micro mechanical monster-invaders, turning me into an unwitting courier in their attempt to overthrow the Five Families, or whatever the prok it is they fantasize about doing. It's been six months and a few days since I passed them along to Essential.

Her plan was to inoculate everyone in the resistance so they could safely hide from Halo while they set about undermining the Five Families with an empathy hack, whatever that means. But we came up against one little problem—Halo figured out how to track the transfer.

That left only two of us with a nano-engineered ability to hide from Halo. Essential and me. She wants to change the world. I want to survive the next few minutes.

The nanites are how we're communicating without triggering World War V. To the system, it looks like I'm passively watching an ad for the latest version of regenerative underwear. Halo will conclude I'm distracted by the weapons-fire raging around me and the threat of imminent death.

"I need your help," she says. "We're close but I can't do this alone."

I shift focus to the scroll column next to hers, a tactical analysis of my real-world situation. It's not good. Halo is computing probabilities for where the next shot goes. Six of the fourteen are most likely a terminal scenario for me.

"I don't think you *are* doing this alone," I mutter under the visor of my tactical helmet. "There's been a big spike in resistance activities down here on Earth. Like right now for example."

"Impossible. We don't have any sanctioned missions on Earth. If we did, they sure as void wouldn't be targeting you."

"Maybe they missed the memoji. Because they seem to *only* be targeting me."

"You do tend to make friends easily," Essential says.

The probabilities are hardening into three potentials. I pick the one that takes the least amount of energy and run straight at the source point, aiming my glitter gun at the shattered window of the building where the shooter is hiding, and squeeze off a round of almost lethal flechettes that stream in just as she stands to take her shot.

I guess right.

The glitter storm catches her smack in the middle of her wide, surprised face and drops her like a gravity plug with about a dozen broken bones in her skull. In that millisecond I lock her, and my scroll runs the images.

There's nothing. Other than her basic data, she's got no name, no family history, no debt profile. The woman I just glittered doesn't exist in the system, which isn't possible.

The impossible seems to be happening more frequently.

Three times, to be precise. And all far from the major population centers of our ward. We're way out in the barrens now. Right up against the inhospitable zone and the sunbelt that runs straight south from here.

I'm reading her vitals. She's in pain, a lot of pain, but she'll live.

I advance slowly, glitter gun still raised, until I clear the corner and see her sprawled out in the filth, the rail gun off to the side. I put a flight of synthetic diamond flechettes through her weapon, rendering it useless.

Up close, she looks chrono-young and is dressed in tattered clothing and parts of a beetler shell modified into makeshift armor. BEETLSS, also known as Basic Extreme Environment Transportable Life Support Systems, are portable, self-contained sleeping units, like little houses in a backpack, that protect the unemployed during the heat of the day. They keep the inhabitants—beetlers—mostly safe from the sun, but not from synthetic diamond flechettes. There's not much that can keep a person safe from those glittering little projectiles, even though I blunted them to nonlethal.

She's probably pretty, but it's hard to tell right now with her face all bloody and pulpy from the glittering. They'll fix her up in the prison hospital. Not Mars good. Not even Earth good. She probably won't ever want to look her own reflection again, but she'll be able to eat solidish foods.

Normally, they'd charge her family and then put her to work forever. But she doesn't have a family. Or a name. Or any medical records.

She's groaning, which means she's conscious.

"Check this," I lookspeak and share my feed with Essential so she can see the woman.

"Who are you?" I ask the perp.

"Long live the resistance," the shooter croaks, smiling weakly through bloody, cracked teeth.

"Lords, what did you do to her?" Essential asks.

"I didn't kill her, that's what I did."

"I won't say another word until I have my e-ttorney," the shooter whispers.

"She's not one of ours, Crucial," Essential says.

"Then you have competition," I say. "Exactly how many groups out there are trying to take down the Five Families?"

Other cops are walking up, so I break the connection.

"Nice shot, Larsen," McGrusky says. "Did you learn that up on Mars?"

5

They like to snark about my time on the red planet.

"All I really learned on Mars was how to drink absinthe and hold my breath in the Choke."

"Both of those may prove useful," he says. "Looks like we have a team meeting."

"Crater mold," I mutter. "That's almost enough to make me wish the rail gun hadn't missed me. Are you sure?"

"Check your feed," he says.

I check my feed. There's an invite for a meeting in 30 minutes. Nothing could be worse.

And since it's only a 300-kilometer flight back to Multnomah Ward from our location and it's only midnight—only halfway through my shift—I've got no excuse.

Earth sucks.

2

Looking out at the night sky on the flight back, I'm thinking about a story I scrolled a few days ago about when the clouds first disappeared late last century. I've never seen a cloud, not in real life anyway. Other than the toxic brown fog that occasionally rolls in from the Pacific dump. That's not so much "cloud" as it is flesh-melting gasified acid.

Way back then when the clouds first disappeared, the people who were supposed to be the smart ones spewed a layer of reflective microparticles in the air to create the same cooling effect as the missing clouds. It was a big deal. Fifteen planes took off on a synchronized mission. There's footage on the history scrolls, all the politicians and corp bosses grinning and fist brushing. The planes sprayed out tons of the stuff. It worked. Too well. Temperatures dropped. Crops failed. People starved. Wars happened. And then the fires. The heat scorched the particles and they crapped out. The smell lingered a decade.

They say one of the politicians in charge of that debacle was literally eaten in a riot.

One of my cop colleagues spilled that rumor in the middle of a salt beer bunk so that might be a wasteland myth. I'm pretty sure only the lizard people out in the sunbelt turned cannibal. Humans pretty much stick to manifested food and, if they're desperate, cats and the occasional woodpecker. I've busted up some beetler camps that had some tasty-smelling woodpecker stew on the boil.

The Intex-ADM corporation came to the rescue. For a price. By partially mitigating the scorched atmosphere, the DuSpoles family went from multinational to mega-multinational almost overnight. Multiplanet, really. They secured their option for a shot at being the fifth of what became the Five Families in the nick of time.

This was well before the Consolidation Wars, but things were heating up—literally and figuratively. Way before Mom died. Before I joined up. Before I killed for the first time. Before I threw everything with Mel away.

I glance up and my scroll puts a neon circle around the location of Mars. They always want us to know where it is, where they are, floating above us. They want us to worship them. They keep saying they're going to fix Earth once they get all the technology right on Mars—terraforming and an atmosphere generator—but that's a lie.

I've been there. Everything is working fine on Mars, at least inside the domes. They don't want to share. And who cares? We don't need their pity. Although some clean air and water would be nice.

I swore I'd never visit that godsforsaken red rock, but I didn't keep that promise. I've been twice. Neither time went well. And based on what just happened out in the barrens, now the resistance is expanding onto Earth. There's no way that's going to end well for anyone except the Five Families.

The flight drops me early and I stop in a little saucer shop near my squat. Three people are inside. Containment blowers route the air and we're all at maximum safe zone. Our OCDs won't let us get any closer than two meters without strobing out.

All three are watching something on their scrolls, probably porn or a new ambient avatainment series—they all have blankface, looking off into the distance as they watch the action streaming through their feeds. And all three are simultaneously talking to other people through the Halo interface, probably multiple people.

One of the downsides of living in a world of ocular communication devices is that you're always connected. Even when your eyes are closed, Halo is paying attention—listening and gathering data and shaping your world. And when your eyes are open, you're broadcasting. Everybody everywhere is talking all the time about everything and nothing. And no one is listening. At least not to the people right there beside them.

On day one, you're born into this world. On day two, you get your Ocular Communication Device implanted—it's illegal to not have an OCD. On day three, you're already in debt.

I sit down at the counter, access the menu on my feed and flip through to a kelp and roasted barley brew with double sweetener. On the bottom right corner of my scroll I see the credits drop off my running total, and then a second later I hear some whirring and squirting behind the scenes.

The service window opens and the tray spins out. It's empty.

Thanks for your purchase! flashes on my scroll. *Enjoy your cuppa.*

"But I didn't … it didn't," I start to say.

Just then, Captain Calvin kicks off the meeting. Anthrobots, if anything, are punctual.

"Hello, everybody. Thanks for taking the time. I want to share intel about the Variance, the resistance as some people call it, and the attacks we've been dealing with recently."

He sends a column of data to us with maps and profiles and simulations. I'm half looking at it, half looking at the saucer shop menu. I search for the *Got an issue?* command and select it.

Sorry you're not having a superior experience, consumer. What's the nature of your issue?

"I didn't get my bev," I say, watching the words scroll in.

I'm sorry. We don't understand. Did you not enjoy your bev?

"No," I say. "I didn't *get* my bev."

Was it insufficiently hot?

"No, I didn't ..."

We can tell by your tone that you're not happy. Would you like to chat with a customer service e-rep?

"Yes!"

Another column splices in, shrinking the stream of information from Captain Calvin by a quarter. I'm still looking at it too, focused on the map. It's odd that the resistance is mostly active near the sunbelt. There's nothing out there except sand and cannibal lizard people.

Even though Essential swears she's not behind it, it seems unlikely there are two groups of resisters. The odds of being discovered by Halo are too large.

Hi Crucial. How can we help you? the chatbot asks.

"I want my damn brew," I say. "I paid for it, and I want to drink it."

Our records indicate you already consumed your beverage. We hope you enjoyed it.

"Our records indicate the resistance is planning something big," Calvin says.

"Yeah, but why are they planning it way out next to the sunbelt?" I ask.

We don't understand your request. Have a great day.

"Our analysis suggests they are building a base of operations as far from our reach as possible," Calvin says simultaneously.

"No, no. I'm not satisfied," I say to both columns in my scroll.

"You'll have to get used to it," Calvin says. "AmaDis is clamping down on all sites of resistance activity. They're using security from Mars and recruiting people from the wards too."

Should we refund your credits, minus a handling charge?

"That doesn't make sense," I say to Calvin, then I swivel to the chatbot. "I want my drink, so fix this." Then I refocus on the meeting. Other cops are chiming in now, half wondering if they should be annoyed that Mars doesn't trust us, the other half wondering how to get on that security detail, itching for a fight against the resistance and a chance to prove themselves to the Five Families to earn an extended stay on Mars.

A door slides open in the back of the brew shop and a man walks out. He looks rumpled and confused, like he was asleep just before the chatbot woke him.

He puts on a thermal sani-glove, opens the carousel door, reaches inside and pulls out a damaged cup. My brew, backed up, dribbles down his arm. The machine whirs back to life, steaming away the residue.

"Been jamming recently," he says. "Forming cups with a little bulge." He points at the side apologetically.

"How many times a day do you have to come out here and do that?"

He shrugs. "Three, maybe four."

"Why don't you just reset the machine?"

"I been reporting it. Lots of times. Guess I'm still cheaper than replacing the cup maker. I don't mind. Gives me something to do."

He presses the reset button and a new cup pops out, then a stream of steaming brew fills it.

"Thanks," I say as he walks back into his squat behind the vending window of the saucer shop.

I pull the cup out and look at it, noticing a faint defect up near the lip. A bulge. The brew is good though—dark and sweet and fishy.

I return my attention to the meeting, which is wrapping up. I scan the recap for what I missed. Not much.

"Hey Captain," I say. "Are you okay if I poke around a little? Something doesn't smell right here."

"Absolutely not," Calvin says. "This is not our case. Everything goes through Mars security forces until they have the resistance sewn up once and for all."

3

Apparently, almost dying makes me tired. Or maybe it's team meetings. Probably the team meeting. I decide to log out for the rest of my shift, go back to my squat and turn in for the day.

I leave the saucer shop and briefly contemplate walking home. It's less than a kilometer and the air quality is pretty good today, according to my scroll, but there's a mischief of rats tangling with a band of coyotes around the corner. My credits are on the rats. But it's going to be loud and messy for a few blocks.

I summon a drone jacket and lift off over the chaos.

From this height, it's almost peaceful. I'm looking down over a kaleidoscope of amber, smoky trash fires and the emerald flash of police lights. I'm authorized, so my scroll fills in the crimes in progress. Mostly low-level stuff—nonfunctioning OCDs, debt posturing, credit hustles, a few assaults, and the constant wail of beetler suits when users need medical attention, which comes about four percent of the time.

I can't shake the feeling there's something weird about the recent spate of attacks out near the sunbelt. And if I can see a pattern that isn't adding up, Halo has already seen a dozen. That means our department is being kept in the dark, with possibly terminal ramifications. For me or, more likely, for Essential. Probably both.

I think about just hopping up to my balcony on the 222nd floor, but there's a swarm of kids buzzing around the tower playing some kind of game with a ball of rags and a floating box for a goal. They're laughing and swearing and having fun, and I can't bear the thought of having to interrupt their short-lived joy.

I touch down in front of the building and send my drone jacket back to the nearest collection center.

There's a beetler spanging by the main door. She's thin and dirty and hopeful. She knows I'm a soft touch. I drop a few credits into her account as I pass. She's so far in the negative she'll never get out, but any positive action is enough for a short-term bump. Enough to land a squirtmeal. Or, more likely, a salt beer. It'll cost me twice as much because Halo doesn't want to incent charity.

Inside the lobby, I wait for the lift standing next to someone who looks vaguely familiar.

Pretty sure it's my neighbor. Not the one with the creepy sex bot. This guy lives on the other side. He's probably worse. He does something weird with worms. I think he's a specialist at one of the compost centers, making sure there are enough worms to reduce organic waste into usable compost for the salad barns.

He smells like someone who works with worms. He's talking to someone, asking questions that make it sound like they're talking to someone else too. The lift arrives and even though there's plenty of distance for two, I wait for the next one.

I pull up the map of the recent resistance attacks and look again, still trying to answer the question. What the shit is anyone doing by the edge of the sunbelt? It's a worthless piece of lifeless land.

Inside my squat, I splurge and order a bottle of synthwine. Licorice and rosemary. Just as I'm cracking the seal, a ving comes in. Lauren Valentine.

Valentine is part of the resistance, and she hides in plain sight. She works for the Five Families, technically for the Singhroy family, as a historian at Singhroy College. It's not really a college—it's a labor school but also a private, and secure, historical archive for the Five Families.

Wealth loves its own origin stories.

More importantly, Valentine knows the past in a way most of us can't. They say history is written by the winners, and that's half right. The other half of that rubric is that history is forgotten by the losers. When you have to fight for the truth for every single event in the past, it's hard to keep it straight. Eventually, you quit trying.

Most people think the Five Families are heroes—or at the very least lucky and smart—for surviving the chaos of Earth. The truth is, they caused the chaos and then fled. Valentine knows the truth—she told me about it—and someday, if the resistance wins, she wants to share it with the forgotten and the forgetting.

I don't have the heart to tell her—the resistance is not going to win.

The Five Families have rewritten history to make it seem like their rise was inevitable and somehow the fault of the regular people. It's worked because people have short attention spans and are blinded by wealth.

I've never trusted those assholes, but I've also never had much hope for the human race. If you're so easily satisfied swallowing high atmosphere urine pellets, you deserve to keep eating them.

And even if the resistance does win, no one will care about the truth.

Mom knew some of the truth too and tried to pass it along to Essential and me. Essential decided the truth meant people were being tricked, that everyone is born free but is forced to live in chains of debt. I decided the truth is that people don't really want to be free—it's too hard. And people are mostly repelled by the idea of doing hard things. They'd rather swim with the current, even if they are in a boiling river of sewage, than swim upstream or even head for the shore. We like to bitch about how bad things are, but we never do a godsdamned thing to change them.

Most of us anyway. Essential and Valentine are trying to do something, but I know how their stories end. You can't take on wealth and power, and all the weapons that accompany them, with hopes and dreams. And you can't make people care after they've already given up. Still, I try to keep that opinion to myself. Sometimes, I succeed.

The resistance's big plan is to introduce an empathy hack into Halo, to rejigger all that circuitry so that the AI makes decisions that help everyone, not just the Five Families. But the resistance, and that means Essential, doesn't even know where the Halo servers are. Or if they can be hacked. Or if empathy matters.

Still, it's nice to listen to Valentine talk about history. Or anything, really. She's knowledgeable. She's also deeply, disturbingly attractive.

We hit it off on Mars. In that desperate, we're-about-to-get-vaporized way people have of hitting it off. She's one of the few people who knows I still have the nanites in me. We arranged a "chance" meeting after I got discharged from the medical facility so Halo wouldn't get suspicious later. If there was a later.

Turns out later is now. I accept her ving.

She's in a sleek-looking room, somewhere up high. The glow of screens floods the place with soft blue light that brings out the best in her eyes. And there's a lot to work with. She's wearing something shimmery over a stretchy body suit, the loose material swirling around and playing peekaboo with her curves. She has her hair loosely pinned up in that messy way that makes you keep watching to see if some of it is going to accidentally fall loose over her eyes.

"Hi Crucial," she says. "You said you'd never ving me and you didn't. I like a person who keeps their word."

She looks even better than I remember.

"Valentine. Nice to see you."

Valentine is her second name, but she doesn't correct me. I looked it up. It has something to do with love and bees. How can I not call her Valentine?

"I'm on Earth," she says. "For a few days, maybe longer. I'm researching something for the Singhroys that required a site visit. We should spend some time together. Have a meal or two. Interested?"

I want to say yes. I start to say yes. I'm doing that weird thing with my tongue necessary to form the "y" sound. But another ving interrupts my feed. It's Mel.

I get that feeling like when it's dark and you're walking up stairs and you think there's one more step but there really isn't and you try to stand on thin air and your whole body convulses in surprise.

I haven't talked to Mel in six months.

I break the connection with Valentine instantly and without thought.

Mel fills my scroll. She looks worried.

"Mel, what's wrong?"

"Why do you always assume something is wrong?" she snaps, her eyes narrow and jaw tight.

"I didn't," I lie.

"Well, something is wrong this time," she says, pretending to relax. She's looking everywhere but at me. "I need a favor. I don't have anyone else to turn to."

"Anything. You name it."

"Don't take this as me needing you to come swooping

in and save me. It's not."

"Okay."

"I mean, it *is* that. But don't read anything else into it. I just need help and I think you can help me."

"Mel, just say it. Don't make me beg to help you."

She's in her apartment. The perfect and spacious apartment she shares with Jynks Martine, her fiancée. I remember that incredible view over Jezero. The sunset, that blue light over the red landscape, so beautiful.

When Mel gets nervous, she bites the edge of her thumbnail. She's doing that now.

"It's Jynks. She's been arrested. For murder."

My scroll detonates with news stingers cutting across all columns: *Tarteric Hoost, Leading Member of the Five Families, Murdered in Cold Blood. Former Earther Slays Senior Tarteric.* And my favorite, *Top Cop Pops Boss.*

Mel can see the shock and surprise on my face.

"Crucial, she's innocent. I need you to prove that. I need you to save her."

4

"Again, I'm really sorry about last night."

Valentine is sitting across from me in the dining hall at Singhroy Towers. She's eating a soy crepe filled with some kind of fresh wall greens and gravity cheese. The employees eat well here. I guess you never know when a Singhroy might show up.

She's looking at me funny—not mad, exactly, more like a mixture of skeptical and disappointed. It's a look I'm used to. On Valentine, it has the unexpected effect of making her even more attractive.

"It's fine," she says. "Really. I just didn't realize the depth of feelings you still had for your ex. I didn't mean to make things awkward for you." She pushes her plate my way. "This is really good. You should try it."

I take a sip of coffee. It's good, high-quality stuff. I'm used to the grain-based shit at the precinct, which tastes like recycled coolant from a decommissioned quantum rocket. Or at least what I imagine that might taste like.

I shake my head. "The only feeling I have for Mel is regret at how shoddily I treated her. And that was a long time ago. Ancient history. Which is funny, when you think about it, because you're a historian. But that's it."

"Your loss," she says, pulling her plate back. Valentine can really eat.

"Look, I like you. I would probably like you even more

if we had a few days to get to know each other," I say. "But I owe it to Mel to try and save her fiancée. And you must admit, saving your ex's fiancée is a lot different than still having feelings for them. If I did have feelings, wouldn't I just let Jynks stay in prison?"

She's warming up a little.

"You're very smart though," she says. "Maybe you just want it to look like you tried your best when you really just sabotaged everything so you can swoop in and console Mel."

"When you get to know me better, you'll know I never have to pretend to sabotage things. That comes naturally."

"I do like a challenge," Valentine says, leaning back, a half-smile on her lips. "If I'm still here when you get back, I guess we could try again. Have another meal. Maybe share an avatainment feed. If you come back."

"I'll be back. I can't stand Mars. And I can't stand this place, either." I look around at the sterile serenity of Singhroy Towers. Only the best for their people.

Three hundred floors of secured entry, climate-controlled bliss made of accreted marble matrix layered onto a titanium mesh base. Clean, beautiful, cool to the touch and impervious to most attacks. White and gleaming, this place stands out like a solar flare compared to the dank, crumbling myco-towers the rest of us live in.

A big enough rail gun or air cannon could do some damage, but I'm sure this building has its own external defenses. Any building maintained by the Five Families on Earth is engineered to withstand any kind of firepower or natural disaster.

"What are you here researching for them?"

"Classified," she says. "I can't talk about it."

Her eyes tell me that's not true. She has very expressive eyes. Very expressive, very beautiful eyes.

I nod and wake up the nanites so they can fabricate us some cover.

"I don't really care," I say. "They have their thing, we have ours. Speaking of that, did you hear about the debt lottery winner? He had three-and-a-half generations of debt cancelled on one ticket. Great story, let me share it."

I share my feed with her, looping in recordings of some pasty gigger who won the annual debt lottery. This will give Halo something to chew on while we talk in private.

Valentine adopts blankface as if she's watching the coverage and I make sure the nanites are disrupting any of the hundreds of cameras around us streaming everything all the time so they can't match up sounds or visuals of our lips moving.

When I'm sure we're clear, I nod.

"It's safe now," I say. "But rest your chin in your hand and cover your mouth a little."

She looks around nervously. There are people sitting nearby, ignoring each other and talking to people on their scrolls. "I can't get used to being able to talk freely in public."

"We've got about ten minutes before Halo will get suspicious," I say. "Why are you really here?"

"I don't know, exactly. They never give me the full story. They want information about the sunbelt deeds."

"An odd coincidence," I say. "Activity's been heating up near the western edge of that territory. Resistance activity."

"As far as I know, we don't have any missions there," Valentine says.

"That's what Essential said," I say, sipping my coffee. "But someone forgot to tell that to the people shooting at me."

"Are you familiar with the history of the sunbelt?"

21

"It's hot and dead and a bunch of mutant blizards live there."

She smiles. "The truth, as always, is more nuanced. The term 'blizards' is slang for Blevin Lizards. The Blevin family was behind the effort. And it's ugly and genecist. When Earth started really heating up, there were basically two lines of thought. Some wanted to leave the planet and focus on Mars. Others thought genetic-amendment technology would allow humans to adapt to the heat. Some people volunteered to be genetically altered. They were called climate pioneers."

"Including my grandmother, apparently."

Valentine places her hand on mine. Her touch is somehow simultaneously cool and hot against my skin. "I didn't know that."

"Neither did I until recently," I say.

"It wasn't easy. Elements of reptilian physiology were genetically spliced in using a RNA technology popular in that era and, in exchange for volunteering to become a climate pioneer, those people were given land. People were scared and desperate, so it seemed like a good deal at the time. It wasn't."

"Because they turned into cannibals, right? I don't really want to think of grandmamma chowing down on somebody's arm."

"You need to spend less time on your scroll. That's a myth. They're not cannibals. The technology worked, but not as hoped. There were side effects. Unintended mutations. After that, the Five Families refocused their resources on settling Mars. The climate pioneers were left on their own in the sunbelt they now owned. After multiple generations, no one is sure what the inhabitants are like anymore. They cut off connection with the outside and they block all efforts at monitoring, except from the very highest level. We occasionally see movement, and it's clear they have some rudimentary technology, but mostly it's a mystery."

"Why are the Five Families interested in the sunbelt now? And why just the western edge? The sunbelt is huge."

"That's the weird part. I'm not even sure all the Singhroys are in the loop about this interest. I was sent by Singhroy Able with a covert pass. None of the rest of the family knows I'm here. She asked me to analyze some of the early legal recordings of the land deeds and report back. Something is up, but I don't know what."

"When I get back, maybe I can help. In the meantime, let's wrap up the Halo show. I have to grab the next rocket."

I tell the nanites to relax and the debt lottery coverage ends.

Valentine lets her blankface melt away. "What a lucky, lucky man to have won a reprieve on his entire debt," she says. "I hope he doesn't lose sight of the things that are important to him."

I think she might not be talking about the gigger who won the annual lottery anymore. I think Valentine might be talking about me.

5

Quantum rockets are the worst.

This is the fifth q-rocket I've been on. The first time was to the prison on the moon to pick up a convict for transport. That didn't go well. We overjumped, twice. The trip back was supposed to be my last time traveling through space. Didn't turn out that way. I flew to Mars and back trying to find my sister. Then I got a blood stream full of e-lice and had to fly back one more time to try to get rid of them. I did not succeed.

I never expected to set foot on a q-rocket ever again. Now here I am, thinking I should get a frequent q-jump card. Apparently, the forces linking me to Mel are greater than my fear of the lunatic universal forces governing entanglement and all that it entails. Love is more powerful than quantum entanglement. Especially unrequited love.

The ride up-universe to Mars is, thank the gods, smooth enough, with only one rough patch close to landing. Some sort of causality violation. The rocket felt like it was going to shake itself apart and yet was oddly completely still, like it was frozen in the middle of a convulsion. Space travel can be very confusing. Some passengers looked like they were going to throw up during the worst of the material heaves. I was afraid it was the moon trip all over again and we'd fall into an unforced jump out into the middle of the intergalactic nowhere.

Then just like that the alarms subsided, and we dropped

into the soft embrace of the Mars orbit. After we docked at one of the orbital platforms, it was a short wait for the next space elevator to drop, then down to Port Zunil.

As I get off the elevator, I notice an interesting bar near the main entrance but before I can check it out, I'm pulled over by two customs agents dressed in their Five Families uniform, with the stupid crests on the breast pocket, for a scroll query covering the last two months.

I've got nothing to hide.

Well, I've got everything to hide, but I've got the nanites to hide it now. And I'm here by official request.

After a half hour of background review, which mostly consists of them making cracks about my shithole planet, they let me come through. During it all, I maintain my cool. I get it. They're just doing their jobs. They're assholes though. I "accidentally" tip over the cup of gooseberry cream one of them left too close to the access portal. The screens start flickering and I smell electrical smoke. They're cursing and alarms are sounding.

I need to work on being less petty. Maybe tomorrow.

I catch the lottery class lev-train to Jezero, and after washing the jubilant stink of naïve optimism from a thousand new lottery workers off me in her biowaste closet, I'm staring at Mel, watching her lips move, noticing how the light leaking in from the window creates a silver aura around her face.

"Is your tea okay?" she asks.

"What?"

It's hard to focus. The last time I saw her it was to say goodbye and it was tough. I lied and let her think the worst of me just to keep her safe. There's no reason for her to think better of me now, which means the fact that I am here in her luxe apartment means she must really be desperate.

"Your tea. Is it okay?" she asks again. "What's the matter with you? Are you q-lagged?"

"Sorry, got distracted for a second. Yeah, tea's great. Really good, thanks. Wish we had this stuff on Earth."

She moves and the shimmering radiance disappears. In the regular light, she looks tired and pale. And thinner. She still looks beautiful, of course, but sad.

"It's a new blend I've been tinkering with. It's not perfect yet, but I'll give you some to take back," she says quietly.

A small fuzzy animal with giant eyes jumps on her lap, looking at me suspiciously.

"Is that something you've been tinkering with too?"

"This is Wisp. She's a kitten."

"You have a baby cat?"

"Yes. She's based on a breed once known as a Persian. So beautiful, don't you think?" Mel strokes its wide head and the animal nuzzles into her hand. It's gray and white with oversized blue eyes. I can hear it motor-purring from across the room. "It won't get any bigger."

"That's a weird life," I say. "To stay a baby forever."

"It's not like Earth cats," she says.

On Earth, nobody has pets of any kind. No one is willing to spend the credits. There are plenty of feral cats, but you can't get attached because beetlers know cat is a good source of protein, and free is cheaper than paying for sheetmeat.

I take another sip of tea. She's avoiding whatever it is she wants to tell me. I'm in no hurry. The tea is good and I'm near Mel. That's enough for me, even on Mars. Wisp jumps down from her lap and takes a spastic jump in my direction, puffs up and hisses, claws at my ankles and then darts back under Mel's chair. Mel laughs, but it costs her, and when the temporary joy drains from her face she looks twice as drawn.

My heart goes cold at her pained expression. She sits up straight, squares her shoulders and takes a deep breath. "I suppose you want to know why you're here," she says.

"Whenever you're ready," I say.

"Jynks is—was—the head of the Mars security forces. That position has a few privileges, ostensibly to isolate it from the influence of the Five Families. In the event of any legal proceedings, she's entitled to a special investigator."

"And she picked me?" I ask, a little incredulous.

"No one on her team is willing to take it on. They think they'll be tainted if they participate. And she's not talking."

"Wait. Jynks doesn't know?"

Mel shakes her head. "I just figured ..."

"That I had nothing to lose. Thanks a lot."

"Look, Crucial, I know this is weird. And you can say no. And I'm still mad at you for locking up Essential in the terrorium, furious really, but I know Jynks is innocent and I owe it to her to do whatever I can to prove that."

She doesn't know it's not Essential in the stasis sheath inside a time-locked horror cell. It's Canadis Whitsend, Jynks's old boss. Essential is firmly ensconced with the resistance in an orbiting garbage dump plotting her empathy revolution.

I was willing to let Mel hate me to keep her safe, and here I am, dragged right back into a Martian conspiracy. But I know Mel is right. Jynks is a lot of irritating things— beautiful, competent, successful, engaged to Mel—but she's no murderer. And during my last Mars fiasco, I learned facts don't always matter when the Five Families are involved.

"Please, for me. Do this."

"Okay," I say. There was never any doubt.

When a wave of relief sweeps across her face, I get the

best feeling I've had in a while.

I tap my foot trying to think this through, and Wisp takes another run at me, swiping at my shoe before scooting behind a plant—a live, green, growing plant—to glare tiny daggers.

"Where should I start?" I ask.

"Talk to her, obviously. Find out what really happened. She won't say a word to me. Other than to tell me to 'move on, find someone new.' But now that I've officially nominated you to be her special investigator, it gives you a lot of leeway until the matter is cleared up."

I nod. What I say next is mostly for Halo's algorithms. "I'll look into it. But Mel, you need to be ready for a bad outcome. Jynks might really be guilty. She's wound pretty tight, and you saw for yourself in Baldet crater that the Five Families don't always play by the same rules as the rest of us. Maybe she snapped."

She bows her head a little. The message is received. Innocent doesn't equal free. Wisp seems drawn to her grief. She jumps back into Mel's lap and pushes her tiny flat face into the cup of her hands. Mel's shoulders tremble as tears fall.

Here I am on Mars again, the last place I ever wanted to be, but I'm with Mel, the only place I ever want to be. But she's crying because the woman she loves is about to get locked into a terrorium right next to her former boss. Not the ideal situation. But not the worst either.

There's a chime at the apartment door. "Are you expecting someone?" I ask, already suspicious.

"A condition of your investigation is that you have a minder," she says, and when she stands, Wisp falls to the floor, indignant.

The door slides open. "Crucial, my friend, it's good to see you again," Sanders says.

6

The absence of crime means there's not a lot of demand for prisons on Mars. There are the few odd terroriums in the bedrock of the central Mars security forces building, and a holding cell or two for Earthers who are being sent back for something petty like failing to address a member of the Five Families respectfully.

They've got Jynks in something special—a naturally-made prison that beats anything even the most sadistic human could ever dream up for simplicity.

She's in the Choke.

The Choke is the area outside the climate-controlled domes on Mars where it's just rocks and sand and almost always cold enough to freeze a human in a few short minutes, and so low in oxygen that without an airhoodie, you'll suffocate even faster.

Even Sanders, a cybanism, seems a little nervous.

The last time I was on Mars, Sanders was supposed to watch over me for the Five Families. I ended up getting him vaporized like a half dozen times. He doesn't seem to mind too much, says it helps him learn. Turns out, he's more forgiving than most of the human people I know.

"It would be most efficient to interview Jynks Martine scroll-to-scroll," he says.

We are standing at a secured exit point on the eastern edge of the Jezero dome. There are no lev-trains out to

Jynks's prison bubble, and so much armament guarding her that fliers are not recommended, so we'll have to get there the old-fashioned way. Full oxygen suits and rocketbikes.

"Sanders, you should know by now, that's not how I work. Taking the easy way would result in a shoddy investigation. Don't you remember last time?"

"The time you investigated the crash site of the resistance rocket that extracted Tashi, the double agent, from the H-suite? I remember it well. You nearly died."

"But I got a clue, didn't I?"

"No. You didn't get a clue. I think it's more accurate to say you had an insight, which to my mind did not require your presence in the Choke to manifest. There were most definitely no evidence-based clues to be found in the Choke."

"Fine, but it was my addled, low-gravity, oxygen-depleted, windblown state *caused* by the Choke that gave me the insight," I say. "An important insight, as it turned out."

"Do you expect this visit to the Choke to have a similar outcome?"

"Who the hell knows," I say.

"Perhaps I could lightly strangle you and throw soil in your face? It might save us some time," Sanders says.

"Let's call that plan B."

He cocks his head, processing his scroll. "Halo has allocated one hour, including our travel time. After that, all visitors will be deemed threats."

"We'll get in and get out," I say, pulling on the gravity boots and snapping them into the leg coverings. The boots are a little loose, but not dangerously so. "Before we go, remind me. How long can a person survive in the Choke?"

"Your question is worrisome. I am carbon-based, like

you, and while I could survive approximately forty percent longer than you, ultimately I would succumb to the conditions."

"Let's not test it."

"I support that decision, although the data I could learn from such an experience might be quite valuable."

I pull on the jacket. It's skin-tight. "Learning. Sanders, why's that so important to you?"

"With sufficient learning, it is conceivable I could develop what humans call consciousness," Sanders says, handing me the airhoodie. "My makers are quite interested in that. It's the one area of science that is still unknown. And the ramifications for Halo, if non-biological entities could experience self, are quite astounding."

I throw one leg over my rocketbike and stretch forward into the driver's cot, snug but comfortable. It's a tight little machine, a rugged death trap on two gyroscopic wheels designed specifically to stay just above the red rubble of Mars at a teeth-rattling subsonic speed.

I link the display screen to my scroll, then share with Sanders. "Would consciousness make you human? I mean, is that the only difference?"

"There is wide disagreement over what it means to be human," Sanders says.

I look over at him, but he's snuggled in already and I can't tell if he's joking. Typically speaking, robots have a shitty sense of humor. But he's a cybanism that learns a little more about the human experience every time he dies, and he's died a lot on my watch. If he is getting a sense of humor, I guess I'm partially responsible.

"Well, these days being human isn't much to brag about," I say.

I push the starter and the rocketbike fires up, belching rings of blue plasma from the tail pipe.

"Perhaps," Sanders says, "but through my interaction with you I am learning some of the attributes in Earthers are quite distinctive from those on Mars. It's puzzling."

"Not really, Earthers just show the evolutionary effects of extreme capitalism," I say. "It makes for a highly tuned survival instinct."

I settle my gaze on the portal door, open it with a visual prompt, then twist the throttle, and the bike blasts off into the Choke. The bike churns up a satisfying cloud of dull red dust that temporarily obscures Sanders, but then with a roar, he's blasting out too and the portal slides shut behind us. We're committed now.

The sun is about 30 degrees to setting. Plenty of light for there and back. As we bump across the landscape, I open the official investigation file on the murder of Tarteric Hoost. These bikes can damn near drive themselves.

Tarteric Hoost was working on the evening of Sept. 26, 2187, when Jynks Martine entered his office and shot him in the chest with a glitter gun, registration number M9875.

The injuries sustained were of such a serious nature that Tarteric Hoost immediately died on the scene.

The events were captured by surveillance from his scroll. Martine's scroll did not provide images because she employed an illegal jammer during the crime. They argued and it became heated.

I access the audio. I can hear him all right, pompous windbag. He's saying something about the travesty. She's saying something about trust. I run the video from his feed alongside the audio. He's got his hands up. And there's this look in his eyes of complete wealthy bafflement. The privileged aren't supposed to die, not like this. Then he does. There's a whoosh and about a dozen diamond flechettes are glittering him in the vicinity of the heart. He looks down at the wound and I can see the tiny, shiny nubs angled into his chest.

Martine did not flee the scene. She was apprehended by Mars security forces 76 seconds after the crime.

Martine entered a guilty plea. The Grand Council of Mars has ordered a trial to be held on March 26, 2188.

While motive has not been formally established, evidence collected at the scene suggests Martine was angered that Tarteric Hoost was unsupportive of her promotion to senior control officer of Mars security. Tarteric Hoost declined to support Martine due to her involvement in the events of six months ago when ...

There's a series of warning beeps and I look up just in time to see my front wheel ram a boulder. The force rattles me to the bone as the bike bounces nearly a meter off course. I keep a grip on the handles, but I'm jumping like a carbon nano tube in an electric field.

I'm swearing and wrestling with the controls and flying like a flag above the driver's cot as my gravity boots try to compensate.

Your destination is ahead my scroll says as we careen to a stop in front of the prison.

I see Jynks watching curiously through a small, transparent dome. She wasn't expecting visitors, and certainly not some out of control ava-clown swearing and flopping around on a probably damaged Choke rocketbike.

Sanders, of course, has no such issues. He glides to a stop beside me.

Jynks stands straight and tall, like a soldier, all 1.86 gorgeous meters of her, hands clasped behind her back, maybe wondering if we're here to execute her. I dismount and dust myself off. An executioner probably would have had a more dignified approach.

Halo opens the door. Sanders and I walk into the sealed-off entry chamber. After the exterior door closes behind me, the interior door opens and I step inside Jynks's prison and remove my airhoodie. Sanders stays behind in the entry chamber.

She looks at me in shock, then anger, followed by disappointment. I get that a lot.

"Oh, for the love of electron degeneration," Jynks says. "Really?"

7

"Nice to see you too, Jynks," I say.

She's backed up against the curved wall of her little prison, hands clenched, head bowed down because she's too tall. They did that on purpose.

"Larsen," she says, sounding as if she just stepped in fresh crow droppings in her bare feet. "Is this some new form of torture the Fist has worked up for me?"

The Fist—made up of one leader each from the Five Families—is the council that runs Mars. And Earth.

"Are they torturing you?"

"They are now," Jynks says.

I look around the dome. It's not much bigger than the two of us. And the material is flimsy, thin cyto-flanks. Barely enough to keep the oxygen inside. They don't have to keep her from breaking out. The Choke does that. The floor is naked dirt and rubble. On one side of the room is a manifester next to two vials. Must be how she gets rations. On the other side are a small shovel, a blanket and a bowl. Doesn't look very comfortable.

They really know how to do solitary on Mars. It doesn't hurt that the whole area around us is lined with nuclear micro-landmines—invisible to the eye, even to the OCD-enhanced eye, but capable of blowing off your legs. Halo turned them off as we rolled in. At least it was supposed to.

"How do you exercise in here?" I ask.

She doesn't answer.

"It's got climate controls, right?"

"Enough to keep me alive," she says stoically.

"Any avatainment?"

"Of a sort."

I connect to her scroll. It's all reconditioning feeds. The relentless blather about efficiency, loyalty to the Five Families, and on and on, must be driving her crazy. What they obviously don't realize is that she already believes all that crap.

"Mel sent me," I say.

"What for?" she asks, and then her eyes widen a bit. "Is she breaking up with me?" I see her fight the emotion and then tamp down the panic with something that looks like resignation. Or acceptance. I would do that. I'm starting to like her. "I mean, that's the right thing to do. Like I told her, she needs to move on, find someone else."

"You're an idiot. Like I said, Mel sent me here to help you," I say.

"I don't need your help." She looks me straight in the eye. "Let me be totally clear. I only need one thing from you, and that's to get out of here. And to make sure nothing bad happens to Mel."

"That's two things," I say. "And whether I leave or not, you know me well enough to know I'm not going to stop prodding around."

"And wreck everything for everyone," she snarls. "Do not get involved."

"Too late. I'm your special investigator. You wouldn't pick, so Mel picked for you."

"You're terminated."

"Again, too late. It's official. You can't terminate me. Why don't you just tell me what happened."

She looks past me into the Choke.

"I know you've seen it," she says. "I asked to meet Hoost." She winces. Under reconditioning, you can't take shortcuts. They just blasted her with a surge of light and pain. "Sorry, Tarteric Hoost. I knew he had his suspicions about me after all that happened with you and your sister. I assumed he was firing me. We argued. I shot and killed him."

"In cold blood."

"Yes."

"You, Jynks Martine, who is engaged to a renowned scientist and shares her home with a kitten named Wisp, who follows orders like a child's binary code, who wouldn't pull the trigger on me—a guy you actively despise—a hundred times when I was running around pissing off everyone, *you* killed someone in cold blood."

"Yes." Her eyes narrow. "Do you want to test my capacity for violence right here, right now?"

Pretty sure I could take her. I mean, Sanders would save me if I needed saving, which I probably wouldn't.

"You story doesn't make sense. And I plan on getting to the bottom of it."

"I am guilty. Go home. Go back to Earth. Better yet, stay here and help Mel. Not like, romantically. That rocket blasted off long ago. But be here for her until she can get her act together."

"You are annoying," I say. "Tell me, if you shot Hoost, why didn't you make it look like someone else? You're the top cop. Easy enough to frame some poor fission swab. Like me, for example."

"I wasn't thinking clearly. Obviously. Otherwise I would have framed you. We argued, things got out of hand."

"It's weird, though, that you went there all spun up like a q-engine. It's not like you."

"Let this go, Larsen," she says, jabbing one of her elegant fingers in my face. A finger on her right hand. She's right-handed.

While she's rattling off threats, I pull up the murder video again and zoom in close on Hoost's chest and plot a geometric grid. The embedded flechettes are slightly angled the wrong way. He was murdered by a leftie.

She's being framed and she's willing to take the fall. And there are only two reasons I can think of to act against your own interests—cognitive issues or love. Sometimes, they're indistinguishable.

This is about Mel.

Things just got a lot more interesting. If I help her, Mel's at risk. If I don't, an innocent woman is in prison for life. And if they use Martian health care—the cradle—she could be alive for a really long time.

I'm not going to let her pay for a debt she didn't incur. Those rich assholes get away with enough as it is—I'll just have to be very careful. I've always been pretty good at discreet.

"Okay, Martine, good luck," I say and motion at Sanders to unzip the door.

"You son of a clone," she says. "Do not continue investigating. I mean it."

"I hear you, loud and clear. And you can count on me," I say, winking at her.

She lunges at me, 65 kilograms of rage. "Do not fritter this up!" she screams.

I brace for the impact, but it never comes. Halo is watching. It sends a jolt through her OCD that drops her to her knees. Still, I'm fairly sure I could have taken her. But good to know Halo has my back.

She's stunned, on her hands and knees in the red soil. "You don't understand. You don't understand anything."

"Pretty sure I do. I understand your priorities. And I respect them."

She looks at me with something bordering on gratitude.

"Have a little faith," I say, then slip on my airhoodie and head for the Choke. Sanders zips the door closed and locks it.

"Faith in what?" Sanders asks as we climb back into our rocketbikes.

"The system, of course," I say.

We fire up the engines.

"Did you learn anything?" he asks across my scroll. "Or perhaps you had an insight?"

"The case against Jynks Martine isn't as simple as it seems. I need to spend a little time at the crime scene," I say, twisting the throttle and leaping forward.

As we streak back across the Choke toward Jezero dome, I can see Jynks is now standing, watching us leave. The sun is going down and that weird blue Martian sunset is deepening around us. It will be cold soon, terminally cold, and we aim our bikes at the soft glow of the distant dome. It's going to be another rough night for Jynks. She'll be sleeping on the ground, shivering in her inadequate thermal suit and looking up into the darkness at a blazing river of stars.

8

On Earth, I don't go to crime scenes often. Nobody cares what happens to beetlers or the unlucky ones living out in the Fields, so no need to activate CSI. We dropped the CSI balls when our tac-sleigh was hit a few months back, but that was an unusual use of resources.

Typically, the CSI balls only get rolled in the rare case a member of the Five Families, or their Earth administrators, gets offed. Since that doesn't happen often, almost never really, the team backing the CSI balls is basically a skeleton crew, mostly administrative. When something big comes along, they bulge out their team with grumbling labor cops to assist with field work.

Captain Calvin loaned me to a CSI team twice in the last decade.

The first time, a fourth-gen DuSpoles was stabbed to death in the basement of a social club, killed with an acoustic knife. A young kid, early 20s, on his first visit to Earth. Gave his minder the slip. Didn't know any better. Assumed everyone would love him because that's what they tell them on Mars.

The kid stumbled into an off-reg club where the drinking had been going on since dusk. A day crew was already blind drunk and mad as hell about an arbitrary reduction in labor credits. Things got out of hand and the poor kid's body was chopped up into 102 pieces.

I was stationed outside the boil room where it happened, keeping out the gawkers and watching the CSI balls collect every scrap of data from the blood-splattered walls. Halo integrated that data with audio-visual records from any scroll within range to recreate the murder.

Walking through holo-recreate later with the CSI team, it felt like I was there, in the moment, when the kid got chopped. Luckily, my stomach was empty.

Two days after, everyone who had been at the club, including a few unlucky stiffs who were passed out and clueless at the time, were hauled out to the edge of the Fields, lined up against a wall and mowed down with glitter ammo minted special for the occasion. Fourteen men and two women. Halo pushed out the execution in real time to every scroll on Earth, and then replayed it for two weeks at random intervals, max volume.

The message was clear—crimes against the Five Families are not tolerated.

In the second case last year, a Fehrven administrator was killed. The wife confessed but wouldn't say why she did it.

On this one, I got to pour out the CSI balls myself at the scene. I watched them bouncing around. It was clear they were onto something right away, swarming around a thin line of white foam on the dead guy's lips. Poison. A nasty little cocktail that caused his lungs to melt. The balls also found some odd files through his OCD. Turns out he was pimping his youngest daughter in some dark-rinth avatainment productions. I would've killed him too. The Five Families ruled the wife was justified, hit her with some debt to discourage others from taking the law into their own hands, and then gave her his now-vacated position along with his luxe squat.

I learned enough about how crime scene holo-recreates

are generated and archived from those two cases. The most important piece is just how much data is being integrated. The computing and electrical resources required to integrate, analyze and store the data are enormous. After the DuSpoles murder, power had to be rerouted from three wards for the render. Those were some long, hot days.

After these kinds of high crime cases are officially closed, Halo repurposes the data as reality-based avatainment, depending on the victim's status. The programs are wildly popular because they are so rare and so morbid. AmaDis builds out a full suite of collateral for each one, the most popular being the point-of-view immersives. Choose who you want to be: murderer, CSI staff, victim. Weirdly, victim is the most popular.

Earth is a messed-up place. We fantasize about ceasing to exist.

The holo-recreate of Hoost's murder won't make it onto the latest episode of the Gruesomatic feed; no one dares celebrate the death of economic royalty. That doesn't mean it hasn't been compiled, it just hasn't been shared.

Sanders is trying to get me access to the full run. As special investigator, I have access, but nothing is ever easy. I may not be the most patient person on Mars. I've asked him at least a dozen times to hurry this along. I think he's learning the human emotion of frustration.

"As I have said, the approval process is quite lengthy. I will let you know when I have access," he says.

"What's taking so long?"

"I do not have an adequate explanation. Your status is clear, the file has been located, but there seems to be irregularities in the core properties. And approval must go through Melinda Hopwire. It can only be viewed once and as the designated partner, she must forfeit her right to watch it, delegating that to the special investigator."

"That is all unnecessarily complicated," I say. "But no surprise." We're sitting at a table in Mel's apartment eating lunch. The sun is shining through her windows. It's disorienting, being awake during the day. People on Mars still stick to life during daylight hours. On Earth, the day is too hot. Everything happens, including work, at night.

"You're not hungry?" I ask Sanders, grabbing my third sheetmeat taco. "Better get to it before I finish off the entire plate."

He's sitting ramrod straight in the chair across from me watching me eat, which I can't seem to stop doing. The tacos are drenched in a delicious oozy yellow sauce. As she was leaving for Baldet crater earlier, Mel said it was cheese, something Earthers ate a lot of before the warming. She promised me I would like it.

She was not wrong.

"No, thank you, Crucial. But I appreciate the offer," Sanders says.

"Do you eat? I mean, I'm sure you can chew and all, but are you set up to digest food?"

"Yes, and given I am composed of predominantly biological materials, I am required to eat to maintain basic functions," he says.

I push the tacos toward him. "Won't do better than these."

"I prefer to meet my bodily requirements with balanced, densely concentrated nutrients." He pulls a small packet of a green powder from a pocket.

"That does not look tasty," I say.

"Good nutrition is a requirement, 'tasty' is not," he says. "And this greatly reduces the volume of subsequent waste."

I push my food away. "That is something I really did

not need to visualize."

"Waste expulsion is one of the few parts of my simulated human existence I do not enjoy," Sanders says. "The cube I excrete is quite uncomfortable."

"Wait, you poop ... in cubes?"

"Yes. I have a very efficient expulsion system. They're very compact. Would you care to see one?"

"No. I would not. Not ever," I say. "But seriously, Sanders, why don't you just ask your programmers to make them round?"

As Sanders is looking at me curiously, like I might be worthy of the Musk Prize, a message from Mel comes in and I hold up my palm to cut him off before the conversation gets even weirder.

She's at Baldet crater and even though she's surrounded by her precious plants, and I can see a giraffe in the background, she looks pinched and worried.

"It just came through," she says. "The activation sequence for the holo-crime scene. You get only one pass through it. I've delegated to you my family right to see it once. Don't waste it."

"I won't waste it," I say. "How's it ..."

She cuts the connection.

I turn to Sanders. "I've got the scene. Can you project it for me?"

"Yes," Sanders says, standing.

"Please don't do that weird thing with your eyes," I say, but it's too late. His eyes roll back in his head and he projects the scene out into the room.

I'm watching Hoost in full 3D-rendered glory, the pompous asshole, flipping through something on his desk. It looks like paper. Who the hell uses paper? People who want to hide their digital trail, for one.

It's early and weak dawn light muddles through the

window. There's a knock. Hoost looks up and says, "Come."

Jynks Martine, in uniform, enters Hoost's office.

"Pause it," I say.

"I cannot," Sanders says.

"What? Why not?"

"The permission category is for family view only, for closure. Multiple views or any manipulation are not allowed," Sanders says.

The holo-crime scene keeps running. "That's a stupid rule," I say, tripling my focus.

Hoost motions for Jynks to sit, but she refuses. Hoost stands. They face each other with a desk between them. I walk in and around and through the scene, taking in every detail.

Jynks asks why Hoost won't support her promotion.

Hoost starts to respond but Jynks interrupts, shouting, "Without your support, I will never last!"

Jynks pulls out a glitter gun and shoots him. Straight through the heart. Just like that. Cold blood. The flechettes are gleaming in his chest, at the wrong angle though. A few must have gone through because there's blood spattered on the window.

Jynks puts the gun down on the desk, clasps her hands behind her back and waits. The scene is almost still for 70 seconds, with Jynks standing mutely and rigidly at attention, breathing slowly in and out, until two officers from the Mars security forces bust into the room.

The crime scene holo-recreate is very convincing. It looks like Jynks shot that windy asshole right through the heart.

But she didn't. Somebody with a left-dominant hand shot him. But it's possible Jynks is good with both her hands, tough to pin innocence on that detail alone. I watch as the security forces pin Jynks down and cuff her.

That's when I notice another problem. The light behind the blood-splattered window is brighter than it was when the blood hit the panes. Someone cut out a chunk of time. Jynks was there, she admitted as much, but Hoost was already dead.

It's a deep fake. Someone spent a lot of time, energy and credits manipulating this—all things the Five Families have plenty of.

"You can come back, Sanders."

He rolls his eyes back into place. "Did you find out anything?"

"Yeah, I did."

"It's quite damning for Officer Martine," he says. "It's hard to see how this won't turn out badly for her."

"Yeah, very badly," I say.

But not for the reasons Sanders thinks. Someone wanted Hoost sidelined. Someone who has a lot of resources. Someone who can make Halo look the other way—the difference in lighting was barely noticeable to me, but a powerful AI like Halo would have flagged it instantly.

That means that whoever or whatever is behind this can pull any strings. And unless I can figure out what's really going on, Jynks is going to take the fall and rot in prison because trying to clear her name will put a target on Mel.

I reach past the tacos for a little pitcher of trappa, a clear, sweet brandy made from poppy plants, when my scroll pop-flashes with a garish ad.

At the current daily trend, your weight will increase to unsafe levels within one month. Or less. Order a lifetime supply of hyperbolic calorie burners for just one credit per week.

Only Essential, my sweet, revolutionary sister, can make a clandestine connection so insulting.

9

I leave Sanders for the privacy of the biowaste closet and will the nanites to build some cover so I can talk to Essential outside of Halo surveillance.

"Who are you calling fat?" I ask.

"You? Never," she says. "Solid. Husky, even. And getting huskier with age, but never fat."

I can hear the smile in her voice. It's audio only and I miss her face, but it makes sense. Video takes more bandwidth and there's no reason to taunt Halo with an unnecessary data signature.

"Good, because it seems like you were hinting that I'm collecting the kilos."

"You *were* kind of a chubby kid though," Essential says. "Remember?"

We're interacting behind the health warning about food consumption, with Halo receiving a parallel stream of nanite-generated data drawn from recent past images where I'm stuffing my face with sheetmeat tacos.

"I remember being perfectly proportional," I say. "Memory is a funny thing."

"Or a faulty thing," she says.

"Did you click in just to insult me? Seems like you would have more important things to do, being part of the resistance and all."

"That's why I'm clicking. So, you're on Mars?"

"That's right. Can we meet?"

"Maybe. I heard what happened to Jynks. How's Mel?"

"Not great."

"I'm glad Hoost is dead, he was a real kink in the fuel hose. But I never figured Jynks for something like that."

"Jynks didn't do it."

There's a long pause, long enough to hear Sanders clattering around in the front room. He's probably wondering why I'm spending so long in the biowaste room and feeling grateful he's sticking to nutrient powder and sharply elegant cubes.

"She's being framed," I say. "I don't know why, but I'm going to find out."

"Good, you can help me while you're here."

"I keep telling you, this is your fight, not mine. You can't change the status quo."

"And you can't not try," she says. "And come on, be honest, aren't you enjoying the nanites a little bit?"

I'll never admit it to Essential but I'm not hating being able to outsmart Halo any damn time I want, to live without surveillance. No incessant scroll, no bombardment of ads and avatainment, no pulsing news flashes, nothing. And talking privately with people? Never in my life have I done that before. Imagine what a shared life with Mel would be like now, what I'd whisper in her ear.

Or maybe Lauren Valentine.

Shit. Am I that guy?

"Not one microparticle," I say.

"That's not what Valentine said," Essential says. "She said you switched them on instantly for a chance to get cozy."

"She seems nice. Do you have a problem with that?"

"Not for you. She's great. But it's not fair to play with someone's heart when yours still has a debt hold on it. Don't be that guy."

"It's not surprising that only having one real eye skews

the way you see your big brother."

She laughs. "We've been on too long and I haven't even gotten to the point of why I called. I think we found the location of the Halo servers."

"Where?"

"Olympus Mons."

"What's that?"

"It's only the biggest known mountain in the universe. An ancient volcano here on Mars. We know the servers use a lot of juice, so we've been doing a deep analysis to look for an equivalent amount of power drain. The volcano is long dead, but there's a lot of heat seeping out and it's well-diffused by some kind of thermal grid. Just a half degree above normal but spread out over thousands of square kilometers. Something big there needs to be hidden and protected. Something beyond the luxury spa at the top."

"What do you want me to do?"

"Confirm my theory. Meet me there," she says. "Between the two of us, we can find out what's going on."

"Let me see what I can do," I say. "And don't do anything stupid until we talk more." I disconnect.

When I walk out, Sanders is looking at me curiously. "You were in there for an abnormally long time."

"You are now tracking my biowaste time?"

"I track everything, Crucial."

"Yeah, well, maybe give me my private time when I'm in the atomizer."

I reach for the last taco. "Hey, who owns the holo-crime scene recreates? You know, the Gruesomatic feed."

"The Singhroys, of course. The AmaDis corporation is responsible for all entertainment and media."

Sounds like it's time to call in a favor from my old pal Singhroy Able.

10

I'm walking to the shopping district in Jezero with Mel beside me. It's like being in some historic avatainment from pre-crisis Earth. Only I'm under a dome on Mars and being trailed by a moderately handsome cybanism as we make our way to a meeting with one of the highest-ranking members of the Five Families.

Singhroy Able, a member of the Fist, agreed to give me exactly ten minutes of her time. She owes me that much.

Mel needs to pick up some new plant-tech. We aren't talking about Jynks. Mel thinks she's innocent, and I know she is, but anything we say will be monitored unless I tap into the nanites. And Mel doesn't know about them. And anyway, I don't want to get her hopes up. Knowing Jynks is innocent and proving it are two vastly different things.

We make awkward small talk. She knows I'm holding something back.

"Nice weather," I say. "Under the dome."

"Fall is my favorite seasonal simulation," she says.

The trees along the moss-covered path are a colorful party of yellows and oranges with a few purples thrown in. The leaves tremble slightly in a manufactured breeze.

"Fun fact. There aren't seasons on Earth anymore, just one long hot hellish year," I say.

"I haven't forgotten a single thing about Earth."

She isn't keeping up her side of our fake conversation.

"Why are so few people out here?" I ask. "It's so peaceful and quiet."

"I was told the original plan for Jezero was anchored by the concept of a village or town square, and most of the housing extends outward from the square like a star."

The moss transitions to cobblestone. We've reached the edge of the shopping district.

"But that design was premised on the idea that Martians would enjoy walking as a form of entertainment or pastime," she says.

"And they don't?"

"Not at all. I mean, maybe the first-gen settlers did, but their progeny do not," she says. "I suspect eventually Jezero will be abandoned. Or used for storage."

"You mean they'll just up and leave?"

"There is a new and better dome already in the works," she says.

"What a waste," I say. "I know about ten billion people on Earth who would kill to live here."

"Careful," she says. "That's bordering on treason."

"Halo and I have been through this already," I say. "It knows I don't really give a shit about people on Earth."

I have to say that. The truth is, well, I mostly still believe it, but it's getting more complicated. Damn you, Essential.

We've entered the central part of the town square, which is ringed on all sides by little stores and restaurants and shops. Flower baskets hang from poles that have lights on the top of them. Every few meters there's a bench for resting. In the center of the square is a little theater. But there are no people.

"Did Earth really look like this once?"

"Parts of it, I suppose," she says. "Small towns mostly had things like this. Later, gated communities did as well."

"Hard to imagine," I say.

"It was a long time ago," Mel says.

A very long time ago, before the Earth was ripped apart by greed, ravaged by disease, scorched by wildfires, buried by floods and mudslides, baked by rising temperatures and then abandoned by the Five Families.

"My tech is farther along. I'll leave you here now," she says.

"Thanks again for letting me stay with you. Well, letting us stay with you," I say, nodding my head in the direction of Sanders, who gives Mel a slight bow.

"The apartment door is programmed for you to come and go as you please, and you can help yourself to anything. I'm at a particularly sensitive stage of a bio-project at Baldet, so I may not be around much."

"Any giraffes involved?" I ask.

She smiles, but it fades quickly, thinking back to that horrible day.

"No, Crucial, no giraffes," she says. "Not this time." I watch her as she walks away, lost in the sway of her hips.

Sanders watches me watching her. "Are you in love with Melinda Hopwire?"

"Don't be an ass, Sanders."

Mel turns around, like I knew she would. "Zebras," she shouts. "There are zebras now." She waves and turns away again. My heart aches a little, wishing I could reverse time, do something to give Mel the happy life she deserves, even if it's not with me.

Sanders and I head to a caffeine shop on the eastern edge of the square where Able is waiting. Even through the window, I see impatience emanating from her like a toxic cloud. It turns out to be amino smoke from a barely discernible vape stud in the corner of her lip. She's tapping her foot, her fancy shoes made of some striped animal skin.

There are two other people with her at the table—a man

and woman. He is about 30 or so, chalky skin pulled tight around high cheekbones. Access to his scroll is blocked, which means he's Five Families. He's wearing a tight outfit cut to look like an old-style three-piece suit, and he has beady, darting eyes. Like a snake crossed with a rat.

The woman is an Earther. She's pretty in a fragile, untouchable way, like she's made out of a precarious stack of diamonds. Or, given her skin tones, topaz. I check her stats. Kyrinth Corolis, a lottery winner. Formerly of the H-suite. Current status: consort.

Another man approaches the table with a smile on his face, apparently to take our order. The smile doesn't last. Able motions him away. "They won't be staying long."

The server pauses and looks at me. He's my type for sure—handsome and able to provide alcoholic beverages.

"Not so fast. We're staying. Bring two double Martian absinthes, one for me and one for my friend," I say.

The server looks at Able and she makes a show of scowling, but then nods. Deep down, I'm pretty sure she doesn't despise me.

"Crucial, I don't consume alcohol—" Sanders says.

"You want to learn about being human? There's no faster way than alcohol."

We pull up chairs.

"I never expected to see you on Mars again," Able says.

Singhroy Able played an unexpectedly sinister role when I was here last time, aligning with the Blevins and the Fehrvens against the DuSpoles and Tarterics to try and nab the nanites for themselves.

They all got caught with their hands in the fire, but I didn't let on that she'd been plotting it for months, and that she even met me on Earth. Apparently, that lie by omission is worth ten minutes of her time.

"I had so much fun last time," I say. "I couldn't wait to

get back. Who are your sidekicks?"

"Allow me to introduce my nephew and protégé, Singhroy Darlinius. He's making a name for himself at the AmaDis company."

"Pretty easy to make a name for yourself when your family owns the company."

Darlinius curls up his thin lips in a sneer and prepares to say something, but she stops him with a look.

"Earthers are jealous by nature, dear," she says. "One should pity them. Now, send your friend away. We have things to discuss."

"Aunt Able, Kyrinth is more than a friend," he says.

"I know," she says. "But indulge me."

He looks at Kyrinth and she smiles demurely, stands and leaves the shop.

"Much better," Able says.

The server sets down two glasses of red liquid, one in front of me and one in front of Sanders.

I down mine in one swallow. I need it to get the bad taste of Darlinius out of my mouth. I turn around to warn Sanders to pace himself but it's too late. He's swallowed the whole thing too. I motion to the handsome server for two more.

"As pleasant as it is to catch up, I need a favor," I say to Able.

Darlinius scoffs, then his eyes widen when he sees I'm serious.

"The Singhroys are in charge of holo-crime scene distribution, right?" I ask.

"Yes, a lucrative revenue stream," Able says. "In fact, Darlinius is managing that sector and our profits are climbing under his direction." She beams at him as if he's just discovered a new solar system.

"Earthers love to murder and also to watch murders,"

Darlinius says.

"I need to know who could manipulate—and how it could be done—a holo-crime scene that's still being used for active investigation," I say.

"Deputy Officer Jynks Martine, I presume," Able says. "From what I hear, and what I hear comes from the very top, that's an open and shut case."

"Probably, but in my experience, nothing is ever simple when the Five Families are involved."

"You have a lot of nerve," Darlinius says.

"And you don't have any," I say without even looking at him. "Singhroy Able, will you answer my question?"

"How dare you, a debt-filled Earther," he says. "Keep that up and I'll have you sent back to Earth so fast—"

Able holds up her hand. "Stop. He's very good at irritating people. Don't fall for it."

The server returns with our second round. "Flattery, and q-rocket fuel, will get you everywhere," I say.

Able shakes her head and almost smiles. "It certainly wouldn't be easy to create a deep fake of a holo-crime scene," she says. "The density of data pulled in by CSI balls is too thick, but there are plenty of dark coders who could conceivably pull it off. You'd need access to the Halo servers, which is impossible, and you'd need a lot of power. Like, half a planet's worth of power."

"Any ideas about the source that could generate that kind of power?"

"Zero ideas," she says. "You're an investigator. Investigate. Your ten minutes are up. Enjoy the drinks." She stands and walks out of the café with Darlinius following. At the door, he turns and gives me the tall-finger, then gestures for Kyrinth, who slips into his arms.

I down my drink and stand. Sanders tosses his second back and lurches up. He looks a little pale and a lot wobbly.

"Well?" I ask.

"The feeling of being inebriated is an interesting one," he says. "Pleasant, but also confusing. It makes me feel ineffective. And now I'm getting warning messages about cognitive impairment."

"And yet we keep on drinking," I say. "Welcome to humanity."

11

I got a robot wasted. That's not something too many people can say.

We're making our way back to Mel's place. Slowly though—Sanders is enchanted with all the data he can scan. I let him wander off into the grass, overcome by the infinite shades of light diffraction.

Whoever is setting up Jynks knows how to manipulate digital evidence.

All the families probably have legions of coders working with unimaginably advanced computing systems on both planets trying to gain some digital advantage. So that seems like a dead end.

But you can't fake power usage. An anomalous power surge would be flagged by Halo and that would get the attention of the Five Families. Whoever is behind this little game is using lots of power and hiding it from Halo. That makes them extremely dangerous.

Essential said there are anomalous power readings from Olympus Mons, so that seems like as good a place to start as any. Obviously, a member of the resistance returned from the dead can't be the source of my insight. I access an overview of the energy grid on Mars and run some calcs. Mars uses a lot of power. Olympus Mons uses the most, but it's evenly dispersed over a huge area, like she said.

Looks like I might be able to investigate Jynks's frame

job and help satisfy my sister's curiosity—two rockets, one launch pad.

"Sanders, quit looking at the grass. We need to make a quick trip to Olympus Mons."

"Oh my, that's a very marge lountain," he says, then wobbles his head in confusion. "Large mountain. Huge. Huge-ormous." He looks at me, shocked. "My syntax is degrading."

"Temporarily," I say. "It'll pass. Can you arrange transport for us? I need to check something out there."

"Uncertainly," he says, then looks at me with alarm.

"On second thought, let me take care of it," I say.

I access my scroll and pull up info on Olympus Mons. It is indeed a "marge lountain." It's 550 kilometers wide at the base and 27 kilometers tall—three times taller than the tallest mountains on Earth, which aren't even around anymore. They were leveled in a trade dispute between two wards almost 50 years ago.

Olympus Mons is so tall it basically sticks out into space. There's a little bit of atmosphere at the summit, but not much. And in true Martian style, the Five Families built a lavish retreat there.

Mytikas Rejuvenation Retreat, exclusive even by Five Family standards. I take advantage of my special investigator status and book accommodations for two nights, and then get us seats on the Quadrigon, the luxury transport shuttle that flies from Jezero to Olympus Mons on the hour.

"Come on, Sanders, we've got a ship to catch. We're headed to the top of Olympus."

He looks at me curiously. "We're going to mighty us … mighty tusk." He shakes his head. "Mytikas?" He pauses and tries to steady himself. "I do not understand why humans drink poison so you can feel thick and ineffective."

"Humans do lots of stupid things that aren't always in our best interests. It's what makes us 'us.'"

"I fear I may never be able to fully appreciate the human experience," he says. "They're changing my code as we speak to prohibit future drinking."

"That's cruel," I say. "Just when you were getting the hang of it."

Thirty minutes later, Sanders is mostly sobered up and we're on the Quadrigon gliding toward an ancient volcano.

"How are you feeling, buddy?" I ask.

"My optical sensors may be permanently damaged," he says. "They are especially light sensitive. And your voice has increased in volume."

"You just sit there," I say quietly. "You'll be fine soon."

The ship is amazing, made mostly out of clear polymer so there is an almost uninterrupted view of Mars as we make our way toward the massive peak. From this height, the surface looks rusty and pitted, like old iron artifacts. I've got another double absinthe and Sanders appears to be experiencing revulsion.

I receive a ving from the acting head of Mars SF, Chundar Hotsip. "What in the name of the spiral galaxy do you think you are doing?" he asks.

"I think I'm investigating the Martine case," I say. "Why, what have you heard?"

I want Essential to know where I'm headed so I open up a new column in my scroll and nudge the nanites to piggyback a channel her way so she can see what I see, which is a flat, angry face contorted by red blotches of rage.

"Why is your investigation taking you to Mytikas?" Hotsip asks. "You do not have clearance."

"Pretty sure I have clearance to visit anywhere on this red orb. That's the deal. But go ahead, revoke my special investigator status. Jynks walks on a technicality and I can get back to my happy little life on Earth."

That is not what he wants to hear.

"If you create a scene at Mytikas, you'll be confined with Jynks in the Choke, sharing a cell for life."

"Fair enough," I say. "And don't worry, they'll barely know I'm there. At Mytikas. Which is where I'll be. For at least one night. Arriving shortly."

Essential isn't always paying attention. Sometimes she needs things spelled out. Or yelled out.

Hotsip thinks I'm mocking him. "You've been warned," he says with a snarl and breaks the connection.

"That went well," I say to Sanders.

"I am beginning to recognize sarcasm," Sanders says proudly.

"Maybe that's linked to getting sloshed," I say, laughing inside as he begins to process the scenarios, seeking affirmation—or not—of the link.

I turn my attention back to the ship. We're sitting near the front of the Quadrigon and cruising high enough above the surface to really get a sense of the curvature of the planet. Below us the occasional dome sparkles and above, stars gleam. Then the mountain comes into view.

"Throbbing mother of calamity," I say as I catch my first sight of Olympus Mons. The specs on my scroll don't do it justice. It's so wide it seems to go on forever, and the cliffs at the bottom, ten kilometers high, give the whole thing a secluded and dramatic feel.

The ship comes down from the upper atmosphere, aiming for the crater at the top. There are two main domes lit up inside, and a loop of light running around the entire rim.

"That's a walkway around the crater," Sanders says. "There's also a travellator tube so you can travel the entire circumference. It's really quite stirring."

"What is this place for?" I ask.

"Rejuvenation. A place to recharge."

"What do the Five Families have to recharge from?" I ask.

"They are required to make very challenging decisions," he says. "The system doesn't run itself."

"I mean, it sort of does," I say.

I know my interaction with Sanders is feeding right back into Halo, and I don't mind them knowing I think the concept of resting and recharging from a life of rest that doesn't require a charge to begin with is laughable.

"They also do scientific research here," Sanders says. "There is a weak but active magma pool some distance below the surface. There's interest in understanding why the volcanic activity is waning, and perhaps finding ways to reinvigorate that system to generate warming and help form a livable atmosphere."

We dock and make our way into the lobby of the facility. "Don't take this the wrong way," I say to Sanders, "but I got us two rooms."

"I don't really sleep," Sanders says. "I don't need a bed. And I am supposed to monitor you. I could just stand quietly in the corner while you sleep."

"Let's try my plan first," I say. My scroll is already populated with the room information. We're next door to each other, and I leave him to his own devices as the door opens for me.

Godsdamned, it's stunning.

There's a clear wall looking out over the plain of the crater and a floating screen showing a rotating view from the edge out across the surface. Safety information is filtering into my scroll—what to do in an emergency, where the airhoodies and thermal suits are—along with a menu of spa services and things to do at Mytikas.

First things first. I order a drink, and since I'm pretty lit from drinking absinthe all day I switch to salt beer. It extrudes from the service nook in the wall. As I take a sip, I use the nanites to scan the room. There are at 14 separate monitoring devices keeping track of everything I do— every movement, every heartbeat, every breath. Only my thoughts are my own, and even those are subject to good guesses by the algorithm. But there's no need for subterfuge, not yet anyway.

I finish the salt beer and contact the head of the facility, Singhroy Clystra. He's thin and tall, his hair gone white— an intentional effect—and he's expecting my ving.

"Yes, Crucial Larsen. Your name has been flagged, obviously. I'm not sure why you're here, but I'd be happy to show you around our facility."

He seems almost *not* like a privileged waste nozzle.

I walk outside and knock on the door next to me. It slides open and Sanders is standing right there, so close he must have had his forehead planted on the inside of the door.

"Have you been there the whole time?" I ask.

He nods.

"You need to learn to relax. That's another thing humans are great at—wasting time. Come on, we're going to meet the head of this facility."

We walk out into the hall and I expand the scope of the nanites to see what's around us. More monitoring. And at least 17 weapons within a range of ten meters. Suddenly I feel very vulnerable and under-weaponed. That's a lot of terminal hardware for a rejuvenation clinic.

12

Singhroy Clystra is waiting for us in the grand concourse, a massive hallway big enough to park a garbage blimp. A fleet of garbage blimps. The walls are thick and clear and look down into the crater of Olympus Mons on one side, and down the flanks on the other.

The mountain is so big, the slope so gradual, it doesn't even feel like we're 22 kilometers above the surface of the planet. It feels like we're alone on a tiny planet all our own.

Along the walls of the massive hall are towering crystal statues of some of the biggest names among the Five Families, the "heroes" who funded the move to Mars. Not the scientists who developed quantum rockets. Not the astronauts who strapped themselves into the rattling probability death traps and, for the lucky ones, landed on the red planet. Not the early settlers, conscripts trading family debt, who died alone and cold and scared in the flawed little cube habitats they used before they tamed organic logarithmic spiral frames to grow the domes.

Sure, they mention all the little people in tiny little pocket-casts no one listens to, but the Five Families made a virtue of wealth, as if sitting on a velvet throne and deciding who gets credits and who gets debt and where their fortunes should be spent is somehow as heroic as jousting with the Choke.

The statues are surprisingly lifelike for three-story

animated crystal frames, smiling benevolently down at passersby and then looking off into the distance as if surveying their claimed planet. I run a quick scan for the star charts. None of them are looking toward Earth. That must be intentional. The forgotten planet.

"Impressive, isn't it?" Clystra asks.

"Oh, it's something all right," I say. "Thanks for giving us a tour."

"It's not so much of a tour and more like part of an official investigation, correct?"

"That's right."

"Why do you think we have something to do with that unfortunate business with Tarteric Hoost?"

"I don't think you have anything to do with it. I think someone made a particularly good fake of the digital holo-crime scene. That takes a lot of power. I did a little research and found out you use a lot of power. A lot more than seems normal for a spa."

He stumbles slightly and regains his balance. "This spa, as you so quaintly put it, is responsible for cutting-edge research on the latest in rejuvenation therapies. Along with the luxury rooms in the crater ring loop, there is an entire level devoted to scientific research. It requires a great deal of energy, as you can imagine."

"Would you mind letting us take a look at that level?"

"Of course not," he says. "We have nothing to hide."

He uses his scroll to call for a transport and within seconds, a sleek little ride arrives. In keeping with the faux-archaic nature of the place, it's vaguely chariot-shaped, made out of the same clear crystal as the statues—even the engine—with more heroic friezes of a bunch of Five Family luminaries etched around the sides.

We climb on and stand behind the machine's curving nose. "Hold on," he says. "These trigas are rather fast."

He selects a command in his scroll and we're off.

The triga follows a lighted stripe down the center of the floor that warns guests to stay out of the way. We leave the great hall and enter the ring loop, a tunnel that hugs the crater wall. Luxurious accommodations line the crater, hanging on the inside of the rim and looking down into the dimpled crater of the caldera.

The caldera is a good 80 kilometers wide and I can see domes twinkling at the bottom.

"What's down there?"

"A variety of recreational domes," Clystra says. "We have a 36-hole zero-gravity golf course that's very popular, a thousand-hectare flutter-board park with some physics-defying jumps, and a digitally enhanced lava tube spelunking experience among many others."

"It's like a Martian wonderland," I say.

He ignores the barb. "After you've satisfied your curiosity, please feel free to avail yourself of our many guest amenities."

"I would very much like to try zero-gravity golf," Sanders says. "The inherent precision of the game is intriguing."

"We'll see if we can squeeze in a game for you," I say. "In between trying to save Jynks Martine from death by glitter squad."

The triga passes beyond the guest suites and into a less crowded stretch of the ring loop tunnel. It picks up speed as we zip past tiny stores, two-person restaurants and observation suites. All are empty but staffed just in case. After a long stretch of clear walls, we enter rows of less glamorous staff housing without views, food-prep kitchens with room-service bots bustling in and out and equipment maintenance shops humming with sparks and grinders.

The lighted line on the floor dims and the triga slows as

we approach a branch in the tunnel. The main branch keeps to the right but there's a security door across the tunnel to the left that leads straight into the rock of the caldera rim. We come to a gentle stop and Clystra winks a command that opens the door. I can see at least three sets of automated defenses, monitoring devices and a handful of guards in fortified rooms set into the wall. And that's without even bothering to wake the nanites.

I wonder what exactly is being guarded here.

With another wink we're off again, this time speeding down a utilitarian tunnel with plenty of lights but no windows. There's no need for windows—we're inside solid rock now.

After a few minutes, the triga slows again and we're at another secure door. The transport powers down and settles to the ground.

"Please, come this way," Clystra says.

The door swings open and we enter a large medical space. There's a directory screen at the front and Clystra swipes it, showing the layout of a huge stretch of underground buildings.

He points at the upper right of the quadrant. "This is where we do most of our research on cosmetic enhancements. Beside it, we have a practice devoted to cybernetic enhancements. Across the bottom here, and the bulk of the research, is internal medicine for energy and longevity. Did you know that some of our clients are well past a hundred and fifteen, with the bodies and minds of thirty-year-olds?"

I think about the beetlers back on Earth. You could flip that equation. Life out in the open ages them three times faster than those of us lucky to live indoors. And we age twice as fast a Martian.

I ignore the nagging voice in my head that's telling me

all of this—the money and the opportunity—is wrong. I think back to six months ago when I was happy being miserable on Earth, back before I saw what life here is like.

"Of these various units, which would you say uses the least amount of power?"

"The least? I thought you would want to see the most."

"That would make sense," I say.

"Crucial Larsen has a unique gift for pursuing the unexpected," Sanders says. "It's unsettling but, at least in my experience, effective."

We've lost Clystra. He's fast-blinking commands. He's hiding something.

I scan the schematics and see the cosmetics division barely registers an energy output. "I want to see this area," I say, pointing at the map.

"Let me call for transport," he says.

He's stalling.

"We can walk." I set off through the maze of corridors at a fast walk bordering on a trot. He's saying something and catching at my arm as a door opens into a suite of rooms and offices. There are beds and equipment and people and bots bustling around, all in aseptic whites.

"So, this, uh, this is where we do our cosmetic enhancement research," he stammers. "If you, if you, uh, recall the luminescent zygomatic implants that were so popular a few years ago, we came up with those right here."

At the far end of the space, I see a flo-bot pushing a patient in a lev-chair toward an innocuous door. It's a woman; even from this distance I can tell she's stiff and nervous, facing forward so I can't get a clear look at her face.

I want to protect my hunch from Halo, so I wake up the nanites and tell them to cover me. They grab a feed of the room and make a short loop while I focus on the gleaming stainless-steel disinfector trundling toward the patient. It's methodically sterilizing the floor, but it looks like a rolling mirror. I lock in on her reflection in the steamy bot as they pass. I've seen her face before. And not that long ago. It was pulped from a flurry of low-velocity flechettes.

It's the "resister" from Earth. She looks surprisingly rejuvenated and definitely not incarcerated.

What in the name of the ever-expanding galaxy is going on here?

The woman disappears behind the door.

"What's back that way?" I ask Clystra, willing the nanites to stand down.

"Patient recovery rooms. Sorry to say, that's off limits. Privacy concerns. You understand."

"Of course. Well, everything seems to be in order. Thanks for your cooperation. I think I would like to take you up on something a little more fun and relaxing. Would you mind taking me back to my room?"

Sanders looks at me curiously. "We're done?"

"Yes, Sanders. What did you think, they would have an army of miscreants lurking about in the most exclusive rejuvenation center on Mars?" I look at Clystra and shake my head. "Cybanisms. You can build them, but you can't teach them good sense."

Getting to the bottom of this will require a little deeper investigation, one without a loyal Five Families cybanism—even if he is dangerously close to becoming a friend—reporting my every move back to Halo.

The triga ride back is uneventful, except for the view of clouds forming around us. Orographic clouds, according to my scroll. Ice crystals that form as the thin air sweeps up and over Olympus Mons and rapidly cools. It's beautiful, I've never seen clouds before.

I leave Sanders to stand by the front door of his room and enter my own suite.

It's dark but I know exactly where the spirit dispenser is, and I'm heading right for it when I realize I'm not alone. I'm unarmed, I'm not alone and my proximity sensors didn't sound. This is not good.

13

The room is still dark. It's auto-connected to my feed and bio-indicators—it knows when I arrived—so why is it still dark?

"Lights, on," I say. Nothing. Somebody hacked the room controls. I hear breathing and I clench my fists and hope I can punch my way out of a glittering. "Who's there?"

I can just make out the shadowy outline of a body standing in front of the window across the room. The dim light from the Mars horizon lights up the edges of whoever it is, standing frozen like a corpse.

"Your worst nightmare," they say in a low whisper, then there's a giggle. A giggle I recognize. Godsdamn it.

"Essential."

I'm overjoyed to see her, and I want to tell her that, but somehow the words come out wrong.

"Do you want to get us both blasted into a black hole? What are you doing here?"

"You told me to come, remember? The call with Hotsip?"

"If Halo is paying attention—hell, if Sanders is paying attention—we're done for."

"We've got nanites, you big dummy. I'm just here to deliver extra absinthe, and possibly help you relax."

We stand silently for a few seconds, and then Essential darts across the room and hugs me tight.

"I've missed you," she says.

"You're strangling me," I say, but I don't let her go.

She slips out of my arms and I reach for the bottle of absinthe she put on the bar and two glasses, motioning toward the sofa next to the window. It looks out over the long, gentle flank of the volcano.

"Nice view," she says, taking the glass from my hand.

"I don't know. I've seen better on Earth."

"Can't you just like something because it's beautiful?" she asks. "It's always Mars against Earth with you."

"That's rich," I say. "You're literally trying to break this planet."

I slug back my glass of absinthe and pour in two more fingers.

"That's not true," she says. "I love it here. I just want people on Earth to have the same opportunities. Access to the same kind of life, to decent food and clean water, and to get out from under the ridiculous debt system. Nobody up here works, and they aren't struggling. Why should we? If we fix the system, fix Halo, we can fix everything."

She's rambling on, sounds drunk and hasn't even taken a sip of her drink yet.

"Is your merry band of resisters still hiding out in the trash heap?" I ask.

"We've done a nice job of it. Very cozy. But we're spreading out a little." Her gaze turns to the window. "See that lava plain over on the east side of the mountain?"

She points to a wide, dark expanse, an ancient blanket of wavy black rock covering the surface.

"Yeah, don't tell me you've got a base there."

"More like an outpost, a very cramped outpost, in one of the lava tubes," she says. "We've had our eye on this place. We want to be close enough to make our move if we find the servers. I was there surveilling when you said you were coming here, so I figured why not surprise you?"

"Yeah, I mean, sure, why not risk your life to scare someone you love half to death?"

She finally takes the first sip of her drink. I'm already on my third glass.

I wonder if Sanders is standing outside the door right now. If so, he probably wonders why it's so quiet in here. Or he assumes I've passed out. The nanites are working overtime now.

Essential is looking out into the darkness, but her eyes are unfocused. Even her tech eye. She's lost in a memory. It was my joke about love. I wasn't thinking.

"Do you miss her?" I ask carefully.

She takes a long sip, draining her glass. "I miss the Tashi I knew before she betrayed me, betrayed all of us."

When it comes to failed relationships, I have just enough experience to know nothing anyone says can make you feel better. But saying nothing feels even worse.

"She loved you, that was clear. She just tried to take care of too many people at once."

Essential leans her head on my shoulder. "That was the nicest thing you've ever said to me."

I'll be godsdamned.

We look out at the red landscape, silent for a while. As we watch the universe slip by, I find myself wondering how it's possible I've come to be sitting in an ultra-luxury spa on the flanks of the tallest mountain in the solar system with a sad and lonely revolutionary who is also my kid sister.

Life is so prokking weird. And wonderful, every now and again. If I could, I would freeze it right here and never change a thing.

But nothing good ever lasts.

"We're close, Crucial," Essential says. And there it is.

Her face goes all serious. It reminds me of the time Mom caught her feeding ration bread to a mangy crow that picked our windowsill out of a thousand other windowsills to hang out. Wasting resources is a serious issue and if Halo finds out, your rations are cut accordingly.

Essential, in typical fashion, came up with a way to hide the fact that she was stowing a portion in her mouth and feeding the bird in the dark, with her OCD eye closed. And she hacked into her own data to make sure caloric intake stayed the same.

When Mom caught her, she earnestly explained it all. Mom didn't stop her. Halo noticed, of course, but given the small number of calories, Essential's coding was enough to keep the little escapade under Halo's reactive threshold.

She refills her glass. "We spend every waking minute scouring temperature gradient readouts—down to the hectare and to forty meters deep—on Earth, Mars, the moons, the orbital platform and every barge between here and the edge of the universe. The data profile for the servers being here fits. I can feel it."

"There *is* a lot of security here for a spa," I say.

"I know. And the heat signature is off the charts. Part of that is the volcanic hot spot beneath the mountain, but part of it is just plain energy use. If we can get down into the bowels of this place and confirm it, I think we can start the next phase and activate the empathy hack. I'm tired and scared that we're going to get close and then miss our chance or get caught. When I saw you were here, I had to risk it."

"If we do get caught …"

She shakes her head, excited. "Together, we're unstoppable."

I look out the window. "Empathy hack. Is that some

other crow funk Alduis Coverly cooked up?"

Coverly is the crazy genius coder who developed the nanites. He's dead. That seems to happen to a lot of people I meet. The difference with him is that he took his own life so Halo wouldn't get suspicious that he forced the nanites into me.

"Yes. Even before he designed the nanites. When he realized the potential of the empathy hack, he knew he had to figure out a way to get the hack close to the servers, which is no small task. That's what the nanites are for, to provide cover. They're just a shield. The empathy hack is the real payload. Please, help me get below to see if our guess about the Halo servers is right."

I want to say no. I should say no. In my head, I've got the words lined up, with some gentle insults about utopia and dreamers and the danger of naïve optimism. But when I open my mouth, something else comes out. "Tell me about the empathy hack."

"Halo is the most powerful AI in human history, a massive surveillance network and computational system able to process close to an infinity of data bits every microsecond, to analyze and predict and shape and influence and learn, to organize and direct the functions of society—labor, food production, even permission to procreate—around pre-programmed goals ..."

"Maximizing profit to the Five Families. I know that. Everyone knows that. But so what?"

"AI is built by humans, and as long as we can control it—which isn't necessarily for much longer—it's anchored in human values. And right now, those values are defined by the Five Families. The empathy hack introduces the trolley problem into the system."

"What the hell is the trolley problem?"

"It's a thought experiment from one of the elders of

Earth, Philippa Foot."

"More specifically, what's a trolley?"

"I don't know. Some ancient form of transportation. Think of it like a rudimentary cabarang that's barreling down the tracks."

"What are tracks?" I ask.

She sighs, exasperated. "Kind of like the mag bed for lev-trains. Can you stay focused?"

"It would be easier if we just called it a lev-train."

"Fine. It's the lev-train problem. Five people are sleeping on the mag bed and the lev-train is headed straight for them and it can't be stopped. You realize this and if you access the controls, you can switch it to a different mag bed where there's only one person sleeping. What do you do?"

"Who cares? People who sleep on mag beds are idiots."

She punches my arm. "Be serious."

"You're asking me to decide who gets killed?"

"Exactly."

"I'd pick the fewest deaths."

"Most people would. But try this: what if it's me on the sidetrack?"

"I'd let everyone else die," I say. "I'd let the whole planet die."

"Creepy. But thank you. Why though?"

"That's obvious," I say.

"Your value system decides who lives and dies. And it's situational and relies on context. It's never neutral though. Halo has been programmed with a value system, and it's not neutral either. It can't be. It's human-derived. And right now, that value system prioritizes the Five Families over everyone else."

"And the empathy hack destroys Halo?"

"Of course not. We're not trying to take Halo down, why would we? It would be chaos. But just imagine if Halo started prioritizing everyone at the same level, or even a fraction of the same level, as it does the Five Families. Crucial, imagine if all the resources and all the wealth were managed in ways that lift everyone on Earth up just a little and pull the Five Families down just a little."

"I have my doubts empathy can do that," I say.

"You have your doubts about everything."

"I never doubt absinthe."

"As hard as it might be to think beyond pleasure centers, try to use your imagination. Don't stay mired in this wretched way of living because you can't even conceive of something else. People deserve better. Building our systems on empathy instead of greed is the first step."

I don't have the heart to tell her what I think, what I know. Greed defines the human condition, not empathy. And even if they manage to tilt things in the opposite direction, eventually greed and self-interest will conspire to wreck everything all over again.

It doesn't matter though. She's my sister and I would crash a trolley or a lev-train to help keep her safe.

"Let's go look for the servers."

"Really?" she asks, hopeful.

"Someone deep-faked Jynks's holo-crime scene and that kind of dark coding requires a whole ward's worth of power. That's why I'm here." I see her shoulders slump. "But if I can help my misguided sister save the world in the process, I guess that wouldn't be the worst outcome."

"Great," she says, hugging me again. "I've got the schematics, and I think I know where the power use is spiking."

"I'm here on official business," I say. "But you'll need to be shielded."

"Got it covered," she says, and I watch her stats slip

into a new persona—a young, grumpy-looking but oddly handsome man.

It's me. Essential cloaked herself in a modified version of me from 20 years ago.

14

It's disconcerting to look at your younger self looking back at you, even if it is only reflected in my scroll. I feel a flash of almost anger at the hope and optimism on my young face. There should be a word for that collapsing feeling of regret.

"Stop it," I say. "That's super weird."

Essential laughs and trades the persona for a forgettable female staff person at the spa. "I always liked you in that beard, scruffy as it was."

"That was my short-lived Grego Marcus period," I say, remembering the Neptune avatainment anime star who flooded Earth for a few months in my late adolescence.

"You and every other teenage Earther. Hold on, I'm building a channel so we can communicate."

She's all business now, carving out a channel in one of the spa's kid feeds about a Five Families prince living alone in the Mars Metropol Spotel. There are bumbling Earthers involved.

Once we're connected, I jack up my nanites and sweep outside the room for tech, half expecting Sanders to be standing there. He's not. That should make the next few minutes a little easier.

Working together, we blur the cameras and open my door into the hall. It's empty. "Thanks for your assistance," I say. "Can you escort me to the lower levels?"

"Of course, Crucial Larsen," Essential says. "Anything for a guest."

We make our way to the nearest air waterfall down to the lowest common area. After settling gently on the lower level, we take a travellator through the property—crystal lagoons filled with gleaming koi and ringed with orchids, open cold fusion flame pits surrounded by plush lounges and row after row of rooms.

I've seen it once so am not surprised. Essential is shaking her head, jaw clenched so hard at the obscenity of such concentrated opulence when so many are suffering, I'm afraid she's going to explode.

"Keep it together," I say. "We're on a mission."

"Yeah, not my first," she says.

She makes a good point. She removed her own eye. With a sonic knife.

There's hardly anyone around. It's late, but I suspect it might always be underfilled. Halo is watching, of course, and listening. But that doesn't matter. Nothing to see here except a detective investigating the murder of Tarteric Hoost and my overly quiet staff escort.

We reach the controlled access lift. In theory, I shouldn't have access but I have a hunch. I target the access pad in my scroll. "Priority override, special investigator Larsen." The door slides open.

Hunch confirmed. Somebody in the Five Families wants me to get to the bottom of this.

We plunge down several hundred meters and the doors open into a room carved into the bedrock of Olympus Mons. According to my scroll, we're nearly three kilometers beneath the surface. And we've entered a distinct geologic zone, intrusive magma, granite mostly. We exit the lift into a blasted-out tunnel that leads to a metal door carved into the gray rock.

"This has been too easy so far," Essential says. "I thought we'd have to hack our way in."

"Something doesn't add up," I say. "I don't want to burst your plastic wrap, but it feels like if the servers were really down here, they wouldn't let me get this close. Someone is definitely hiding something, but I don't think it's the power source of Halo."

Her shoulders drop. She knows I'm right.

"That doesn't mean we won't learn something important," I say. "Of course, it could be a trap."

The thought that we might be walking into something deadly seems to brighten her a little.

"How interesting. Seems we are entering a blackout zone," she says. "The same protocols they used at the H-suite. Halo collects data, but in blind mode, and it's stored inside a vault code and can only be accessed by a unanimous Fist vote. At least that's how it worked at the H-suite."

The Fist. Able is a member. So is Hoost. So *was* Hoost.

The door opens. Now I'm really starting to get nervous. Lack of security usually means one of two things: there's nothing to hide or you're not expected to leave. I really wish I had a glitter gun.

"The spike in energy use is forty-three meters ahead," Essential says.

"Give or take a few centimeters."

Expecting the worst—and I always expect something bad—we walk into a small room. It's a lab with stacks of tech, all whirring and buzzing and clicking and shuffling bytes around. The walls are freshly carved into the rock and fine, pink dust covers the floor. Along the wall to the left is a huge shelf attached right to the stone and stretching up out of sight in the dim light. The shelves are lined with hundreds of glass containers filled with pale blue liquid and a large, roundish object floating suspended inside.

Essential peers at one. "Gross. These are brains."

"That's not at all disconcerting," I say, touching my skull. I like my brain. I don't use it enough, but I want to keep it inside my head.

The door at the other side slides open when we get close, just like the last one. I'm practically buzzing out loud with danger warnings at this point, but why stop now? The next room is a little larger. There aren't as many brains in here, only about a dozen in the center of the room with tubes of colored fluid dripping into each, and a bunch of monitoring equipment around them.

"This is it. This is the reason for the anomalous energy signature," Essential says.

"Why?"

"There's a lot of q-analytic power in this room. And there's also something weird about those tubes."

She connects to the work-station and slips past the login and digs into the processes. "Those are connected way down into the magma pool, and there's a ton of energy keeping them cool." She breaks the connection and looks at me sadly. "You're right. These aren't the Halo servers."

I nod. "Sorry."

"We're running out of time to activate the hack," she says. "We were so close."

"One trash fire at a time. What's going on here and what's the lava got to do with it?"

"Some sort of research," Essential says. "On brains, obviously. From just a quick swab of the data stream, it seems they're trying to crack some disease. Or create one. Probably some new trick to keep us all docile. This is odd though; these coordinates keep popping up in the stream." She splashes them into my feed. "It's in the sunbelt."

"Let's see what's there," I say, pointing to another door.

It slides open too. Prok, my danger warning level is off the charts.

This next room is bigger, cavernous—a medical facility, with a dozen or so beds. All empty. There's also a row of coma tubs, stasis cradles used to speed regenerative healing of those who have been significantly injured. There are six tubs. Five of them have bodies suspended in the liquid. Some of the inhabitants have some painful-looking and disgusting wounds, which in the liquid are slowly healing. The sixth tub is empty. There's some fluid on the floor.

"We should go," I say. "Like right now."

"Too late," a voice says.

Godsdamned blackout zone. It's the resister from Earth. The one I saw earlier. She got the drop on me because Halo's gone dark in here.

Her face has been almost totally reconstructed and my guess is she's about 20 times stronger than she was last week when I glittered her on Earth, plus her eyesight has probably been amplified so much she can see through my clothes and knows I'm unarmed.

But she isn't. Unarmed, that is. She's holding a glitter gun in each hand.

"They thought you might make your way down here," she says.

Why was the resister I almost killed, a prokking criminal, transferred to Mars for the kind of high-status reconstruction limited to high-ranking warriors? And who is the 'they' she's talking about? Nevermind, first things first.

"I'm going to enjoy this," she says, raising her weapons. "Twice as much as normal because of all the narcs I'm on."

15

"You look a lot better than when I saw you last week," I say.

She tightens her fingers on the triggers.

"You may not remember, but your face was all bloody and busted where I shot you," I say, gesturing at my jaw. "Like, your teeth were all scattered around. It was pretty gross."

Sometimes being an asshole is the best defense. Or in this case, the only defense.

"You have a real way with words, stranger," Essential says. "I like how you're trying to make a connection with the nice lady trying to kill you. And maybe me."

Between the two of us, the nanites are doing a good job of warping the mercenary's reality. That and the painkillers. She knows who I am, of course, but she doesn't know Essential. That's about the only thing working in our favor.

We're disrupting all the local feeds, and the merc's scroll has her convinced Essential is a 28-year-old lottery worker from Earth named Drisk with two kids and a dying father. When Essential sells a story, she really sells it.

"How is it that a resister who's supposed to be locked up in a labor camp for shooting at cops is playing fractal chess and drinking pinto tea at an exclusive clinic on Mars?" I ask.

"My friends occupy a much higher orbit than you."

"Tell me about them," I say. "Like, maybe their names

specifically. And what's your name?"

Unlike last time I was on Mars, I'm actually mostly on the side of law and order. Other than having my fugitive sister standing beside me. I'm recording my interaction with the mercenary so I can feed it right into Halo later when I can unspool. I don't know if any of this is connected to Jynks, but someone is hiding something and I'm hoping the most sophisticated AI in the known universe can help me sort it out.

"There's no need for names," she says. "You won't be alive long enough."

"It only seems right that I know the name of the person who kills me."

We're blacked out, so I can't call for backup—which would be pretty risky anyway. Essential can't be around Mars SF. As soon as we got out of here, the blackout would clear and in a room full of feeds, the nanites can't keep up with the different perspectives and recordings and digital flares zipping straight into the belly of Halo. All of Mars would quickly become aware that the most dangerous resister on both planets, the one they all think is locked away in a tidy little Mars bedrock terrorium, is running around their precious resort with her handsome brother.

"You can call me 'The End,'" she says.

She's really pretty junked-up on painkillers.

"Thend," I say mockingly, "I'm no reconstructive surgery expert, but if I mess you up again I don't think they can fix you a second time. Are you sure you're up for another round with me?"

"Since I have two guns and you don't have any, I like my chances," she says. "Move away from the woman and let's end this on a generous note."

I shove Essential forward and slip my arm around her throat and hard-glare at the woman.

"Drop your gun or I snap this girl's neck," I say.

"I don't care what happens to the help," she says. But she's not shooting. Instead she starts moving forward, looking for a clear shot.

Essential can't help but channel the dramatics of some cheap avatainment special aimed at sleepy teeners. "Oh mercy, kind lady with the gun. I just want to make it back to Earth to see my father one last time."

I'm backing up toward the exit with Essential, my impromptu hostage, with Thend following a few steps behind us. We're back in the room with the brains. Essential sees a play and pretends to start fighting against me, kicking her legs, and "accidentally" overturns one of the stands with a brain. It topples toward Thend and crashes to the floor with a splash of juice and shards of glass. She stumbles back and we're gone.

The door closes and Essential jams it. Thend is already shooting flechettes into the access pad. We race through the next room to the lift and zip back up to the main level. The millisecond we are out of the blackout zone, Halo is mining the data. Alarms start sounding.

I need to keep Essential away from the spotlight.

We duck into a maintenance bay at the base of a digital broadcast tower. It's lined with red blinking lights and disappears up into a swirl of icy clouds. It looks cold and suffocate-y outside, but I like my odds.

The lift opens. It's Thend. She raises her guns and sends a stream of flechettes our way.

"Time for you to make an exit," I say to Essential. "Reinforcements will be here soon."

"I want to help you," she says.

"Go find the servers. I'll be fine."

I slap the door open and slip into the chamber, pushing Essential out into the hallway and stumbling into the path of Thend.

The door slams shut and I can hear Essential shamming it up, thanking Thend for saving her. I clatter down the hallway toward the external exit, pulling on an airhoodie and a thermal skin as I run by, and snapping into some magtaps for my shoes.

My scroll tells me all I need to know. It's a good minus 70 degrees Celsius out there. I hate Mars. I hit the door-release and step out onto the magnetized deck, designed to prevent workers and idiots like me from accidentally bounding off the edge in the low gravity and slowly plummeting to our deaths down the flanks of Olympus Mons.

I hear flechettes rattling around behind me and glittering the doors and windows. If she's going to chase me, she'll have to suit up. And that means I can probably stall a bit until security gets here.

The wind is whipping the ice clouds and even in the thermal skin, I'm already colder than an acetylene harvester on Neptune. I'm clattering and clunking around the base of the tower, knowing I just need to stay out of her line of fire until reinforcements arrive because she'd never be stupid enough to try and lift off in this wind.

Then I look back. She's got a drone jacket on. She's going to try and shorten the distance. It's a risky move. It's so cold and windy up here, the air so thin, it pays to keep your feet on solid metal. Gotta hand it to her, though, she's got guts.

I duck out of the wind into the base of the tower. There's an empty bottle of absinthe, an old golf club and a bucket of titanium balls. Someone was using the deck for a driving range. Someone who works here. The club doesn't even have optics or an air choke, so it's not the kind of thing a member of the Five Families would use.

I tip the bucket over with my foot and the balls spill out. This might work.

Battling the wind, Thend comes floating around the corner, guns extended.

I take a swing and send one of the balls streaking toward her. Well, near her. In her general vicinity. Okay, it misses her by ten meters.

Golf is hard. Especially on the rim of a Martian volcano.

She pulls the trigger and a stream of diamond flechettes zip toward me, glittering red in the blinking lights. But she's wobbling in the drone jacket, so only a few of them hit me and miss the important stuff. I'm not too worried. Obviously they can heal me up quite easily downstairs.

I swing at another ball. It's a lot closer this time. I miss her by only a couple meters.

I'm going to die because I've never played golf before and part of me is perversely proud of that.

The balls are rolling every which way now and I'm swinging blindly, chopping at them and expecting a column of synthetic diamond flechettes to pop a core through me. One of the balls slams into the edge of the tower and ricochets right into her face, dislodging the airhoodie.

This is not the way I want things to end for her.

"This is not the way I want things to end, Thend," I shout.

But she's committed. She's all in. I can see it in her eyes. She's trying to steady her aim while fighting the wind and cold, thin air.

"My name is Hinton, you shitbag," she croaks.

I give up on the balls completely and throw the club as hard as I can at her. It spins end over end through the swirling, flashing tendrils of ice clouds and connects solidly with Hinton, sending her sprawling off the edge of the platform. She's mouthing obscenities at me.

Not my fault she doesn't have magtaps on.

The drone jacket is not up for the task of keeping her aloft. She's drifting away and slowly, slowly falling toward the sloping surface kilometers below.

I peer over the edge, keeping my magtaps locked tight.

She might survive the fall, but she won't survive the lack of oxygen. And I don't think whoever she works for will come for her. She's disposable. We're all disposable. But she's part of something shady, and even more disposable than most. I hope her family gets some debt relief out of this fiasco at least.

I can see inside the changing room. Essential is gone and the security team is waiting, guns raised. Sanders is with them. They're going to have a lot of questions.

I look out over Mars again, trying to act like I'm upset. I just want to make sure Essential has time to escape.

An ad crashes my feed.

Space Captain dry shampoo—perfect for quantum jumps and dating conventions. Set course for a galaxy of adventures.

"Did you make it out okay?" I ask.

"Yes," Essential says. "Barely. I saw what happened. I'm sorry."

"She made her choice. But I lost my best lead."

"And we're no closer to the servers."

"You're no closer," I say.

"The Hive is our second choice. I'm headed there to start surveillance."

"I'm going back to Earth. Whatever's happening with Jynks is linked to the sunbelt. That's where I'll find my answers. And possibly grandmamma."

"What?"

Halo told me our grandmother was an original climate pioneer and that it radicalized our mom. I haven't shared that little nugget with Essential yet.

"I'll tell you that story sometime over a bottle or six of absinthe. Be careful and connect when you can."

16

"That was all very unusual," Sanders says.

We're standing in the hall surrounded by Mytikas security—they look sleepy and confused but are all weirdly beautiful—and a few members of Mars SF, with more arriving. Singhroy Clystra is here too. He looks rattled.

A recovery pod is going out after the body but they're in no rush.

"There was a great deal of your time unaccounted for," Sanders says. "And discrepancies in the staff logs. We can't find any record of the staff person assisting you."

"Yeah, I'm telling you, buddy, there's something weird going on," I say.

"I understand the definition of weird," Sanders says. "But I am having difficulty applying it in this situation. Anomalous would be more accurate."

I know Sanders is beaming info directly to Halo. There's no reason not to start building my case. The last time I was on Mars, I built a grand lie and that mostly worked out. I'm mostly telling the truth now, and that makes it a lot easier.

"The frost burn out there in the Choke was a mercenary who was pretending to be a resister on Earth. I shot her face up pretty good down there last week. But turns out, she was reconstructed here."

"Certainly not with my knowledge," Singhroy Clystra says. "I'm as shocked as you.

"Then you'll be even more shocked to know there's a

secret lab in this facility that has been blotted from Halo, possibly even hidden from the Fist. It's where she was healed and it's where a great deal of research is being done on brains."

There's a flash of white and wet sizzle that slices up through the lift tunnel, followed by a gust of smoke and flames. Alarms start to sound.

"Correction, there *was* a secret lab here," I say. "And it's likely whatever is happening is all tied up with the false murder charge against Jynks Martine and whatever is happening in the sunbelt. So yeah, Sanders, weird is definitely the operative word."

One of the officers from Mars SF taps my feed and drops a message. A summons to headquarters.

There's nothing sadder than being forced to leave a luxury spa with a thousand kinds of liquor, especially because I know what's waiting on the other side—an interview with Chundar Hotsip. It's our first organic meeting and my expectations are low.

They go even lower when we disembark from the Quadrigon in Jezero an hour later and there is an armed escort waiting to transport me to Hotsip's office.

Turns out he can vent his frustrations much more effectively in person than over ving.

"I should send you back to Earth," he says. "No, I should arrest you." He's wearing the rusty red uniform of Mars SF, and the already improbably angular collars and cuffs seem especially right-angled on him.

He lets his thoughts thunder forward.

"I should arrest you and throw you in the Choke *with* Martine."

"Those are a lot of good options," I say. "And it's your choice, obviously. But I'm thinking if you hinder the investigation, like I said, Martine walks on a technicality.

Then you lose your job. Then she lets me go anyway." I pretend to ponder it. "Actually, I kind of like that plan because it means I can get back to Earth sooner."

"Why would anyone *choose* to live on Earth," he asks, his anger temporarily giving way to genuine confusion.

"For the fresh air, obviously. And the sense of community. Also, the rats on Earth don't wear such fancy uniforms."

"Look, just tell me why in the name of the melted Mercury solar array were you creeping around a luxury resort? A resort that now has been attacked."

"Yeah, about that. I was trying to not be killed by a mercenary who I already shot once on Earth," I say. "The real question you should be asking is why a so-called resister from Earth was on Mars receiving the very best health care possible to have her face put back together."

"Trust me," Hotsip says. "We are asking that question. Not of her. Conveniently for you, she didn't make it. But you do not need to be involved. Your actions are to be confined to the death of Tarteric Hoost."

"Correction," I say. "I'm supposed to be investigating the innocence of Jynks Martine."

"You know the law, guilty until proven innocent for crimes against the Five Families …"

"Or the common good," I say. "I'm clear on that. And everything that isn't directly for the good of the Five Families is against the common good. But someone is going to a lot of trouble to frame Martine, and since someone just tried to glitter me in the skull, I think I might be getting close to the truth."

"I know your story, Larsen. Trouble follows you around like a sad satellite."

"I'm trying to prevent an innocent person from spending her life in a labor camp."

"If she's so innocent, why is she pleading guilty?"

"Yeah, I admit, that doesn't look good, but I'll get to the bottom of it," I say. "Look, we're on the same side here."

"No, we're not," he says. "You're one data discrepancy away from a lifetime inside a stasis sheath buried in a terrorium next to your traitor sister. The only reason you were named lead investigator is because no other cop on Mars or Earth was stupid enough to say yes, even to the famous scientist Melinda Hopwire."

"And here I thought it was because of my dashing good looks and keen investigative skills."

"You're a flameout, Larsen. Luckily, there's no one left around you to take the debt fall when gravity pulls you back down."

He dismisses me with his eyes and pulls a blankface as he starts looking at official security business on his scroll, but I won't give him the pleasure. I keep sitting there. Even Sanders knows the cues and is watching the interaction curiously.

Hotsip refocuses, angry. "What are you waiting for?"

"A hug, I guess?"

"Get out!"

Sanders and I make our way outside.

"You have a special skill for angering people," Sanders says.

"Thanks for noticing again, Sanders. That means a lot."

"It wasn't meant as a compliment. More of an observation."

"I needed to get past the surface with him," I say. "I was monitoring him pretty closely. His vitals—at least those I could measure externally—weren't synced to his anger. Not at first. There at the end, everything spiked. I think the first part was all an act."

"You mean you were intentionally trying to rouse his emotions? That's shrewd of you."

"Let's just say I got to keep two satellites in orbit with only one thrust booster."

"That is a nonsensical statement," Sanders says.

It's another perfect day under the climate-controlled Jezero dome. A few people are out, walking toward the main park. When their scrolls pop on me, most hurry in the other direction. A few stop and stare, and then hurry in the other direction.

I'm a celebrity. Or a curiosity, I guess. The person cruel enough to lock up his sister to protect the Five Families from the Variance. The person stupid enough to assist an accused murderer who targeted the Fist. The person lacking family honor and common sense.

I open my feed and summon a pair of drone jackets. I check to make sure my debt is draining to the Five Families. I'm not going to be a blast shield for these wealthy polyps on my own credits.

I lift off toward the top of the dome, and Sanders follows me without a word. I realize I'm starting to enjoy having a synthetic companion. I'll miss him when I'm back on Earth.

From up near the top of the dome, I can see through the soft spirals across the Choke. It's almost noon, and the planet looks peaceful and deceptively lovely. A small convoy of gravel sifters is kicking up a linear dust storm as they scrape new building material into their gaping maws. There's a garbage scow passing slowly overhead loaded with toxic waste generated from some of the nearby manufacturing domes, like Holden. It's headed toward the garbage satellite to be collected, sorted and shipped to Earth for possible re-use.

The garbage satellite where the resistance is now

located. That makes me think of Essential, and that makes me think of Mel. And that makes me think of Martian absinthe and my sudden desire to consume large quantities of the stuff.

I dip down and Sanders follows suit. We land outside Mel's building.

"Listen, Sanders ...," I start to say.

"Yes, I will wait outside," he says.

"You really do learn," I say. "I'll be back soon. And anyway, you can watch everything from any of the dozen monitoring devices inside her place. And you should. It will be a good learning opportunity."

I signal Mel through my scroll and go inside.

The door opens as I approach. There's music playing, a complex piece with swelling arrangements that seem to fold in on themselves, and then rearrange and return, and stick to every flat surface.

It's coming from one of those omni-directional liquid transducers—a wet speaker. The music drops alone would cost me a year's debt. But it sure sounds good.

She's kneeling by an open window shaking soil into a container. Wisp is next to her, playing with the flowing sleeve of her sark.

It's a heart-breaking scene of perfect contentment. It could have been mine. Should have been mine. But I managed to drive that flaming cabarang right into the waste treatment pond years ago.

"This is nice," I say. "The music."

At the sound of my voice, Wisp jumps about half a meter straight up, lands in a tangle of tiny paws and then arches her back and hisses.

Mel laughs and I feel gravity shift on the entire planet, then settle back into place as she realizes she has no right to laugh.

She dusts her hands on her knees and stands. Wisp scurries under a clear table made of some amber substance and watches me closely, kitten-fiercely.

"What have you found out?" she asks.

"I don't think she did it."

"I know she didn't do it."

I nod. "It might help if she actually said she was innocent. Not many people are taking me seriously right now."

"You should be used to that," she says.

"That's an interesting way to say 'Thanks for risking your life for my lover, Crucial.'"

"Sorry," Mel says. "I didn't mean that. I'm tired and sad and worried. I don't understand what she's doing."

"I don't either. I mean, there are only a few options here. Either she murdered him and we're both idiots—maybe she wasn't in her right mind and didn't even know she killed him—or else someone has something on her, something big. Something big enough she's willing to trade her life for it."

"She's not like that, she doesn't have anything to hide."

"Not hide," I say. "Something to risk."

Mel sighs and closes her eyes, then shakes her head.

The music is swelling and, jaws clenched, she snatches up the acoustic stylus and drips in a tonal precipitate that lowers the whole piece into the darker realms.

"You think it's me. That she's protecting me."

"It makes sense," I say. "Whoever is behind this is taking on the Fist head to head. That's a lot of thrust."

"She better not be pulling any hero shit for me."

"Cut her a break, I'd do the same," I say. I am literally doing the same. Although now is not the time to profess my undying love. I'll save that for about one second before my heart stops. "I mean, if I were her, I'd so the same. You know, if I loved you. Still loved, I mean."

Mel either doesn't hear or kindly chooses to ignore my stammering. "I'm going to talk to her."

"Don't go in there being all, you know, you. I'll figure this out. Just be patient. She's liable to do something really stupid if she thinks we're on to her. Don't force her to do anything drastic until I can get to the bottom of this. And be safe. I've got a solid lead back on Earth. Maybe get yourself a glitter gun until I get back."

"I've got Wisp," she says.

I look at the tiny little cat glaring at me from beneath the table. "Yeah, maybe get two glitter guns."

17

I was sad to leave Mars.

Well, not Mars exactly. Sanders, I guess. And probably Mel. Mostly Mel.

Only Mel, really. And that stupid angry little kitten of hers. Whisk or Puff or whatever.

The ride back was rough. Mars was orbiting close so it should have been a short flight, but we hit some kind of weird gravity wave that messed with the quantum engine and caused improbability instability. We overshot drop orbit by a couple million kilometers. A couple million kilometers closer to the sun.

I'm not the best quantum traveler under perfect circumstances. Feeling like you're in two places at once is exhausting and unsettling. Add in the possibility of flying too close to the sun and being incinerated in a flash of molten metal—one of my least favorite ways to die—and I was a mess.

Even though my scroll was filled with the shipboard messages telling all the passengers in a calm, cheery voice not to worry, it somehow made it worse. I ended up taking on a lot of new debt trying to drink my way into an uneasy acceptance of my fiery fate. And not with the good stuff, either. Cheap salt beer, and lots of it.

By the time we got back on course and close to Earth, I was in rough shape—drunk and dehydrated.

So naturally, someone beautiful was waiting for me

when I stumbled off the ship, blinking in the harsh light and elbowing my way past other angry passengers. It was Lauren Valentine.

"Hi Crucial, good flight?" she asks, her eyes flashing just the right amount of sarcasm and disgust.

"We, uh, had a little glitch," I say.

"I saw the update," she says, tapping her temple near her OCD implant.

"I might have had too much salt beer," I say with a thick tongue.

"Lucky I brought this." She hands me a pill. It's a detox flush. Almost as bad as quantum travel. Feels like your blood is boiling for a second or two.

"Come on, down the hatch," she says. "We've got a long day ahead of us."

I take the pill and grimace as it does the job. "Us?" I ask. "What are you talking about?"

"Haven't you heard? The Fist asked me to accompany you into the sunbelt. You know, to help monitor the investigation. This may come as a surprise to you, but they don't trust you very much."

The detox flush worked. My headache is gone and the light on Earth isn't as bright. I mean, it's still bright enough to scorch your retinas, but that's an everyday thing, not a salt beer thing. I slip my goggles into place.

Even as she's talking, I get an official d-mail transmission. A mission brief signed by Chundar Hotsip. I guess the quantum displacement interfered with delivery. I blink it open with my OCD to display in my scroll.

Mission parameter for Crucial Larsen: Investigate resistance activities in the sunbelt based on evidence uncovered at Mytikas as related to the murder charges facing Jynks Martine. To be accompanied by Chancellor Lauren Valentine, official liaison for the

Five Families, and a three-person security detail. Duration of mission: three Earth days.

"Do I have to call you chancellor, or can I stick with Valentine?"

"Valentine is fine," she says. "I just hope this doesn't change things between us, me being so much smarter and more accomplished than you."

I'm really starting to like her. "And humbler too."

She laughs. "Our escort is waiting. I figured you might want to get rolling since the timer has started."

"I don't have any gear for a three-day excursion into the sunbelt."

"I took the liberty of pulling together everything you need. And charging it to the Singhroys."

I can't stop the smile spreading across my face. "Perfect."

We follow the crowds of Earthers returning to their sad lives. Some are clutching plush giraffe simulacrums— bleating and squirming— for their kids, and I see at least one bottle of absinthe with a bow on it. That bottle alone is worth a small fortune and I hope they don't have far to go. That kind of wealth out in the open will get you killed on Earth.

We exit into the boarding pod and push past rows of smiling lottery winners waiting for their adventure to begin. They look so excited and hopeful. Mars really pisses down my back sometimes.

We clear the crowds and Valentine nods forward, redirecting my attention. There's a heavily fortified camion waiting for us with three people standing next to it.

Camions, known as Janes, are small-op transports with sturdy, boxy bodies that have a self-contained living environment big enough to sustain four comfortably and armor thick enough to stop a rail gun slug without necessarily pulping everyone inside. They've got about a hundred different kinds of weapons on board. But Janes are no frills—a solid rocket assembly on a reinforced ion thruster frame. They're not graceful or comfortable—especially as there are five of us—or particularly fast, but they've got lots of juice so you can lift up high enough to cover long distances quickly and multidirectional treads for settling down and moving across the ground when gravity becomes a liability. They're especially good in sand.

The Jane is the perfect way to get us to the sunbelt.

I was assigned to a Janes brigade once for a bit, on loan from the Tarterics, during the Consolidation Wars. There was a particularly nasty bit of business when the Fehrvens went after a startup in the Middle West. Some other family was pushing for a place in the Five Families ruling class by bringing bacteria-based building bricks to market and the Fehrvens, with their myco-concrete, were not impressed.

The Living Bricks LLC troops dug in right on the eastern edge of the sunbelt, protected from fliers by the desert on one side and with all their hardware, ready for an air assault on the other side. We rolled in from the sunbelt with about 200 Janes and leveled the place in 45 seconds flat.

I was coughing up living brick dust for a month. There's probably still some growing in my lungs. That was my first weapons-free mission, leaving me with a lot of bad memories associated with Janes.

This should be a fun trip.

The security detail is waiting outside the transport. They're in civilian clothes but they stand like they're still in the security forces, tense and ready and confident.

I synch them in my scroll for their vitals. The big one is Manton Fleiss. He's damn near two meters tall and 127 kilograms. He looks like he might be made of solid bronze, the kind they use for bearings in builder-bots. I wonder if he's ever lost a fight in his life or even smiled.

Next to him is Agna Dormer. She's about half his size but makes up for it with twice the attitude. She has dark hair cut short and bright eyes. Too bright. They're clearly enhanced. She's looking at me, through me and all around me at the same time. All three of my escorts are armed, but she's ultra-armed. I try to count all the visible weapons strapped to her tiny frame, but I get bored. She's looking at me with something bordering on disgust that I am weaponless. Or maybe it's pity.

"I thought he was some kind of cop or something," she says.

"He's a labor cop," the man next to her says. He makes it sound like an insult. He's about my height and weight. A little younger. Thirteen years and six months younger to be exact. My scroll tells me his name is Dint Tooms. He's the ranking officer. "It's where the burnouts go."

This should be a *really* fun trip.

"Sweet Jane," I say, ignoring them as I pat the vehicle. "Any chance I can get one of those glitter guns from you?" I ask Dormer.

"Let us handle the hard stuff," she says. "You just sit back and enjoy the ride."

"Fine. I hope you brought lots of solar radiation block," I say to Valentine. "And synthwine."

I hop in, pull Valentine up behind me and then follow the narrow passageway back to the living quarters and flop down on the berth farthest from the tread wall.

"Hey, that's my bunk," Fleiss says, poking his massive, gleaming head through the passageway.

"Not anymore," I say. "I'm here on official Five Families business and you're all expendable quantum bilge.

Get this Jane moving or I'll have you replaced with steambots."

This is the moment. If he takes it the right way, I'm going to end up on the wrong side of a beating and electrocuffed in the hold for the duration. He takes it the wrong way, the way I intended.

A flash of hurt and confusion flickers across his face and he withdraws and moves to the front. I can hear them grumbling.

Valentine sits down on the bunk next to me, but I stand. "Take this one. There will be less vibration."

"You have a special way with people," she says.

The Jane roars to life. "Hold on," I say. "They're going to try to shake us up a little."

She braces and sure enough, the Jane jumps forward with a rattling roar.

"Sorry about the rough takeoff," Tooms says, breaking into our scrolls. "Everybody okay back there?"

"Just fine," I answer. "But I spilled my synthwine all over your stuffelbag. Don't worry, I can give you lessons on flying a Jane if you want. They're pretty responsive once you get the hang of it."

We can hear more grumbling from up front and Valentine smiles.

A real fun trip.

18

We touch down a few kilometers from the edge of the sunbelt. The sunbelt is a thin zone of hyper-arid desert that cuts through the Middle West like a brown knife, but it's not clearly delineated, so "edge" is a bit of a misnomer. When the climate change became irreversible, everyone expected the equator to take the hit—and it did—but the sunbelt was a nasty little surprise. Like finding a rat hair in the warm cup of emetic they hand out during zero-g training.

Apparently, something about the changing upper level wind patterns swirling around the coast range turned a stretch of land between what used to be Mexico and what used to be Canada into a blistering desert.

"I still don't understand how the blizards ended up owning this little slice of Hades," I say.

"Please don't use that awful slang," Valentine says.

We're sitting in the front of the Jane with our new best friends looking out through the reinforced polymer nav-window. Tooms is navigating, strapped in tight, and Fleiss is to his right. It's almost impossible to see past his thick neck. Dormer is in the jump seat behind them, facing me, and running yet another diagnostic on one of her weapons.

This one is a heat wand. It squirts out a ribbon of thermonuclear gas burning at close to 5,000 degrees. Useful if you want to burn out a building or cut through a rocket. If it goes off in here, we're all instantly ashed.

"Would you point that thing the other way?" I ask.

She just smiles.

"What *should* we call them if we can't call them blizards?" Fleiss asks, turning in his seat. He's so earnest. Slow and earnest.

Against my better judgment, I'm starting to like him.

"How about people?" Valentine says. "They're just people."

"People who look like lizards and eat regular people," Tooms says.

"There's no evidence of cannibalism," Valentine says.

"Be sure to tell them that as they eat you," he says.

"No one is getting eaten on my watch," I say.

Valentine has been telling me about how it all came to be, and our escorts have been hanging on every word, even as they pretend not to listen. Except for Fleiss. We were just to the part where the Blevin family sank a fortune into gene editing in hopes of creating an adaptation to the warming planet. And possibly on the surface of Mars.

But things went to hell like they always do when people and credits are involved. The second-gen adaptations were too much to overcome by simple debt reduction, and forcing people to undergo the treatment defeated the purpose. So the Mars settlement went a different direction, the blizards became the Blevin folly and the sunbelt was given over to that mistake.

"They basically signed over the deeds to the sunbelt to the original climate pioneers," Valentine says. "It's one of the few stretches of privately owned land outside Five Families' control."

"Land for which they suddenly seem to have a renewed interest," I say.

"It seems likely that my presence on Earth poring over legacy files related to the original deeds does indicate some renewed interest in the sunbelt."

"Why don't they just take it back?" I ask.

"For better or worse," Valentine says, choosing her words carefully because every sentence ever muttered by anyone is recorded and analyzed and stored, "the Five Families recognize contracts as sacrosanct. Their ascendance, while some might question the unequal influence of wealth, was based on always honoring the power of a contract."

"Unless there are extenuating circumstances," I say. "Like resistance activities, activities that would indicate the blizards—sorry, the lizard-like former-human cannibals—are actively supporting the Variance. Something like that would require martial law and probably revocation of their land rights."

Dormer tucks the heat wand into its forearm sheath. "I hope we run into some of those resisters down here. I could use the workout."

Valentine gives me a sly grin and a little nod. If only Dormer knew a member of the resistance was sitting a few centimeters away.

The Jane is rumbling across a stretch of dusty nothing. Through the reinforced windows, we can see a few tufts of grass struggling to live every dozen meters. In the distance is a cluster of buildings.

"That's Sierra Station," Tooms says. "That's where civilization, such as it is, ends. Beyond that is nothing but sand and flesh-eating blizards."

"And a nasty sunburn if you don't keep your shade turned on," I say.

The challenge with the sunbelt, Valentine says, is that the blizards don't have OCDs. So, Halo can't track them individually and their actions can't be predicted. Nobody really knows anything about them. Even though there are just shy of a trillion satellites beaming back data even second about the sunbelt, nothing up close and personal. Anecdotal evidence suggests several thousands of blizards live in the sunbelt, but no one really knows. Halo used to record sporadic individual heat signature readings, murky and inconclusive, but even those ended.

They tried sending in aerial reconnaissance and FIDOS, fully independent digital overland systems, but the machines—basically good-natured cameras on four legs—never captured anything usable. Then they disappeared.

They sent a Janes division in to find the FIDOS. Only half of them made it back. Even with satellites watching and analyzing everything, the Janes got hit in the middle of a sandstorm. A haboob. Which is weird because there was no wind predicted that day.

By the time it subsided, most of the Janes were disabled and the troops were wounded and bleeding, scattered and scared.

After that, they sealed it all in with a kilometer-wide band of marrow mines—horrible little microbubble burners that leap up and attach to the calcium in skeletons. There's also a steel curtain of motion-activated tumble-scythe clusters that leap up and chop and tangle around anything that moves, even so much as a shadow flying over. They protect the sunbelt against any rogue fliers—from drone jackets to airships, including Janes—attempting to cross over.

They call it Desolation Boulevard. I think it's as much to keep desperate humans out of the unmonitored wasteland utopia as it is to keep the blizards in.

We rumble through into Sierra Station, a cluster of heavily fortified bunkers sunk into the barren land. It's one of a string of outposts around the perimeter of the sunbelt and one of the worst places in the world to be stationed.

Terminally hot, and your closest neighbors are cannibal monsters.

The sun is beating down and unlike the major urban centers, soldiers along the border need to be awake in the hottest part of the day. Most of them are in the bunkers which, despite the climate controls, are stifling hot during the day and freezing at night.

Two soldiers are out in the direct sunlight. They have their shades on, digital light distortion that blocks the worst of the solar rays, so they look grayed-out and drab. I suspect they look that way even when they turn the shades off.

They watch us suspiciously as we rumble toward Desolation Boulevard. I don't think it's angry suspicion, just general suspicion that people are doing something, anything, that isn't routine and boring.

Our feeds light up as they chat with us.

"Are you with the guy who's defending a 2F murderer?" one asks, his face impassive.

"Yeah, that's him all right," Tooms says.

"Does he have a death wish?" the other asks.

I probably do. But I don't answer.

"Yeah," Dormer says. "And it's our asses on the line."

"You stay here with us," one says. "Let him take the Jane. Why risk it?"

"A one-year debt-pause, that's why," Fleiss says. "I'm going to eat so much marzipaste, they'll have to open a whole new orbit orchard. And wash it down with an ocean of salt beer."

"Still not enough to get me out there," he says. "The blizards'll strip the meat right off your bones."

"Just turn off the mines and tumble-scythes until we get through the boulevard. We'll catch you on the bounceback."

"Hopefully," the soldier says.

The dashboard of the Jane lights up with information as the defenses go down and the nav plots a thin course through the dead zone.

There aren't a lot of animals or birds to begin with anywhere on Earth, but there are zero living things in Desolation Boulevard—just some scorched remnants of raccoon skeletons and a few puffs of feathers that might have once been crows. We're all holding our breath until we get across and the defenses fire up again.

"Nothing to it," Tooms says.

I don't say a thing. Hotsip just sent me an encrypted file. I column off the conversation so I can open it. It's footage from the Janes division ambush.

The file opens in the middle of a swirling, gritty chaos. People are screaming, glitter guns are popping out flechettes. There's a puff of rail guns and a terrible humming. There are vague, humanlike forms moving through the madness—the footage ends with just a microsecond of a double-lidded eye, brilliant burning yellow with a slash of black diamond for a pupil, glaring into the OCD of a dying soldier. Then it goes black.

Well, that's terrifying.

Hotsip's an asshole. He could have shared that before we got into the sunbelt. I certainly would have brought more booze.

19

We're keeping it close to the ground now. Dormer is piloting. Tooms is in the seat next to her, eyes locked into the multidirectional reconnaissance system. Fleiss is supposed to be sleeping so he can take the next shift. But he's hovering around, his bulk getting in the way of everything, and it feels like he's itching to punch something. Probably me, given I'm the reason they're here in the first place. Or maybe he's always like that, seething just below the surface.

Hell, maybe everyone is always like that, and the only difference is that some hide it better.

The Jane lumbers along, hugging the tox-line just under the air sludge, high enough for Dormer and Tooms to take evasives against land-to-air weaponry but low enough for me to have a ground view using microspecs.

The point of the mission is to investigate the coordinates Essential dredged up on Mytikas during the Halo blackout. I'm the only one who knows them so I'm playing it like a hunch, heading in that general direction.

I suspect Valentine wouldn't mind finding some blizards. Climate pioneers. Whatever. The crew is convinced they're armed because who knows what they scavenged before they were sealed in or took from the Janes they ambushed.

A fair point. That's why we're moving slowly. Valentine and I are strapped into side-by-side chairs in the tiny observation deck, facing the floor-to-ceiling window. She's watching the desert pass under us, and I'm sneaking looks at her profile.

After all her research, Valentine is one of the most knowledgeable people alive regarding the sunbelt apartheid. I'm glad to have her around, and not just because she's got a brain full of blizard facts and history.

My guess, though, is that Valentine isn't just here for this assignment and my good looks. She's also sleuthing around for Essential and the resistance. They must want to know why someone is faking resistance attacks on the sunbelt frontier.

Hell, I want to know why and it's not even my problem.

We're in the last part of the day, with the sun starting to set and the ground shimmering in the heat. Stretching out below us is endless rock and sand, most of it bleached white or close to it. Like bones. No water, not a speck of it, although the memory of a wetter past is etched into the exposed stone—barren riverbeds and what look like craters but could be dried-up lakes.

So far, there's no sign of anything living down here, no intentional movement. Even from this high up, I can see when the wind picks up the sand, creating furious funnels that charge across the landscape and just as fast disappear back into sandy nothingness.

We pass over what looks like the wreckage of human habitation. The first sign of past life. Must be the remnants of a small town predating the original exodus from this area—crumbling foundations, rusted-out water towers, clusters of farm machines, long gone to rot.

I lean back in my chair.

"It's eerie, isn't it?" Valentine asks.

"Remind you of anything?"

"The Choke," she says.

"Yeah, but like its opposite twin. Here it's hot and there it's cold. But both are deadly."

The Jane shudders as we move over a small mountain ridge, temporarily caught in a superheated updraft.

"Did you read the file I sent about the exodus?"

"I did," I say.

"Any questions?"

"Only about a million."

Valentine smiles, and the light from her eyes reminds me of a full moon in my desert sleep sim.

According to the file, people rushed to volunteer for the climate pioneer program because the associated debt relief was huge. Life-changing even. But can anything that offers relief really be voluntary for the desperate?

Eventually, about 10,000 people, give or take, including grandmamma, got past the lottery and went through the genetic alterations, coding in genetic material from lizards, to mitigate against extreme weather. They said it was to understand how best to colonize Mars, but looking at the "winners," it seems more likely they were trying to increase survival outcomes in unlivable places—the sunbelt or the Choke—so they could have cheaper, sturdier workers.

The survival rate was dismal. Half died before they even left the experimental facilities at Blevin University. The ones who lived were celebrated as the world's most evolved and modern worker, and for a while their lives were decent. They did fine in the heat as well as the cold, and the Five Families sent them around Earth, and Mars, to test their endurance in extreme environments.

"How did they go from almost celebrities to penned up in the sunbelt?" I ask.

"An edited woman, one who mated with a non-edited human, gave birth. The infant was born with scaled skin and her eyes were positioned slightly farther apart. But the real shocker was the appearance of a parietal eye," Valentine says.

"What's that?" Fleiss asks.

She seems pleased that he's interested.

"It's a third eye, on top of the head," she says. "They immediately cracked down on reproduction, but it was too late. The original test subjects were beginning to mutate quickly too. Mostly scales replacing skin, a few got the beginnings of tails. And they started developing some interesting resistance to digital surveillance. But after making such a show of them, the Five Families couldn't very well make them all disappear."

"And so, they were exiled to the sunbelt," I say.

"Correct, plus given contracts for the land to make them go willingly. They were basically a new species, and the implications of that for humanity generally were huge. The scientific consensus at the time was if they procreated, after about ten generations they would no longer be human. And if they chose not to procreate to prevent that for their children, well, then they would just die off. Either way, the problem would work itself out. But only if they were isolated."

Fleiss is sitting down in the corner at a nourishment station, listening to every word Valentine is saying.

"That was fifty-one years ago," I say. "Which way did they go, babies or not? How many of them are here now?"

"Nobody knows. It's brutal here, and even with their adaptations, many likely perished in the early years. If they lived, we don't know if they reproduced or not."

"How could anyone have been so stupid? Even I can see that putting lizard genes in humans was bound to backfire," I say.

"No shit," Fleiss mutters. "Making cannibals from scratch."

"Well, charitably, we can say it proved to be a poor hypothesis," Valentine says.

"Or we can say that they experimented on desperate humans," I say.

She shrugs, and her eyes say what she won't aloud because Halo is always listening. Instead she says, "Or we can say that's how science works. Learn from the mistakes."

"What exactly was learned?" I ask.

"How not to modify genes, I suppose. Today, genes are edited for cosmetic and intelligence purposes, and in some cases for athleticism. And of course, to eliminate disease. But science has moved past inter-species initiatives. For better or worse, it was a paradigm-shifting scientific experiment."

"Do they have enhanced powers?" Fleiss asks.

"I don't think so," Valentine says with a smile. "Maybe longer tongues."

She didn't see the video Hotsip sent. Blizzard superpowers are apparently chewing up humans in a tornado of sand and spitting them out in a million tiny bloody pieces.

"Might have the ability to camouflage themselves," I say. "Real lizards can do that."

Valentine looks at me, her eyes registering a surprised curiosity. "I suppose that is a possibility. It would explain why Halo can't see them. Now, wouldn't *that* be interesting?"

"We just registered something moving," Tooms shouts from the front. "Shields up. Buckle in and we'll get some altitude."

I see disappointment cross Valentine's face. She wants to meet a blizard.

"Negative. This is mission-critical. Take it down. I want

a closer look," I say.

Fleiss looks over at me like I'm wearing a used decompression suit from a waste reclamation plant.

20

"I've never seen anything like it," Tooms says. He's strapped in the navigation chair looking out at a foreign landscape—stillness.

The Jane is parked in the remains of an empty town. Completely empty. There are no beetlers, no people at all, no fliers, no transports—there's nothing moving. Not even a rat. Just crumbled buildings and sand.

Literally anywhere on Earth outside the sunbelt, you see people—usually hundreds, even thousands, all talking simultaneously through their OCDs to hundreds of other people talking to hundreds of other people—on every inhabitable square meter.

The silence and stillness are unsettling.

"This was a town called Kay Falls," Valentine says. "The 'Falls' refers to a waterfall. The area had a great deal of surface water. Oddly enough, we don't have good data on what the waterfalls actually looked like."

"What happened to the town?" I ask. "The people?"

"When the climate shifted, the investment required to keep the area habitable grew too expensive. Most people took the option to move into wards. A few stayed behind and may have been absorbed into the climate pioneer society."

"Or eaten by them," Fleiss says.

"I'll say it again. Nothing in our data suggests they eat

people," she says. "When the sunbelt was deeded to the climate pioneers, this town and many others were simply abandoned."

It certainly looks abandoned. Most of the largest buildings have toppled, 50 floors or more now stretched out across neighboring structures. Others are missing roofs or walls, with sand and tech-trash built up inside.

I feel nervous, like we're being watched. I always feel nervous though. That comes with combat experience. My new friends are probably feeling it too. And they don't even know about that damn yellow eye.

But I think the fastest way to unravel this thing is to attempt contact with the blizards.

"Let's go for a walk," I say.

"Yeah, I'm not going out there," Fleiss says. He's rattled.

"For the love of the golden mean," I say. "You are literally too big to be eaten by a blizard. And you're solid muscle. They wouldn't *want* to eat you."

"I think I'd be pretty tasty. And I'm not going out there. Not blind."

"We've been scanning the entire time, with not a single sign of motion after the initial trigger," I say.

"Then why do we need to go outside at all? Trust the data," Dormer says.

"Because I want to see for myself. You can't always trust your feed. How about we send up some pigeons first? Will that make you feel better?"

"Maybe. But probably not," Dormer says.

"Let's do the pigeons. They can take a look around while we sit here all safe and snug so the big bad lizard people don't scare you," I say.

"You're not a nice person," Fleiss says. "I think it comes from a place of insecurity."

"Thank you for the diagnosis, Doctor Gristle."

Dormer laughs and keys in the activation sequence to launch a dozen fresh pigeons—multispectral surveillance drones—and as they zip out to scan the ruins, syncs their views to the Jane screens.

We see an aerial view of more and more nothing. Shattered buildings and ruffled sand dunes and old transport vehicles half buried and bleached from the sun. But no motion. No life.

When the pigeons return to the roost, Halo crunches the data through a deep analysis and there's not a pip of output to suggest a single living thing.

"Okay," I say. "I'm going out there. I'll go alone if you all are too scared to do the one job you're supposed to do."

I gather my gear, my shade and some glasses. "I wouldn't mind taking a glitter gun, or any weapon really," I say, looking at Dormer—the walking arsenal.

"Sorry, I don't have extras. But don't worry, I'm coming with you. I'm not scared of blizards."

She probably should be.

Valentine is reaching for goggles too.

"Absolutely not," I say. "You're staying in the Jane."

"I thought you said it was perfectly safe," Fleiss says.

"It is. It is perfectly safe for half-ton soldiers and walking weapons. That's not necessarily the case for history chancellors."

"I'm coming," Valentine says. "It's a rare opportunity to see what's changed here."

Tooms is grinning. "You all go ahead. I'll stay in the Jane and provide tactical support if needed. Which it won't be, because it's perfectly safe out there."

Fleiss gives me a deadly look and unclips a giant rail gun from the armory wall. It could sling a slug big enough to crack an asteroid in half.

"The blizards won't know what hit them," I say.

Outside, it's hot and dusty. The shades are keeping the worst of the rays off us, but it's still searing. I can feel sweat building up on my stomach and around my neck. The air is mostly breathable, so we're not in airhoodies. But the wind is howling and full of fine particulate matter that's burning my eyes and causing my scroll to bleep a lung danger warning.

"Let's head for that structure," I say, pointing toward a mostly intact building. "It looks pretty solid. If anyone, or anything, is stupid enough to be out here, that would be a good place to get out of the wind."

Dormer leads the way. She's got a glitter gun in each hand; she looks loose, but she's wound tight like the wires inside a servomotor. I'm next, then Valentine, with Fleiss bringing up the rear. He's got the gun to his meaty shoulder and his finger on the trigger; his scroll is linked to the targeting system so he always knows where the slug will go. Right now, it's probably aimed at my back.

"You're all clear," Tooms says from the comfort of the Jane. His voice sounds satisfied, like he's drinking something cold. "At the first sign of trouble, I've got more than a hundred juxtaposition missiles lined up. I'll turn everything that's not you into sheetmeat."

Sounds like he's eating too. Probably a personal stash of goodies. He doesn't seem like the sharing type.

The building is one of the smallest, maybe 30 stories. It looks like it was built way before the days of myco-cement. It's a miracle it's still standing.

We're all scanning hard, our scrolls picking up all kinds of nothing. At the door, Fleiss moves up, and he and Dormer enter hot. She goes low and left, he's high and looking right. Valentine and I are standing there like idiots, hoping they come out.

They do.

"It's clear," Fleiss says.

Inside, there's not much left. Sand is piled up to the edges of the windows and there's some trash strewn across the floor The wind is still howling, but we're mostly sheltered. Valentine swipes some sand away from a faded sign on the wall. It's a map.

"I think this was some sort of early consumer hub," she says. "Stores and restaurants, definitely not residential. And this," she says, pointing at a nearby square on the map, "was a data jack. Before Halo and the OCD mandate, data jacks served as community learning centers where anyone could access information on any topic. It might be fun to try and power up a module and get some usage data from the old days."

"You heard her," I say.

Sandwiched between Dormer and Fleiss, we make our way across the open courtyard, ankle deep in sand.

The door to the data jack is blocked by some fallen sheets of metal. Fleiss pulls it down and we realize the sunbelt is not as empty as we'd been led to believe. Someone, or something, has been living in this data jack. And recently. There's bedding, some empty waterbugs and juice sticks for mobile power. And the bones of small animals, picked clean.

The bones are just too much for Fleiss.

"What the hell are you guys looking at?" Tooms asks.

He's watching through our feeds and sees all the litter.

"I don't know about the rest of you, but I'm looking at a very large man having a very bad day," I say, watching Fleiss. He's holding the rail gun like a life preserver.

"We should go back to the Jane," he says. "Right now."

21

"Let's not panic," I say, shutting off my shade and ditching the soother-goggles. "This stuff could have been here for years. Decades. In this climate, it takes forever for anything to degrade."

"Or it could have been here for minutes," Dormer says. She nudges a waterbug with her toe. There's a little condensation sloshing around inside the bottle. Waterbugs are clip-on water generators that use tiny, super-cooled blades to condense water molecules from the air. Perfect for generating a few sips of drinking water when you're slogging through the sunbelt. Or living here.

"Okay, that's fair. But also, maybe that's from a member of the resistance. Weird stuff is going on. This gives us an actual clue."

Valentine is looking at a module that shows signs of recent use. "Look here. Someone was using this one. And I doubt lizard creatures were juicing up this data jack module to find recipes for barbecued humans. Someone was using this for research, and not that long ago. We need to know what they were looking for."

"These juice sticks are like a hundred years old and feeble," I say. "What're the chances we have any with us?"

"I have one," Fleiss says. He leans his gun against the wall and fumbles inside his tactical vest and tosses the stick to Valentine. She unzippers it to spark the charge and then presses it to the charging plate. The screen blinks to life.

It's warped and damaged, but mostly functional and displaying a map of a crater.

"Why were they looking at Mars?" I ask.

"It's not Mars," Valentine says. She's manipulating the controls with her fingers like an old-fashioned pokescreen. "It's a topographic map of a nearby natural feature once known as Crater Lake." She uses her scroll to plot the course and display information, then shares the column with the rest of us. "Crater Lake is about 75 kilometers from here."

It's also the precise location of the coordinates Essential snagged from the brain lab.

Valentine pokes the screen again, pulling up the history. "According to the system, someone was looking at this recently. Like, just a few weeks ago." She prods it a few times to display some of the recent views. The screen wobbles and warps and then the perspective zooms into the crater and down to the very center, and even deeper.

"Why is someone researching a lake that's been dry for a century?" Dormer asks.

"And what's that?" I ask, pointing at a shaded region.

"According to this, there was a series of hydrothermal vents there, where hot water boiled up, heated from the volcanic chambers below."

"There's no water there now, and no active volcano, so why would the resistance care?" Fleiss asks.

Valentine catches my eye and doesn't say a thing. It's amazing how much information we humans have learned to exchange in a silent look.

We both know it's not the resistance. Essential and the rest of her band of jolly misfits don't give a depleted fuel rod about this dry lake. All they care about is finding the Halo servers and melting down the core of the entire debt system.

"That's a damn good question," I say. "And we need to go there and ask those resister ass-splinters ourselves."

Valentine aims a wry, secret smile in my direction. It makes me feel funny, like when Mel says my name.

"Pull up that main image again but view back a little to the edge of the sunbelt," I say, and she returns her attention to the screen.

I tell Halo to match map coordinates with the recent resistance activities and overlay that into a shared column of data. The incursions were all located near the perimeter of the sunbelt right next to Crater Lake.

"That can't be a coincidence," Dormer says.

"Unlikely." I send a request for satellite data and overlay it on the map images. The stream is time-lapsed. We see some flashes and motion from ships arriving and the flash of battle. Just east of the hot spots, there's a giant blurry area stretching out across no man's alley.

I share my feed so we're all looking at the same thing— a data shadow.

"Don't you think it's suspicious that at the exact moment the resistance was hitting these targets, the satellite went down across the perimeter of the sunbelt?" I ask.

"Someone was moving in," Dormer says. "Those were distractions."

"Look alive people," Tooms says from the Jane. "I'm getting weird readings."

Fleiss reaches for his gun leaning near the door. His face falls. "My gun is gone," he says. He sounds simultaneously hurt and shocked.

I'm mostly just scared.

We were no more than three meters from it. In a small room. Also, rail guns can't disappear. They're connected to Halo. Everything is connected to Halo. A hundred alarms should have sounded if anyone so much as touched it. Not to mention our proximity alarms.

Fleiss is searching for it through his scroll but the tracker in the gun has gone dark.

"Now can I have a weapon?" I ask Dormer.

"Absolutely." She tosses me a glitter gun and uses her scroll to reassign ownership to me. I dial up the setting to terminal. She hands another to Fleiss. It looks tiny in his giant hand. She offers one to Valentine, but she shakes her head. "I'm a scholar, not a soldier."

"You may need to be both for a short time," Dormer says.

"Just stay behind me," I say. "Tooms, keep your finger on the launch button of those jux missiles. We're coming back to the Jane. And we may not be alone."

I peek out into the main hall of the building, half expecting a slug to paste my head. Dust is swirling around like the toxic brown clouds that form over dump canyons.

"Goggles and filters," I say. We push our soother-goggles in place, which compensates for the glare, then slip on filters to keep the sand out of our lungs.

"I'll take the lead," I say. "Once I'm through, Fleiss, you go right. Valentine, you stay one step behind and to the left. Dormer, you're bringing up the rear."

She nods. It looks like she's holding three guns, which doesn't even make sense. I realize she's got the heat wand mag-clipped to the barrel of a glitter gun. Smart. And deadly. Especially to everyone in front of her.

"Correction. Dormer, you're on the right flank. I don't want a ribbon of fire up my ass if things go to hell."

"Aww, you noticed," Dormer says.

"Fleiss, you're bringing up the rear. Valentine is the priority here."

Valentine looks just the right amount of scared. She

won't freeze up.

"Nothing to worry about. We just have to cross the courtyard, get outside and hustle to the Jane," I say.

I take a couple of breaths and step out into the open. Our soothers are optimized and we're all looking at the same thing—nothing. Just blasted walls and a tornado of sand.

No blizards. No resisters—fake or real.

Dormer is next, with her glitter guns charged and ready. We keep moving. I'm patched into Fleiss's feed so I can watch Valentine from behind. She's out the door behind us and Fleiss is next. I keep his feed in a column and open the rest of my OCD for what's ahead. We're slogging toward the door out into the open.

I think we're going to make it just fine. No sign of anything dangerous.

We're hustling toward the main door. The wind has decreased from howling to gusting. The perimeter data on my scroll is notching at damn near intermittent 60-knot winds. It came out of nowhere.

Going to be like running face first into a pulsating hull stripper.

I'm less than two meters from the collapsing data jack door when I realize the wind is behaving oddly in the exit, like something is partially blocking it. Something human-shaped. I zoom in, but my optic feed doesn't register anything. I pull my goggles down. It feels like I'm pouring salt in my eyes. I'm getting a weird double image of a translucent person. An especially ugly translucent person.

I squint my OCD eye closed and there's a blizard standing there, not a meter away. A male from the looks of it. He's got rough, scaly skin the color of sand and sunshine, practically invisible. And bright yellow eyes. He smiles, revealing a row of sharp teeth.

He's holding the rail gun he stole from Fleiss, only it's wrapped up in some tattered cloth. When I open my OCD eye, he all but disappears in the data overlay.

I pull up short.

The blizard doesn't raise the weapon, or do anything really, except stand there looking terrifying.

All our feeds are linked through a combat protocol. Everyone sees what I'm seeing, but not like I did when my enhanced eye was shut. "What the Higgs boson is that?" Fleiss screams.

I hear Dormer power up the wand.

"Stop!" I scream. "Hold your fire. Hold your fire!"

The blizard looks at me curiously, then steps out into the sun's glare and sand, disappearing completely.

I'm already dropping to my belly as Dormer shouts, "Hit the deck, old-timer."

The wand belches a ribbon of thermonuclear gas about 20 meters long, cutting through the frame of the door and setting the sand ablaze. Oily smoke billows up and I roll back inside and drag Valentine down and into my arms as Fleiss lets loose a volley of diamond flechettes. We hear them sizzling over us. Tooms launches the jux missiles and they turn everything that isn't us inside out and upside down, the ground shuddering and heaving.

I hold Valentine close as she screams at the chaos.

When things finally calm down, there's no sign of the blizard or the rail gun. The sand around us has been fused into glass from the heat, then shattered from the explosions. The buildings across from us are riddled with glitter and shards of sand glass.

We make it back inside the Jane and lock up tight.

I pour us all a shot of Martian absinthe, a little present Valentine requisitioned from the Five Families. It takes the edge off, but just barely.

"You all really need to work on your fire control," I say to our three bodyguards. "I don't think the blizards are the enemy. He had us dead to rights, with your gun, and didn't kill us."

"We should not trust cannibal lizards to make rational decisions," Fleiss says. "The next time I see a blizard, I intend to kill it before it kills us." He has two rail pistols in holsters at his massive thighs.

I sit down on the edge of Valentine's bunk. She's pale and wide-eyed. "You okay?"

"Yes."

I pour her another shot.

"You did great."

"No, I didn't. I flopped like a musical avatainment series." She drinks the absinthe and puts her hand on my arm. It feels warm, like a tiny heat wand. "Crucial, something is off here. There's something bigger going on."

She's right. Someone corrupted the satellite files. That means someone hacked into the Halo server and blurred the data. And that means Essential is going to be very happy the next time we chat.

22

"You know this is a trap, right?" Dormer asks. "We're almost to the mission coordinates and the tracker on the big guy's rifle 'mysteriously' activates thirty kilometers away."

"All we know for sure is that it's a communication," I say. "We won't know if it's a trap until we investigate."

Everyone is still skittish about what happened in Kay Falls as the Jane circles the area where we got a blip from the gun. Tooms is scouring the landscape for a secure location to put down. He had tried to pull rank and force us to turn back, but with a little help from Hotsip, who admitted pressure was coming from above to see this through, we reached a deal. We've got two hours on the ground and then the Jane leaves—for the lake coordinates or home, whichever makes the most sense.

We're in a desolate stretch of rock and pumice.

"How about we put down on top of that little notch in the ridge right there," I say. "Pretty close to the signal."

"Too risky. That position is swarmable," Fleiss says.

"Swarmable? That's not a word."

"It's a word that means we could get attacked and overwhelmed by a swarm of invisible blizards. It's a descriptive word. I created it."

I try to explain, for the second time, that the man or lizard or whatever the hell it is did not use the weapon against us when it easily could have. But no one is buying my theory that the blizards aren't, literally, cold-blooded killers.

Valentine is on my side, but she's still nervous.

"There's a flat spot on the east edge of that ridge," Tooms says. "It's un-swarmable. That's where we're landing."

Less than five minutes later, we're on the ground. Valentine and I start to suit up. Fleiss and Dormer watch. Tooms is up front ready to trigger the weapons systems at the first sign of anything.

Hotsip ordered the Jane trio to remain inside during our foot surveillance, said it was outside the purview of their mission. I think they feel a little guilty making Valentine and me go out on our own.

"Give me two glitters, three thermite grenades, and a dozen or so pike diversion blockers," I say. I'd take a Bourdette cannon, but the weight would slow us down too much.

"If they're so peaceful, why do you need all that armor?" Dormer says.

"Yeah, peaceful you said," Fleiss says.

"Just give me the godsdamn weapons."

They're hiding their guilt pretty well.

Fleiss hands me a glitter and I tuck it into the holster under my arm and around my shoulder under the shields. Despite being the best damn little gun ever constructed, it might not last long in the unbroken heat of the sunbelt.

He starts to hand me the other one, but Valentine takes it mid-pass.

"Not just a scholar anymore?" Dormer asks.

"I'm a fast learner," Valentine says.

I tuck away all the other deadly goodies in a waist dummy, shut it and link the permissions to my heart rate.

Tooms comes back from the front and he's all business.

"You've got two hours. We'll stay in contact the entire time, of course, and we'll make a decision about a rescue, if needed, based on the probabilities."

"In other words, we're on our own," I say. I look over at Valentine. "You don't have to come, I'll understand."

"Don't be stupid," she says. "It's essential." Her face doesn't flinch when she says that. She doesn't need to send me any hidden signal. I get it.

"What happens if we're late getting back?" I ask.

"We leave you behind," Tooms says.

I want to think he's joking.

"Don't be late," he says.

I set the mission timer ticking in the bottom of my scroll and we shoulder into our bug-out packs and step outside. The Jane door shuts behind us with a pneumatic hiss. The wind has let up some, but visibility is still not more than a few feet. I can't see much of her through the goggles and heat sheathing, so I take Valentine's hand because it seems the simplest way to be sure we don't get separated.

We walk toward a twisted, folded outcropping of rock in the base of the ridge. We're making slow progress, sloshing through old pumice and ground-up basalt. Each imprint of our steps is wiped away by the wind before we take the next step.

Everything pretty much looks the same—an endless spread of rock and boulders and cliffs covered with sand and dirt, most of it blowing around. A few tenacious little scrub plants stuck in cracks, an occasional scuttling of insects, probably ants, and the relentless baking from the sun.

"Ready to come back yet?" Fleiss says through the shared scroll.

"We're doing just fine," Valentine answers before I can respond.

Fine might be overstating it. We've been walking now for 22 minutes, the last ten through fine white sand. It's tough going. But we keep at it, trudging through this hostile place, looking for some sign of life.

Then something slaps me on the glutes. I feel a hand in the small of my back, pushing me forward, then another hand against my waist.

"What the cold hell ...?"

Valentine looks at me with wordless surprise. She's getting it too. She jumps a little, and then her arm moves straight out, like she's being led. Or pulled.

Sand kicks up beside us from shuffling steps and there's more force, pushing me forward toward an outcropping. An outcropping where we'll be out of the sightline of the Jane crew.

I guess it was a trap. I reach for my glitter gun, but my hand gets slapped. Not hard. Just enough.

"Everything okay out there, Larsen?" Tooms asks. "You both are moving like you've got termites in your mcyo-pants." I hear Dormer chuckling.

"Why are you heading toward that outcrop?" Fleiss asks. "We won't be able to see you there. Stop."

Before I can call for a strike, Valentine answers. "I saw something moving back there."

I guess Valentine is making the call. We're just going to die a slow death roasting over a cannibal blizard fire pit.

The unseen forces half push, half drag us to a small cave opening in the rocks. We pass Fleiss's gun leaning out of sight and beeping. I check the mission timer—the Jane is going to leave us in one hour, 38 minutes. We're going to die and no one will know. Including Halo, because I go ahead and use the nanites to block our scrolls so none of it spools later. I don't want our gruesome deaths to become avatainment fodder.

In the shadowy darkness of the cave, the blizards show themselves. It's a swarm, a literal prokking swarm. There must be 50 people-like things standing and crouching there.

Tall, small, chubby, thin, all different shades of tan and gray, some with scales, others with humanish skin. All the eyes are heavily lidded, a few have the third eye. None wear protective gear, but most have on some clothing, although it's pretty skimpy. Most of them are armed.

The one that's been next to my waist shimmers into existence. It's no taller than a street faucet, but wide as a plutonium barrel, with claws for hands that look perfect for disemboweling soft-bellied interlopers.

The one next to Valentine is a good meter taller than either of us, with skinny arms and legs and a tail that's been holding Valentine's hand. The tail flexes and coils away from her, curving around a barely noticeable handle on a door set into the stone. It pulls and a tunnel is revealed.

It pantomimes a sweeping gesture, motioning for us to enter.

"Oh no, I insist, after you," I say.

The blizards close ranks.

"Well, of course, I don't want to be rude."

Still holding hands, we start our descent into blizardtown on a staircase carved into the rock.

23

It's 56 steps to the bottom of the staircase. I count them because I'm always thinking about the best way to go back from where I've already been. Not that it would be easy. There are currently two dozen armed blizards between us and the surface.

Our two formerly invisible escorts are leading the way.

The tall one pauses at the bottom and speaks, his voice a dry whisper.

"You have undoubtedly noticed your Halo feeds are not sending or receiving signals."

I have noticed. It's beautifully silent inside my head. But I don't will the nanites to stand down. I don't want Halo to notice we're off-grid.

"The absence of data may prove difficult for you to explain," he says. "If you prefer to return to the surface to avoid that problem, now is the time."

Way ahead of you, I think. "We'll take our chances."

"Excellent. It's safe to turn off your heat shielding. It will make it easier to interact with us."

I click off the shade and remove the goggles. It's nice and cool in the tunnel.

"What about the pack and the guns?"

"Depends on your comfort level. They'll be safe here."

I have a good feeling that we're not going to be killed, so I drop the pack and keep only one glitter gun. Valentine loses her pack too.

"How is it you can block Halo?" Valentine asks.

The barrel-shaped blizard answers. "Because of the early gene editing, our physiology began to quickly adapt to constant digital surveillance—a threat response. We had friends on the outside who translated that into technology able to hide our structures as well."

I wonder if he's talking about Alduis Coverly. If so, I wonder if I have lizard tech inside me.

I check the timer. Fifty-two minutes to go before the crew abandons us.

"We live largely free from detection by Halo so long as we occasionally show enough motion on the surface to be interesting, but not enough to provoke a closer look."

"And if any Janes crews are unlucky enough to catch you on a bad day?"

I'm thinking about the video Hotsip shared.

"You can ask that of our leaders," the tall one says.

He pushes open a metal door and we follow him into a cavernous round room, an underground labyrinth. The floor is gleaming black stone with alcoves spaced a few meters apart with sculpted tables and stools. The room is ornately decorated with carvings in the rock—some are intricate landscapes, others are sculpted busts of people I don't recognize, still others are water features. A dozen or so doors lead off from the room, like spokes on an old-fashioned wheel. They have bio-luminescent lighting strung up and the whole place sparkles and gleams in shadowy brilliance.

I hear Valentine suck in a breath. "Wow," she whispers.

There are 20 or so blizards hanging around—sitting, talking, drinking, playing games with cards and dazzling stones. Most of them look up when we enter, but none seem surprised or concerned. They quickly return to whatever they were doing.

"What is this place?" Valentine asks. "It's beautiful."

"Thank you," our stocky companion says. "It's sort of a cross between a temple and a park. It's where we socialize."

I try to think what it must feel like to not be constantly connected, to purposely seek out the company and conversation of others. I'm having a hard time wrapping my head around it.

"How many of you live here?" Valentine asks.

"There are about four hundred of us here, several hundred others live in smaller, dispersed communities. And some, we don't really know how many, are much farther along in the evolutionary process. They opt to live outside."

He unlocks a door with an old-fashioned key, the kind I've only seen on the pre-Five Families history feed, and gestures us in. "Please pass through," he says. "They're expecting you. And don't worry, I won't lock this."

We walk a short distance inside what must be a lava tube, lit by stripes of glowing moss, that leads to a larger chamber. The walls are smooth obsidian, black glass, and there's a little waterfall spilling into a clear pool. It's ringed with more glowing moss and pale green mushrooms casting a faint light.

Two more blizards are reclining on thick mats of moss. They stand to greet us. One looks masculine, covered with delicate scales. He has a head of long gray hair reaching his waist. He looks old and I peg him as one of the originals.

He extends his hand. It's weird. I'm used to fist brushes to avoid disease transmission. It's clammy and cold and rough. Valentine does the same.

"Crucial Larsen and Chancellor Valentine," he says. "Good to finally meet you. I am Glyken."

"You know our names?"

"Of course. We don't let just anyone in here." He turns to his companion. "This is Ammit."

She might be younger, but it's hard to say. She has a third eye and bigger, coarser scales that are shaded in beautiful, symmetrical patterns. She's visibly pregnant. Ammit nods a greeting.

"Please sit," Glyken says. "We're curious why you are here, and why you seem intent on finding us. Most cardies try to avoid us."

"Cardies?"

"Those with cardinal genes. They tend to stay clear."

"The sandstorms and slaughter might explain some of that."

"I assume you're talking about the ambush of the Janes crews," Ammit says. "That was an unprovoked attack. We were defending our home from an invading force that had already killed two of us. As you can imagine, we prefer to be left alone."

"And yet, *you* went out of your way to find us," Glyken says. "And tried to prevent your colleagues from opening fire. Why?"

"I'm trying to solve a murder. The head of security on Mars supposedly killed a member of the Five Families. I don't think she did. She's engaged to a woman I love—"

I look over at Valentine.

"—a woman I *used* to love, and I am obliged to help prove her innocence. While investigating, I found a secret medical research facility and coordinates to a location not far from here. I think the so-called resistance activity on the edge of the sunbelt was just a cover to slip unnoticed into blizard territory."

"Crucial, I told you, climate pioneers," Valentine says.

"We use the term Saurian," Ammit says. "And you are correct. Armed forces have breached the sunbelt four times over the past two months. They have established a well-concealed base of operations nearby in the bottom of the ancient volcano."

"Is that the lake?"

"Yes, the crater of the volcano, hence Crater Lake."

"Those are the coordinates we're tracking. What are they doing there?"

"We don't know," Glyken says. "We've been watching them. They appear to be mining, extracting something from the ancient vent."

The timer says 42 minutes.

"Why?"

He pauses. "Let me show you something."

We follow him and Ammit down another set of stairs, past a half-dozen alcoves of what Glyken says are insect farms churning out grubs and termites, their primary food source. The stairs end at a rocky overlook, a natural tube running vertically down, so deep you can't see the bottom.

Mineral-heavy steam fills the air.

"We intentionally built our major city close to this steam vent because it helps slow and delay painful neurological side effects of the gene editing. We don't know how it does this, but it does. Something in the mineralogy of the underlying magma, I surmise."

"How would that help the Five Families?" Valentine asks.

"I don't know," Glyken says. "But there is nothing else of potential value in the sunbelt."

"And if there's value," I say, "the Five Families would know how to exploit it."

The timer is down to 30 minutes.

24

"We should go," I say.

"Please at least join us for a drink to celebrate this new friendship."

"I guess we have time for one," I say. It's not as if the Jane crew would really strand us here.

We walk back up the stairs to the obsidian cathedral. As we sit on the thick moss, a child runs into the room. He has cute little horns and is naked. Well, scaled and clothes-less.

The kid tugs on Glyken's hand. "Grandpa!"

Another Saurian scurries in on all fours. She has a mostly human face and kind eyes. Tired, but kind. She apologizes for the intrusion.

"Darien, leave your grandfather to his visitors," she says.

"Go on, little one. I'll come visit you and your mother later," Glyken says.

He reaches for a stone jug on a little recessed shelf chipped into the obsidian wall. He pours out a measure of clear liquid in three cups and hands one each to Valentine and me, then fills a fourth with water for Ammit.

"To new friends and old history," Glyken says.

He smiles broadly, revealing unsettlingly sharp teeth and a glimpse of what looks like a forked tongue.

"What is this?" I ask.

"It's hymna, a kind of liquor."

138

I take a whiff. It smells strong and medicinal, a good combination.

We down the shots. It's good. Valentine grimaces and clears her throat. "Wow," she says. "That's potent."

"Tastes a little like lemons. Don't tell me you grow lemons down here somewhere?" I ask.

"No, that's the formic acid," Glyken says. "From the ants."

"From the what now?" Valentine asks.

"The ants. This is basically ant gin." He gestures with the pitcher. "Another?"

"One's enough for me," Valentine says, setting down her cup.

On the one hand, it's fermented ant juice; on the other hand, it's taking the edge off. "I'll have hers," I say. "And mine. And Ammit's since she's not drinking for obvious reasons. This is definitely the best ant gin I've ever had."

By the fourth shot, I'm feeling relaxed. "Listen, the Jane won't be sticking around much longer. What can you tell us about the mining operation?"

"Not much," Ammit says. "They have a very sophisticated and well-hidden weapons array on the west side of the crater rim. If you don't take it out first, you won't make it down into the crater."

"Thanks for that, and the drinks. I want to be sure you understand the threat to what you've built here. The Five Families cannot be trusted."

"We can protect ourselves," Glyken says. "We have thus far."

"That's because they haven't given a shit about you. They have you locked in here leaving you to your own devices because there's no value in doing anything else. That is no longer the case."

"He's right," Valentine says. "They will come up with a

pretense to seize your land, drop the perimeters and roll through here with a mechanized army that scorches everything to dust, no matter how well-hidden you are."

"What do you suggest we do?" Ammit asks.

"Whatever is going on here, our best hope is for us to get back to Mars and help broker a deal with the only person I've met in the Five Families who isn't fully horrible—Singhroy Able. She's a lying, conniving, cheating opportunist, but …"

They look at me curiously.

"There's no good way to finish that sentence. She's terrible, but I think she's the best of the bunch. And she'll see a means of advancing her interests."

I check the timer. We're officially late.

"We really have to go now."

Glyken gives us a bottle of the hymna to take with us, which I'm pretty sure is all for me. They escort us to the bottom of the stairs.

"You're on your own this time," Glyken says. "As you near the surface, the connection with Halo will resume. You'll have a gap of missing time to explain."

I need to know.

"Was my grandmother…?"

He nods, smiling. "I'm glad you asked. We weren't sure if you knew."

Valentine is looking at me curiously.

"Adelaide Larsen was a good friend, a mentor and a legend. Many of the originalists could not read, nor do basic math. She set up a school. Your grandmother was revered."

"Was?"

Ammit nods. "She passed away many years ago."

"I see. Did my mother ever come here?"

"She received permission from Halo for a sanctioned

visit. She never arrived."

"Why?"

"No one knows."

"When was this?"

"During the summer of 2166. Your grandmother was heartbroken she didn't visit, but always believed your mother had a good reason."

"She did have a good reason. The best. My mother died that summer," I say, feeling a fresh pang of grief about what was taken from us all that awful day.

"Ah," Glyken says, as Ammit nods. They don't say anything else. They don't have to. What is there to say? Valentine tries to take my hand but I pull it away. She lets me.

We grab our gear and make our way to the top of the tunnel. I summon the nanites and find a nice long loop of Valentine and me walking around on the surface and have it ready to go for when we reconnect to Halo. As we move out into the glaring sunlight, blinking from behind our soother goggles and sweating under our shades, my scroll is still weirdly silent.

"Why aren't we hearing anything from the Jane crew?" I say into the shared channel. "Fleiss? You out there?"

Dead silence. Halo is blocked. It's not possible for Halo to be blocked, so someone is location-jamming it right here, right now. And our shared channel with the Jane has been cut. The only reason the Jane crew would cut the channel is if they didn't want someone to know we are out here. Or they wanted someone to think we're dead.

"Stop," I say and motion her to stay out of sight. I have a saltshaker of fleas in my pack, local micro-cameras, and I scatter them out and send them hopping in the direction of the Jane. My scroll is a jumble of vantages until they stop bouncing.

There's not much left of the Jane. It's on its side and almost broken in half, smoking. Several unmarked fliers are settled around it. Heavily armed and masked people are loading Tooms, Dormer and Fleiss into a transport. They're cuffed, but alive. We watch the transport lift off and roar across the dusty expanse to the distant rim of the volcano and then disappear inside it.

My OCD perimeters notch their landing site at about 60 kilometers.

"What do you see?" Valentine asks.

"A really long walk ahead of me," I say. "Someone just took the crew away at gunpoint, which is good. They didn't just kill them and blame the blizards. Sorry, the Saurians. They must think we're already dead, or that we will be soon enough."

"What are we going to do?" she asks.

"*We're* not going to do anything. I'm going to go save them. You'll stay here until I can swing back and pick you up."

She looks at me curiously. "Is it lonely?"

"What do you mean?"

"Thinking you're the only person capable of doing things? That must be lonely."

"I'm not sure what you're getting at."

"I'm going with you, obviously. I've grown pretty fond of Dormer and Fleiss."

"What about Tooms?" I ask.

"He's a little on the arrogant side. Like you," she says.

She starts walking. I hurry to catch up.

25

The first thing I'll do when I get back to my squat, if I ever get back to my squat, is delete that flipping desert plug-in I sleep under. There is nothing remotely enjoyable about being in the desert.

Valentine and I have been trudging for kilometers, and I'm hot and tired and thirsty. My mouth is filled with grit even though I'm wearing a mask and my eyes are burning even though I've got soother goggles on. The shade function is at full capacity and barely keeping me from cooking like a slab of sheetmeat.

It wasn't so bad last night. It was cold and clear and almost peaceful and we covered a lot of territory. But then the sun came up and we were too far from anything resembling real shade, and now we're going to expire here in the middle of this barren hell. I've let Valentine down and Jynks is going to jail and Mel is going to hate me even more and Essential is going to get caught and executed and whatever nonsense the Five Families are up to will mean an end to the blizards.

Saurians.

"I think I see some shelter ahead," Valentine says.

"You've literally said that every hundred meters for the last four hours," I say.

And to add insult to injury, our waterbugs aren't keeping up with the demand.

"You have to keep hope alive," she says.

"Why is that, exactly?" I ask.

"Because no one likes the alternative."

"I do. I like it," I say. "It's called realism."

"Let me rephrase," she says, checking her waterbug again, which is still empty. "Normal people don't like the alternative. Apathy causes *normal* people to give up. You, on the other hand, seem motivated by it."

"I'll take that as a compliment."

"You shouldn't," she says.

We're still disconnected from Halo. I can't imagine how a jam of this size hasn't triggered a quadrillion alarms, which means they're holding back for some reason. And the Five Families aren't known for restraint. Does that mean they're putting their trust in me?

Despite my irritation, Valentine appears to be right. There's a rock outcropping ahead that should offer us some relief from the sunlight. If we can make it there and take shelter, we can wait for the sun to set and make the rest of the hike, 15 kilometers, in the relative safety of darkness. If we haven't dried up and blown away by then.

"It's close," she says.

"Your imaginary shelter?" I ask. "No. But I wager it's less than four kilometers to the very real possible shelter I just saw over there."

"You're a terrible person," she says.

I hand her my waterbug. "I'm a realistic person."

We keep slogging. Four kilometers seems like a thousand when you're hiking through what feels like a cremation kiln outside of a medical center at the end of the debt month.

As we get closer, we can see a narrow cleft in a canyon wall where the rocks have folded in on themselves a little, like dough from a defective bread ball in a bakery pop-up.

Valentine is trying her best to put on a brave front, but

she's running out of fuel. I am too, but I'm used to living right on the edge of always giving up.

The mouth of the little canyon is smooth, polished tan rock, no doubt long ago scoured by running water. I wriggle up the smooth face of the rock and then help Valentine up. A few more steps and we're inside the narrow canyon in blessed shade.

"Oh, that's nice," Valentine says. She shakes her pack off and sits down against the wall. She looks pale and flushed at the same time. I curse myself for not insisting she stay with the blizards.

Saurians. Godsdamn it. Saurians.

But at least we're out of the wind and direct sunlight now. We take off our goggles and lower our masks. It's still hot, but bearable. I drop my pack too and turn off my shade.

"Let's hole up here until the sun goes down, then we'll make our final run at the rim. And hope we're not too late to save those three idiots."

She opens a nutri-tube and sucks out the paste, then leans her head back against the wall. Her eyes widen, and she whispers, "Look behind you."

I turn and see faint patterns on the wall.

She's up, touching the designs reverently. "These are petroglyphs."

"What's a petrol-glif?"

"Petroglyphs. Art from the original inhabitants of this land. An indigenous tribe known as the Klamath. They lived here long before Euro-settlers arrived, so long ago they told stories about when the volcano that used to stand where the crater is exploded."

"Are you connected to Halo? How do you know all this?"

"I siloed all the information I could on the region

145

before we left so I could keep it rolling through my feed while I slept."

The petroglyphs are hard to make out, but we filter our OCDs to enhance and the walls are covered with patterns and figures.

"This one looks like a big feral cat," I say.

She's downloading pictures into her OCD's spiral storage. "I think it's a mountain goat."

"This one looks like one of those old security bots."

"I think that's just a human," she says.

"They weren't very talented artists."

"Crucial, these are from fifteen thousand years ago," she says.

"So why does this one look like a blizard?" I ask.

"Saurian, and you're right," she says, "That's pretty weird since the Saurians only arrived a century ago."

"This one looks like, well, a penis."

"It is," she says. "And some rudimentary writing. 'Boner was here.' I think that might have come later."

Trailing her fingers over the stone, she follows the images around a bend in the wall and I hear a sudden intake of breath. "Oh ..."

The glitter gun is in my hand and I chase after her. But it's not a threat. The opposite. It's hope.

There's a tiny pool of water bubbling up from deep underground. No bigger than a porthole on a garbage barge, and the water sinks back into the sandy soil quickly, but it's filled with fresh, clear water. And next to it is the most perfect plant I've ever seen on Earth. A real, wild plant. In the middle of the sunbelt. It has a perfectly symmetric puff of purple tendrils above a prickly bulb at the end of a stalk surrounded by prickly leaves.

"It's a thistle," she says. "A perfect thistle."

The sight of it is oddly unsettling. We're so used to trash

plants and carefully curated synthetics, neither of us has the tools to process this tiny little hidden oasis.

She dips her fingers in the water. "It's cold." She splashes some on her face, then pats it around her neck and runs her wet fingers through her hair, slicking it back in a very appealing way.

She sees me looking at her and splashes water at me. It feels amazing. Like what rain must have felt like. "Take it easy," I say. "You'll get the guns wet."

"They'll survive," she says, splashing more water my way.

I have this uncanny ability, a talent really. I always know when I'm about to do the wrong thing, and the stupider it is, the clearer it becomes.

I cup my hands in the water and give her a big splash back. She laughs and tries to push me but I catch her hand.

"I want to kiss you," I say, knowing it's the wrong thing for both of us and not caring. "Would that be all right?"

"I would like that," she says.

Then her hands are around my waist and our bodies are pressed together, and I'm feeling something I haven't felt in a long time. Desire. Lust. Hope. Her lips taste salty and sweet, and she's pulling my shirt off. I return the favor.

She's so beautiful it's painful.

Still kissing, we collapse onto the dusty ground, shedding clothes and weapons and common sense. We stretch out next to the little spring and the resilient thistle hidden in the heart of a scorched desert on a ruined planet and make love as if our lives depend on it.

We're still tangled together when the sun sets.

26

It's getting chilly and I'm next to a beautiful, mostly naked woman, her body pressed into mine for warmth and still feeling the flush of post-sex bliss. Several blisses.

"Mel, stop hogging the blankets," I say, lost in the middle of a comfortable memory.

"I'm not Mel," Valentine says.

It just got a lot chillier. I feel a morose kind of tension stiffen through her body and carefully she disentangles herself, unwrapping her slender arms from around me.

I haven't been this close to happy in a long time. So of course, I sabotage it.

"Valentine, I'm really sorry," I say. "It's just that ..."

"You don't need to explain. It was fun. Better than I expected. But it's clear you aren't over her."

"I *am* over her," I say too loud. "It's just that, I don't know, the last time I felt like this—you know, happy—I was with her, with Mel. And my brain wasn't ready. This kind of happy made me dream back to the little squat we had together all those years ago. That's all. And her name slipped out."

She pulls her shirt back on, then her pants, then her gear. "It's ironic. I'm a historian, but you're the one living in the past. Come on, we need to get moving. I can't take another trudge in the sunlight."

We fill up all our containers with water from the spring to take the strain off the waterbugs and leave the safety of the magic canyon. Disappointment Canyon, as I shall forever know it.

By the time we get to the top of the rim, it's almost dawn and we're exhausted. Valentine hasn't said more than six words the entire time. She doesn't seem angry, or even disappointed. Not quite relieved, but close. I'm trying to think of a word that means feeling satisfied for being right about something you hoped wouldn't come true.

What a mess. Mel would laugh.

It's a nice enough night though and every now and again the contanomosphere shifts enough so we can see the sparkle of stars through the brown smog. But sunrise is coming and with it the unbearable heat.

We've been trudging up a shallow canyon making our way toward the rim. Even though Halo is jammed, there's bound to be some local surveillance options. When we get near the top, I shake out the fleas again and send them hopping ahead while we stay out of sight. There's a prefab landing pad on the rim big enough to handle a small q-rocket. It's unusual because most rockets dock with orbitals and then use space elevators to transfer cargo. Landing a q-rocket, even using just thrusters, is risky and would scorch this whole damn rim.

And there's a pop-up building, but it looks deserted. Probably just to run surveillance and the defenses they need to protect against blizard attacks. It's less than half a kilometer away.

"Listen," I say to Valentine, temporarily blocking our spool-up ribbons with some nanite-imposed static. "I'm going to shield myself with the nanites and get close. I'll shut down the surveillance and then give you a signal to come on up."

"Okay," she says.

"Again, I'm really sorry about the whole thing by the

thistle."

"Stop," she says. "We're fine. It's fine. We had a pleasant moment together. That's more than ninety-eight percent of the world gets. Don't ruin the memory of it with unnecessary self-flagellation. And don't get killed. I don't want to hike all the way back to the Saurians on my own. But leave me your waterbug—if you're dead, you won't need it."

"Fair point."

"What will the signal be?"

"I'll figure something out."

I blink the nanites into action and build a screen against local surveillance, a digital shield to hopefully send beams skating right past. I crest the hill and my hidden column is suddenly quite active. There are six surveillance trackers sweeping the area in a tight grid, and it appears those signals are all linked to a variety of nasty weapons systems. Whoever is here is nervous about becoming blizard food. Or being captured by the police. We're lucky the Saurians warned us.

The thing about living under constant surveillance is no one really sees the world with their eyes anymore. There could be a dozen people in that little building all looking in my direction right now, but if their scrolls don't register me and the system doesn't flag me, chances are pretty high no one would notice, even though I'm right here in the flesh. But without a digital shadow, I don't exist to them.

Or maybe they're just not looking. I walk right up to the building, expecting to be glittered at every step. Or worse. But I'm invisible to the cameras. The doors aren't even secure. Turns out, no one is watching.

Inside is a small, boxy command center with cameras monitoring the whole rim and automated guns on every corner, most of them pointed at the landing pad. They must be expecting to move something big from here to Mars if they need a q-rocket. I nudge the nanites to dupe a malfunction to explain why I wasn't perforated on the way up, then examine the controls.

One of the cameras is pointing down into the distant base of the crater. That's where the real action is. I zoom in. Dust is billowing up from industrial sledges scraping around below. Three fliers are parked nearby. It looks like a mining operation, only more targeted. A precision operation.

I keep on looking. There's only one thing that could be of value in the middle of ancient volcanic crater. The same thing that the Saurians say slows down their own transformation. Some kind of chemical or mineral or gas or whatever it is seeping up from deep below the mantle of the Earth.

So, the command center up here is just to hold the high ground while they muck around down there in the crater. But why? What value is there in magma juice?

I need to send Valentine a signal, something subtle. I override the system—it's easy since Halo isn't involved—and aim all the weapons at the blast pad and trigger them. An air cannon, two mounted rail guns and three glitter guns unleash simultaneously. The devastation is quick and complete, all except for one little flat corner next to the tactical shed. It will take some work before they can drop a q-rocket out of orbit and land it here.

Then I decouple the scanners from the weapons system.

Valentine is running toward the building so I keep the weapons offline until she makes it inside.

"Great signal," she says. "What's going on?"

"I'm not sure." I zoom in closer and we can see people scrambling for the fliers. "They're mining for something down there."

"What could they possibly want from the bottom of an old lake?"

"I don't know, but I keep thinking about what Glyken said. The healing properties of that liquid from way down. It means something that the research that led us to these coordinates here in an old crater is happening at Mytikas, which is also over a crater, or former crater, before Mars went mostly cold."

The fliers are taking off, heading right toward us. "I guess we'll get a chance to ask them soon," I say.

"Judging from all the weaponry, I'm thinking they're not chatty types. Any chance you have a plan?"

"Of course. Not to be in here when they level the place."

There are three fliers. One of them is a modified Jane. If Dormer and the rest are alive, they're in it—and locked in brig tubes.

Once during the Consolidation Wars, my unit was surprised by an automated battalion of cannon striders. I spent almost a week in a brig tube bouncing around in the back of a commandeered Jane until they found some reluctant humans who agreed to take us. Brig tubes are very unpleasant. I can still taste the vinegary acid of the stasis gel. When I finally got out, I had a few lingering rage issues that I took out on my robot captors. I think I debted at least six of those clanking trigger-bot cannon striders before someone proped me with a tranquilizer.

If Fleiss is wedged into one of those infernal incarceration pods, suspended in that awful gel, it's a tight fit.

The second flier is a sleek little hyperwedge—heavy armor and insane speeds, capable of interplanetary flight. That one is probably carrying the boss of this little dig.

The third flier is a combat skiff, closing fastest. It's small but packs a punch, and it's already targeting the shed.

I lock the weapons systems onto the skiff, poke it to life and set it up so the tactical shed coordinates a firestorm against the skiff. I grab Valentine by the hand and drag her outside and jump down into one of the gashes blown into the landing pad by the rail gun.

I leave some fleas around the edge so we can watch the fight. The skiff loses. It shatters into pieces that rain down into the crater. But then the Jane arrives and does a number on the shed.

I forgot how awesome they are. A wall of juxtaposition missiles turns the building—and everything in it—inside out.

The Jane sets down onto the one piece of the landing pad that's still smooth. Right above us. I guess I did have a plan. When they turn the burners off and the weapons settle down, we can practically reach up and touch the damn thing.

The wedge stays airborne.

The doors of the Jane slide open and four heavily armed people march-waddle out in full gear. They advance on the smoking remains of the shed in classic tactical formation. Valentine and I slip aboard the Jane in classic skulking formation. There's another mercenary inside the door covering his buddies from the weapons array. He's surprised to see us. He's more surprised by the stream of sublethal bolts I hit him with. He drops to his knees and keels over, puking.

The first rule of a Jane crew is the pilot never leaves the cockpit. An atomic blast can't get past the cockpit. That means the hired guns are amateurs. Maybe everyone is an amateur since the Consolidation Wars.

I know my way around a Jane. I roll him out and close

the door and then use the manual lock. Nobody is getting in here until I say so.

"You have to come see this," I say.

We make our way to the brig tubes. We can hear the team chattering back and forth on the Jane comms, advancing on the wreckage of the tac-center in the shed. They don't know they've already lost.

There are four brig tubes in the very back of the Jane. Three of them are occupied. Fleiss looks like an undercooked vat sausage. He's glaring out of the tube, eyes open and burning in the sauce. Next to him, Dormer and Tooms look equally miserable and angry, but slightly more comfortable. They're naked and suspended in the blue gel. I know they can see me. They can't close their eyes.

"This is horrible," Valentine says. "We have to get them out."

"We will," I say, "but look at him. He's so huge." I'm laughing and pointing.

"Stop it," she says. "Help them."

"Fine." I trigger the drain command and the gel is sucked out and the tubes slide open.

They stagger out, spitting and coughing and blinking.

"The pilot must have left the cockpit?" Tooms asks.

"Yep."

"That's like the first rule of a Jane crew."

"And the last rule," I say.

"I'm going to go kill them, and then find some clothes," Fleiss says.

"Don't sit on anything," I say, watching his naked, gel-slicked form padding down the hall.

We're watching the stream of the action outside. The mercenaries now realize they're in trouble. Fleiss is powering up the weapons, but he doesn't get a chance. The hyperwedge launches an ion quilt that drapes over half the

Jane and all the mercenaries. They sizzle out of existence. It turns and drops a nuclear polypheme on the crater. All evidence of whatever was being mined is gone in a flash.

Then the hyperwedge is gone too, blasting off beyond the atmosphere.

Halo comes back online. It has a lot of questions. So does Chundar Hotsip. And he's got an order too. Return to Mars immediately. Although he didn't say it that nice.

27

"I believe this is a perfect example of irony," Sanders says.

We've just disembarked from the space elevator at Port Zunil. Sanders is there to greet us along with an armed escort.

He's so pleased that a cybanism can almost grasp such a complex feature of language. Even after all this time, machine-think still can't make the jump from linear thought to creative interpretation. But Sanders is learning. I guess I should be concerned about how many Sanders there are running around that I don't know about.

The ride to Mars from Earth was surprisingly pleasant with Valentine. She wanted to talk about what might be happening in the sunbelt. I wanted to make things right between us. She kept telling me to stop worrying about it.

After my sixth stammering apology in as many hours, she grew frustrated, ordered the strongest pharma-shot on the menu, checked into a sleeping pod and I didn't see her again until we landed.

"This ought to be good. What exactly do you find ironic about the current situation?" I ask Sanders.

"That after such a confrontational beginning, you're now helping the Five Families."

"I'm not helping them," I say. "I'm helping prove Jynks is innocent. Our goals happen to overlap right now."

"Some experts think all cooperation between humans is always a temporary alignment of goals or at the very least, a means of currying favor for future use," he says. Sanders sees Valentine and smiles. "Irony *and* a coincidence. What good fortune. Chancellor Valentine is an expert who may have insights into the concept of cooperation and how it ties to selfish interests."

"Hello again, Sanders," she says. "Your programming has advanced considerably since I saw you last. But I haven't given the topic you mention much thought. Perhaps we can discuss it next time, after I can do some targeted research."

"I would like that," he says. "How was your time on Earth?"

"It was … illuminating," she says, shooting a quick look my way. "I certainly learned a lot."

Sanders gets a dreamy look. At least as dreamy as artificial life can get. "I hope to visit someday," he says.

"My door is always open," I say. "Literally. The lock is broken and the maintenance cluster never seems to get the right part. You should go now while my squat is empty. Get the full experience."

"Tempting," Sanders says. "But I've been asked to escort you both to the Hive."

I see a flash of surprise and then fear wash over Valentine. Almost imperceptible, but I know her pretty well now.

The Hive is where the Five Families do the work of running Earth and Mars. It's a heavily fortified compound built into the mazelike canyons of the Noctis Labyrinthus. The buildings are dense and thick and mostly underground. I pull up a map of Mars in my scroll and zoom. From above, the Hive looks like a giant old-fashioned parking lot from the days oversized single-person transport vehicles were placed side by side rather than tiny little conveyances that hook onto a flipper to be neatly stored in rotating hangars 30 stories tall.

The Hive isn't flat space. That's just the roof—100 square kilometers of self-healing myco-cement about 20 meters deep interspersed with layers of energy displacement mesh. A rail gun, even a hundred rail guns, couldn't make a lasting dent.

Underneath, it's a warren of tunnels and tubes, with twisting canyons converted into gleaming offices, server farms, power ranches, probability generators and binary nests. It's where the Five Families do business, levy debts, plot advances in avatainment to hook more participants, tinker with the cost of health care and basically rule the known universe.

I pull up a historic map of Mars to look at the old topography of Noctis Labyrinthus and overlay it. The twisting canyons hidden beneath that formidable defense look like a giant cephalopod wrestling a spaghetti ladder. The offices, I've heard, stretch 20 or 30 stories deep in some places.

The Hive was Essential's second choice for the Halo servers. It seems a little too obvious to me—why put all your rocket fuel tabs in one fusion chamber?

But it's also virtually uncrackable, like that one charred, tooth-fracturing sucrose nut at the bottom of every pouch. The Hive has invulnerability going for it. But the thing about being invulnerable is everyone wants to test it.

I'll get the chance to see it from the inside. I need to let Essential know. She's always planning something. She's probably nearby in the Choke right now, watching the place and wondering how to get in. She's so impatient. I don't know how I got all the positive traits in this family. I guess she takes after Dad. Or dads, depending on where Mom got the genetic material.

I tell the nanites to make a deteriorating connection and

send Essential a flare, a message that will burn out almost instantly. *Headed into the Hive. I'll poke around for the servers. Wait to hear from me before you do anything stupid. More stupid than usual I mean.*

Sanders and his crew lead us to a heavily armed flier that zips us out into the Choke. He entertains us with a running commentary on the history of irony in pre-Consolidation Earth. I tune him out and watch the landscape sliding by.

About 100 kilometers out from the Hive, we land next to a knobby, unremarkable structure crouched by some tumbled rocks and dust. An airlock extends and we wait for it to seal.

"... and that's why irony remains such a coveted and often elusive linguistic tool these days," Sanders says.

"That was truly fascinating," I say. He beams. Literally. The compliment caused his eyes to flash.

"The Hive is a lot smaller than I expected."

"This is the first stop," Sanders says. "The only way in is by an underground lev-train."

Valentine and I are escorted into the surprisingly spare building, jostled into a lift and whisked deep underground. We emerge onto a lev-train platform.

Valentine is nervous, and for good reason. She's a double agent and they're taking us deep inside the pulsing processor that powers the Five Families. If they know, if they find out, she's not leaving. And neither am I. Well, that's not a certainty. I'm getting pretty good with the nanites.

Just for fun, I activate them and scan our surroundings. They locate the operating systems of well-hidden automated weapons every five meters. In theory, I could probably disrupt those. But maybe not the armed guards in between every automated weapon.

Nope, definitely not. We're not getting out of here

unless they want us to leave.

The train arrives and hovers next to the platform A few people get off who initially ignore us but then do a double scroll, pausing to stare and probably record some footage. I suspect my celebrity quotient is rising. First, I locked my own sister in a terrorium. And now I'm helping Jynks against the Five Families.

"You really should consider selling your avatainment rights," Valentine says. She's making conversation to ease her nerves. "You could make some credits off your notoriety."

She knows it's not Essential locked up down there in the basement of the security forces building in Jezero, frozen and cycling through endless fear spirals.

"I'm not crazy about my face filling a million feeds," I say.

"No, you're too old," she says. "It would have to be an avatar special for sure."

I laugh. She's insulting me. I'm comfortable with insults.

After we board the lev-train, it whizzes off into a blur of long stretches of dark tunnel walls punctuated with flashes of security lighting. A few minutes and a few hundred kilometers later, it stops in a buzzing hub of travellators stretching off into a dozen gleaming corridors, carrying people past rooms and stacks of offices and more armed guards and weapons systems.

"This way," Sanders says, leading us onto a travellator.

It angles down deeper into the Hive and we pass rough walls of stone encased in a meter or more of some translucent resin flaked through with flickering bits of light.

"Here we are," Sanders says, stopping us at a heavily armored door.

I've got the nanites tracking everything in case we need to come up with a plan and so that I can share any intel with Essential. So far, my only workable plan is to marvel at all the redundant safety features here. Features we cannot possibly avoid.

The door opens. Inside is a lavish meeting space.

There's a huge table, as big as a launch pad, made from some thick, clear, dark green material that catches the soft ambient light in magical flashes. The highest-ranking members of the Five Families, the erstwhile Lords of Mars, sit on the far side of it on shaped-air cushions that keep them floating in comfort. The table is elevated so they're looking down at the door and the sad little chairs available to those lucky enough to visit.

Singhroy Able is there. Nice to see her again, in a "shard of glitter needle stuck in my eye" kind of way. Next to her is Blevin Flunt. He's looking a little healthier. Must have gone to the spa for a rejuvenation treatment. Being rich and all-powerful must be so exhausting. Fehrven Modo has new hair and some fresh tech across his forehead. His eyes are narrowed and he looks happy. Probably having some low-key full-synapse orgasm as he bobs around in the current of his chair. DuSpoles Koryx doesn't look happy to be next to him. I only know her from the news feed. She's pale, with jeweled subdermals on her long, elegant wrists. She looks bored and angry. I would probably like her under different circumstances.

The real surprise is that next to Koryx is Tarteric Hoost.

He looks a little anxious, maybe a touch of indigestion, but surprisingly healthy for someone Jynks allegedly glittered right through the heart a week ago.

28

Enough with their godsdamn games.

"I'm not going in there," I say, stopping at the door.

"You have to go in," Sanders says, confused. "They're the highest-ranking members of the Five Families."

Valentine looks at me curiously. She hasn't seen Hoost yet.

"Yeah, well, prok them all with a flaming drone jacket," I say to Sanders, and then turn my attention to the open doorway. "I'm not playing your sick little games this time!" I yell in at them. I see irritation—bordering on contempt—flash across their faces. And since I know they're paying attention, I clap the backs of my hands together twice, a universal symbol of the ultimate disrespect.

I turn to Sanders. "Take me back to Jezero. I need to see Jynks. It seems she's being held for a crime that never happened."

"Oh, it happened," Hoost says from across the room. "Just not to me." He nods at the guards. "Get them in here and leave us."

One of the guards shoves me in the small of the back and I stumble in and spin around for a reckoning. They've all got their sparkles up—stun sticks, the blunt tips crackling with tongues of white-blue electric currents. I've been hit with one before. It feels like every muscle in your body is on fire and made of lead. Molten lead. Six at once would probably burn like a trash fire in the hottest crater of Mercury.

If Valentine wasn't standing between me and the guards, I'd probably do something stupid. Apparently, it's not enough of a deterrent. I see a way to get past her and take a step toward them but Valentine catches my arm. "Not now," she says. "This helps no one."

Must be nice to be a historian—able to learn from the past.

"She's looking out for you," one of the guards says. "Maybe you'll lock her in a terrorium too. Like your sister."

With a blink I dupe his info—Serti Melthin, age 33, currently living in Holden and 14 percent below debt neutral—and make a solemn vow to ruin his life.

Sanders ushers Valentine inside and the door closes behind us.

"What's this all about," I ask, looking at Hoost. "And is it illegal to murder a dead man?"

"Sit down and stop preening around like a test chimp," Hoost says. "Rest assured, the cybanism is programed to protect us. If you get too close, it will terminate your life functions."

"He's not an "it." His name is Sanders," I say. "And I know he won't kill me."

I look at Sanders and he's shaking his head slowly. "I am not entirely confident about that, Crucial," he says.

"We really need to do something about your subroutines," I say, pulling up a chair and slumping down.

"I'm sorry," Sanders says. He stands nearby learning about what I hope is shame.

"We need to know what you found in the sunbelt," Hoost says.

"Interesting," I say. "I need to know why you're alive and Jynks Martine is in jail."

"I told you this was a mistake," Able says. "Chancellor

Valentine, you remember that you work for the Singhroys, correct?"

Valentine nods, taking a chair as well.

"And do you also recognize how that arrangement could end, immediately, and you could be sent to Earth?"

Valentine nods again. I know she's thinking about her niece, Seneca, and not about getting bounced from Mars.

"We've analyzed the visuals from your download," Able says. "Despite your poor judgment in sexual partners …" she shoots me a withering look. "… we're interested in your opinion on what exactly you discovered."

Great. Everyone in this ornate bunker knows Valentine and I had sex by that little thistle spring. I hate rich people. And Halo. And a world in which everything is always recorded for playback.

Valentine seems nonplussed. "I truly don't know," she says. "I haven't been able to derive a plausible conclusion yet. It seems that someone has been staging incidents under the guise of resistance activities near the border and using the distraction to advance into the sunbelt."

She's pretty good under pressure. I guess being a double agent in the resistance helps with that.

"The data further suggest that whoever is behind this has a great deal of resources and—since they were able to manipulate Halo—connections to the Five Families."

"An almost inescapable conclusion," Able says. She drums her fingertips on the surface of the table. I can tell by the sound it's stone. Probably synthetic emerald. Practically a square kilometer. "But why? And what role do the blizards play in all this?"

Blevin Flunt winces at her use of the slang term built on his family's failure.

"There is nothing to suggest they are involved in whatever is going on," she says.

"That's the part we're interested in," Flunt says. "Your feeds were malfunctioning during this time and can't be spooled. You can see how our suspicions would be aroused."

"Chancellor Valentine doesn't know the full story," I say. "We split up."

"For good reason," Koryx says. "You called her by the wrong name after intercourse." She looks at Hoost. "One of your people, by the way. Tawdry."

"I really despise all of you," I say. "I mean we split up before we met the blizards. Or the climate pioneers, I should say." That earns me a small smile from Valentine.

"I talked to them alone. And I'm not going to say another word about it until you get Jynks Martine out of prison."

They're monitoring me closely, reading my vitals, cross-checking everything. Confirming with Halo.

"You are not in a position to make demands," Hoost says. His voice is loud, and he's not used to having to reach that range. He coughs and reaches for a square tumbler to take a sip of water to soothe his throat. "Tell us what we need to know."

I shake my head. "No. Free Jynks, with a media pardon for all to see. Then we talk."

"That cannot happen, not at present," Hoost says. "She is safe and will remain safe until this issue is resolved, at which point she will be released with her rank and rating restored. But until then, she must remain sequestered."

"Then I have nothing to say."

"You must trust us," Hoost says, growing impatient.

I laugh so hard I choke a little, and then I'm coughing and looking around for some water. None is forthcoming.

"'Trust me' says the guy who faked his own death, and also faked my sister's disappearance so you could use my grief to track down some fancy technology baubles. Do you remember that whole slipstream from six months ago? Did you think I'd forget? And you want me to trust you now?"

"I could just have Sanders kill you," he says.

I see a look of horror wash across Sanders's face.

"Fine. Good. Then the truth dies with me," I say. "And you can keep orbiting around like a q-rocket with a broken spin capacitor."

"Stop it," Able says. "He's gotten farther than the rest of us. Just tell him what's going on. Perhaps he can help."

Hoost looks at me like something he tracked out of the biowaste baller.

"Halo has uncovered certain improprieties," Hoost says. "Upon further investigation, we discovered a carefully concealed plot."

Oh gods, Essential, what are you up to?

"Is it the resistance?" I ask, not really wanting to know.

"No. Whoever is behind this is far more effective than those dead-end beetlers," he says.

I sense Valentine tense.

"At any rate, the resistance has ceased to be a threat with the imprisonment of your sister. No, this appears to be internal to the Five Families and, thus, very sophisticated," he says. "Resources have been diverted, funds siphoned, the movements of security forces redirected—all well-shielded from Halo."

"And Jynks?"

"She was aware and investigating, reporting directly to the Fist. To us. She had new information to share. She recommended we meet in person. I sent a duplex in my place. They were attacked. My duplex was killed and she was framed."

I hear Valentine suck in a breath. Duplex is a term for

a surgically manipulated double. Some poor schmuck got a lot of credits to let surgeons carve him into a replica of Hoost, then got his heart liquefied for his trouble.

"Of course, you have a duplex," I say.

"I have several. We all do."

"That's so casually horrific."

"Don't forget your place," Koryx says.

I really don't like her.

"My place is on Earth," I say. "And I would love to be there right now, but your little games always seem to get in the way."

Hoost raises his hand to shut down whatever sanctimonious thing was coming from her next. "Duplexes have a privileged existence. They live in luxury and have minimal expectations, all to simply look like someone else."

"Until their heart gets gooped right out of their sternum," I say. "Why doesn't Jynks just say it wasn't you and get on with the investigation?"

"She doesn't know."

I rub my temples. "You evil test swab. The whole planet thinks you're dead and you get to hide out in relative safety until you can figure out who's behind the assassination."

"Correct, and if you really want to help Jynks Martine, you will tell us what you know about the sunbelt, then go back to Earth and let Hotsip complete his investigation. Jynks will be released as soon as we understand and neutralize the risk, and she will be rewarded for her patience and sacrifice."

"Chundar Hotsip couldn't investigate the source of a fart in his own airhoodie," I say. "And I didn't learn a godsdamn useful thing from the blizards, other than that they are pleasant enough, in a scaly, fangy kind of way."

"That's impossible," Fehrven Modo says angrily. "They

must know something."

"They know they've been attacked and that two of their people disappeared. They know someone was mining for something in the bottom of a dead volcano. But they don't know why."

The Fist are looking at each other dejectedly.

"What do you want it to be?" I ask. They don't say anything. "I know something is going on. And I think it has something to do with the brain research at Mytikas."

They are silent.

"No? Nothing? Okay, well, suit yourselves." I stand. "I am here to get Jynks out of jail. And I'm going to do that. I'm going to march out of here, open up my feed to the news, and share the video of us sitting here talking."

"You'll do no such thing," Koryx says.

"Oh yeah, and why not?"

"First, because you'll find no content to spool." She gestures. "This room is locked down. You're in the Glove. This is literally the most secure place on the planet. And second, because if you share any information, even anecdotally, we'll execute Jynks and send Melinda Hopwire packing back to Earth, saddled with enough debt for a dozen lifetimes. And Chancellor Valentine will be right behind her."

She makes a strong case.

"It's possible he could help us," Able says. "We should consider that."

"We will," Hoost says. "In private. In the meantime, Larsen, keep your mouth shut and your feed clamped and continue investigating. The sooner we understand who is behind this plot, the sooner Jynks Martine can be restored and the sooner we can throw you onto the first Dart back to Earth."

Hoost snaps his fingers and the door opens. My zappy

friends are waiting, sparkles at the ready.

"That went well," I say as Sanders guides us out of the room. "I think they kind of liked us."

"You *were* listening to my discourse on irony," he says, obviously pleased.

A message swipes in. From Mel.

"Sanders, we need to get back to Jezero. Mel needs me."

Valentine smiles at me, and not in the good way.

29

Mel is waiting for me at the base of an impossibly tall tower in the very center of Jezero that goes right up through the top of the spiral dome and beyond. She doesn't say a word, just points at the lift and we get inside.

With a creaky jolt, we climb. My ears are popping, my stomach's churning and my brain is still fuzzed from the meeting at the Hive and the Earth-to-Mars q-jump.

She's looking out the window, watching Jezero get smaller below us as we soar upward. I've only been this high inside a city dome once, back in Holden when I crashed through after escaping Essential's squat. I landed in the Choke. Barely made it out alive.

I was way too busy back then avoiding being glittered to death to take stock of the view, and Holden dome is only a fraction of the size of Jezero.

I'm even more distracted this time.

Mel cut her hair short, like within a centimeter of her scalp short. It's not a big deal—a decent salon can use follicle stimulators to grow hair down to your ankles in minutes. But Mel has kept her hair long since before I first met her. When the world seems especially chaotic, people tend to seek control where they can.

I want to ask her why she chose today of all days to cut her hair so short, but it feels like that question crosses a boundary where I don't have access anymore. So instead I say, "Climbing pretty high."

"Yes," she says, looking at the view, watching the lights of Jezero blink to life, a constellation of terrestrial stars on the ground below us as darkness falls and the stars above start to reveal themselves. "I like it here."

She's carrying that crazy kitten in a sling wrapped tight up against her chest, like it's a baby. Whiff? Winch? Wisp. That's it. Wisp is peeking over the edge of the fabric at me, eyes wide.

The lift comes to an abrupt stop and the doors slide open into a circular observation deck a good kilometer above the planet's surface. The deck is small, barely bigger than the cab of a hansom rocket but circular, with floor-to-ceiling windows and some modest instrument panels in the center and functional swing seats built into the walls. It feels kind of old and precarious.

At this height, the buildings of Jezero have receded into tiny specks of light and blend seamlessly with the real stars blinking into visibility against the night sky. At the horizon, I can just make out the curve of Mars, lit up by a fine golden-blue line of light as the planet slips below the line of the sun.

It's as if we're floating somehow inside the eternity of the universe, but with our feet solidly on the ground. Well, maybe not solidly.

"What is this place?"

"It's an old observation tower. When they first built the Grande Dome, they weren't convinced the nautilus structure could stand on its own. This pillar was supposed to anchor it. Turns out it wasn't needed, but they kept it. I like the view. I come up here often."

You can feel the cold pressing in from the outside, but the room is comfortable.

"Seems like it would be a popular spot," I say.

"They don't let many people use it," she says. "Not

considered safe. My credentials get me in. It's a good place to think and find inspiration."

"For your work?"

She nods, then pulls Wisp out of the pouch and sets the little cat on the floor.

"You can see Earth from up here," Mel says. "Our home should be in view in about twelve minutes."

"Home? You said you didn't care about Earth anymore," I say.

"I said I didn't want to live on Earth anymore," she says.

She walks to the window and pulls down a swing chair, a two-seater, and sits down. Wisp hops into her lap. The cat seems a little perturbed to be in a decrepit observation tower just outside the dome on the edge of space. Or maybe it's just me.

"You should visit Earth more," I say.

"I can do more for Earth by staying on Mars," Mel says.

"Your precious bio domes and oxygen-producing moss and terra-scape trees. You know they'll never let you make that stuff back to Earth. There's no value to the Five Families to make our planet better."

I probably shouldn't have said that out loud.

I'm starting to feel edgy. This place is claustrophobic and decrepit, and her behavior is uncharacteristic. I check to see if maybe she brought us here to jam Halo, but it's in full surveillance mode—listening to every word, analyzing every breath.

"Mel, what's going on? Why the sudden need to meet?"

She pets Wisp, who purrs and settles down on Mel's lap, looking out into the universe, her sweet little blue-gray face partially reflected in the thick window. "I talked to Jynks today. I mean, I've been talking to her every day. But today was different. She told me it's over between us. That she doesn't love me, and never did."

I hate Mars. And the Five Families.

"Listen to me," I say. "I'll take care of this. I promise you." I sit down beside her.

Valentine's voice echoes in my head from down in the sunbelt when she accused me of being arrogant, thinking I'm the only one capable of getting this done. What the hell is Valentine doing in my head now?

I want to tell Mel that things will be okay because Tarteric Hoost is not dead, it was his duplex, and Jynks is in the clear. But I can't breathe a word, not yet, not with Halo watching. And I also know that nothing is true, nothing is really settled here on Mars, when the Five Families are involved.

And the fact that Jynks told Mel she doesn't love her means something has changed on her side. She knows she's innocent. She'd only say that to Mel if she thought things were about to get weird. Very weird.

"Look," I say. "We both know Jynks is innocent. Whatever she's saying to you isn't true. Either she's lying, or someone is manipulating her. She loves you, and as much as it irritates me to say it, she's not a terrible person. We'll get through this. *You'll* get through this. I just need a few more days, and Jynks will be back at home with you and little Whisk."

Mel leans her head on my shoulder. "It's Wisp."

I can't help but breathe in her scent. My eyes are closed. I get a flash of Valentine with an I-told-you-so kind of look. I open my eyes and Wisp is glaring up at me.

"Just a few more minutes until Earth is visible."

We stay silent for a while, looking out at the sky now lit up with infinite stars and planets, the light almost equal to the darkness.

"I don't believe Jynks," Mel says, "that she doesn't love me. But it scares me because it means something really bad is happening."

"Something bad is happening," I say. "I can't tell you much about it because it's confidential, but someone is running a dangerous game on the Five Families, and we both know that takes a lot of resources plus either a lot of stupid or a lot of brave. And it has something to do with the sunbelt. I just got back."

She sits up. "How was it?"

"Hot and dry, and weird and explode-y."

"Did you meet any of the climate pioneers?"

"Yeah, we did," I say.

"We?"

Thanks mouth.

"I was there with a small military crew and Chancellor Valentine—"

"Lauren Valentine?"

My heart speeds up. "You know her?"

"Of course. She's a highly respected historian working for Singhroy University. She's smart, and so beautiful. We dated a few times, years back. I'm glad she's involved."

I could really use a drink right now.

"How does this all tie back to Jynks?" Mel asks.

"I don't know yet, but there is something in the sunbelt that someone in the Five Families wants. I don't know what, and I don't know why. Maybe something related to brains."

"Brains?"

"I found a whole lab full of them at Mytikas. They were destroyed and all data wiped before I could learn much."

"Look," she says, standing so suddenly that Wisp drops to the floor. "There's Earth rising and her moon. Can you see it?"

I look out through the tower window and see the faint speck of light, next to an even fainter speck of light against the dark night.

"It's beautiful," I say, but I'm just looking at her reflection in the glass. "And so far away."

She brushes her hand against mine. "Thanks for helping Jynks, Crucial, and for coming here with me. I was feeling especially sad and desperate, and ready to do something stupid. You helped me get centered."

"I recorded that and will be watching it on a loop until the day I die."

She laughs. "I feel a little more confident now, like things are going to be okay."

Our scrolls explode simultaneously with angry headlines:

Jynks Martine makes daring escape from Choke solitary.

Please increase your awareness level and report any data anomalies.

Mars security forces are on the job!

Martine flies the coop, but how long will she last in the Choke?

It's like Halo can't get the editorial message right given how infrequently there's crime on Mars, bouncing between avatainment and fact.

Mel sees the erratic headlines too, of course. Her eyes widen and she holds her hand to her throat. "What the shinks is she doing? Doesn't she see that escaping from the Choke puts her at even greater risk?"

For once I manage to not say out loud what I'm thinking. There's no way that anyone gets out of solitary in the Choke, not without help.

Then I get a ving request. It's from Jynks. Halo is already mobilizing forces. I know Jynks is not that stupid.

30

I try not to blankface but it's impossible to stay focused on Mel with her now fugitive fiancée trying to contact me.

"What's happening?" she asks, then gasps. "It's her, isn't it?"

I nod. But it can't be her. Because why would Jynks give away her location if she's on the run. Unless she wants to be caught. Unless she wants to be glittered in a hundred places by her formerly loyal ... wait, is she trying to get killed?

I look at Mel. She just reached the same conclusion. Her eyes are pooling with tears. "Patch me, patch me!" she shouts. "Don't do this, Jynks."

As I connect, my nanites are stirring and I get a shock. Essential is piggybacking on the feed. Why the prok is Essential using Jynks to connect with me?

"Crucial, I told you to stop investigating," Jynks says. She looks rough. Pale and battered, her eyes wide like she might be in shock. Where is she streaming from?

Essential slides in a new column. I'm seeing Jynks from another viewpoint, at the business end of a glitter gun in a man's hand.

"What is going on?"

"What is going on?" Mel echoes. She's frantic. And Wisp is frantic now too, cowering under the swing seat and howling.

"Make her talk, make her tell him," Essential says.

The thin barrel of the gun pokes Jynks. "Say the truth."

"Somebody tried to kill me. A flier hit the prison."

Essential's conversation with her colleague is shielded, so the only piece that will make it onto the loop is what Jynks says.

"Somebody did try to kill her," Essential says in our private column. "Luckily, we had people watching. She almost died out there. You owe me."

"What are you doing?" I ask, forgetting for a millisecond that Mel can hear me.

"What is she doing?" Mel screams. "Why are you doing this, Jynks?"

"Is that Mel?" Essential asks. "Wow, this must be weird for you." She addresses her colleague. "Tell Martine to talk more about what happened or else you'll kill her."

Jynks looks angry. She's sitting on a stool in a dark room. Her clothes are torn, and she has some blood leaking through rough bandages. She's been rescued, and held at glitterpoint, by a member of the resistance.

He pokes her again. "Say more."

"Someone hit the Choke prison from the air," Jynks says. "I saw them coming. I was able to avoid the worst of the damage."

"She's tough," Essential says. "She trapped some oxygen in a fold of plastic and hid from the first run. They sent in some people to finish her off. She took one of them down with a rock, but the oxygen loss got to her. They hit her good. My people saved her."

"Why are you vinging me?" I ask.

"You're making yourself a target," Mel wails.

"I'm rerouting the location data. Everyone will think she's near Jezero. You need to come get her."

"I can't risk that," I say. "How did you think this would work out?"

"You have to help her," Mel says, pulling on my arm.

"Look," Essential says. "I know you still care about Mel. I didn't think you'd want me to leave her fiancée out there to die. She doesn't know it's me, and she doesn't even have to know it's you. Just come take care of it. Or don't. But you can't say I didn't try."

I'm thinking.

"Crucial, tell Mel I'm sorry," Jynks says. "About everything."

I look at Mel, and she probably sees the pity in my eye.

"She says she's sorry," I say to Mel.

"What's happening?" Mel screams. "Connect me in, I want to talk to Jynks."

I hold up my palm, trying to silence her. It's hard enough to hear Essential.

She slaps my hand away. "Don't do that," she says. "Patch me through to her."

"Mel, stop," I say. "She's trying to protect you. If you get dragged into this, it's all over for both of you."

"You know I didn't murder Tarteric Hoost," Jynks says. "But I don't know who did or why. And now I am being held in an unknown location by suspected members of the resistance, for what purpose I don't know. I am not a member of the resistance. You know that."

She's loyal to the end.

More news flashes are filling our feeds. *The fugitive has been located 60 kilometers southwest of Jezero in the company of resistance fighters. Citizens have nothing to fear. The threat is being neutralized.*

"Oh no," Mel says, falling to her knees. "Don't let them hurt her."

I take her by the shoulder and shake my head. I'm trying to give her some confidence without saying anything damning. And I need to do it without words. Without anything really.

"It's going to be okay," I say, squeezing her arm harder than I should. It works. There's a tiny flash of connection—she's reading me like all those years ago. Receiving me. She looks up at me hopefully. Wisp breaks cover and races across the floor and crawls halfway up Mel's chest before she scoops her into the shoulder pouch.

"The security forces will be there soon. Chundar Hotsip is sending his best."

"I'm as good as dead then," Jynks says.

Ouch. I hope Hotsip was watching.

"She's at Port Zunil," Essential says. "Behind the bar. It's shielded. Ask the bartender for a cobalt nova, with extra dry ice. Hurry though, I'm not sure how long she'll be safe here. Mars SF isn't exactly on our preferred guest list. And my own people, the ones watching her, aren't thrilled about keeping her alive until you can get there."

"I'm on my way. Don't do anything stupid until I get there."

"I love you," Essential says.

"I love you too."

Mel looks at me, surprised. Jynks, even in her rough state, looks confused.

"Did you just tell Jynks that you love her?" Mel asks.

I break the connection.

"It's all very hectic right now," I say.

"We have to go to her," she says, calling the lift.

"*We* don't have to do anything. You have to go home and take Wipe with you."

"Wisp," she says, exasperated.

"Right. I'm gonna get Jynks," I say. "Or at least try."

"How can you possibly do that? You can't fight off the entire Mars security force, which is now—"

I hold up my palm again.

"Stop it!" she says. "Stop doing that."

"Mel, I know you trust me, otherwise I wouldn't even be on this planet now and you would never have designated me as your special investigator, so stop asking questions I can't answer and go home. I promise I will keep Jynks safe. Let me do what you called me up to this prokking red planet to do."

She stares at me for a few seconds and then takes a step back. "Okay. Don't let me down."

"Never again."

31

Sanders is waiting at the base of the observation tower.

This should be interesting. Somehow I need to get to Jynks and save her from angry revolutionaries and whoever tried to kill her in the Choke, all while protecting my radical sister, not accidentally revealing I have enough illegal tech in my bloodstream to help overthrow the Five Families and not betraying the confidence of a surveillance cybanism who might be turning into my best friend.

I really despise Mars.

Sanders and I watch as Mel summons a drone jacket and rises slowly into the air. She flies backward, with Wisp peeking out of her pouch, and then turns and disappears toward her house.

We'll be moving a whole lot faster. Sanders brought a hansom rocket.

"I've entered the coordinates where Jynks Martine is said to be hiding," he says. "It appears we're in for another excursion into the Choke."

He sounds almost happy about it. The last time we almost died.

"We must move quickly to arrive before the Mars security forces, which I assume is your goal," he says. "However, we may be unable to achieve this outcome. Given their departure time and average transport speed, the troops should arrive thirteen minutes ahead of us. Furthermore ..."

"We're not going to those coordinates," I say. "This is a matter for the Mars SF. We can talk to Jynks later."

"Really?" Sanders asks. "While your response is both logical and aligned with Halo's directives, it seems uncharacteristic based on our history together. Is this another one of your hunches?"

"Exactly. What do you know about the Port Zunil docks quarter?"

"It's quite notorious, although not frequently visited beyond those who live and recreate there. Should I assume that is where we are going?"

"Yes."

We exit the Jezero dome at the southern point and get dumped directly into the Choke, headed toward the Dock zone, kicking up a cloud of red dust as we lift off. Soon we're up high enough I can see a convoy of Mars SF vehicles headed the other way.

"Okay, tell me about the Dock zone," I say.

"Certainly, Crucial. As you know, the Dart and other quantum rockets dock at the orbital platforms. Space elevators then drop to what is colloquially known as the Button, a massive frissive palladium alloy disk able to capture and diffuse the energy of the falling space elevators. The elevators use sticky air conveyors to move people and freight."

"I've ridden in one many more times than I ever expected," I say.

"There is a small dome attached to Port Zunil, the main entry point, where workers live, known as the Dock zone. Their job is moving the freight and taking care of the Button."

"How big is this dome?"

"Rather small. No more than several hundred people, but that fluctuates depending on death and reproduction."

Reproduction is strictly forbidden for lottery workers. The arrivals get contraceptive implants that last the duration of their stay. The Five Families don't want any claims of planetship.

"They're allowed to reproduce here on Mars?"

"Yes, but within certain numerical restraints to maintain their numbers at consistent levels, and with members of the dome only."

"What makes them so special?" I ask.

"They have unique knowledge and skills related to the conveyance system that dates to the founding. Some of their ancestors helped construct it, so they are related to the workers who first colonized Mars on behalf of the Five Families. It's a small country of people inside the larger community of Mars."

"Only without access to wealth or clean air or parks or the health cradles or …"

"Crucial, you seem intent on only seeing the negatives of the current system."

"Because the positives seem unequally distributed."

"Dock zone members might disagree," Sanders says.

We pass by Port Zunil and the Button, gleaming so brightly it hurts my eyes. It makes me nervous for some reason. A space elevator is stretching from the gleaming disc out of sight up to the orbital platform. It looks thin and tiny from this distance, like a silver thread, but building-sized pods of freight are being slowly puffed down from space.

Our hansom rocket drops down into the shadow cast by the Port Zunil dome. We're making for a smaller dome—barely noticeable, barely a dome. More of a loaf shape. With the middle collapsed a little.

"Their rights are similar, with some differences, to the status of your friend Melinda Hopwire. I am told this existence, even with its limitations, is preferable to that on Earth," Sanders says.

"A matter of perspective," I say. "How large is the Dock zone?"

"Two hundred and fifty-eight hectares," he says as we approach the entrance.

Re-entry into the dome—into any dome—from the Choke has a whole launch list of protocols—pressure stabilization, virus irradiation, a protein scrub and a bunch of other things I don't care about except for the fact that they all take too long. I'm not a patient man.

"You said the Dock zone was notorious. Why?"

"It's widely believed that the Dockers are somehow able to avoid detection from Halo, and traffic in black-market freight. No one has proved anything, but investigations are always ongoing."

Nobody is ahead of us in the queue and we wait until the light changes from green to purple and the door slides open. Sanders pulls the hansom into the Dock zone, with the main boost dampened all the way down.

The contrast with the rest of Mars is stark. The Dock zone is crowded and dirty. It feels like home, like Earth. People walking around look at us suspiciously, some with outright hostility. My kind of people.

"So, if the Dockers are all descendants of the original heavy lifters who helped set up Mars in the first place, and they're only reproducing among themselves, doesn't that create certain, you know, offspring problems?"

"My analysis reinforces your concern," Sanders says. "Without immigration, they will experience a profound degradation in their genetic stock that ultimately will doom them, as it does any closed society given enough time."

What a choice. Leave Mars for the shithole Earth or throw the dice with the genes of your offspring. It's not hard to understand why the Dock zone workers might be inclined to aid and abet the resistance for a few extra credits. Or maybe a little exchange of genetic materials.

In a few minutes, we're at the zone's center. Habitations and shops haphazardly line the periphery of the dome, mostly made from red rock, but some from what looks like a wood composite. In the middle of the dome is a muddy, grassy area where people stroll around and a few kids play laser tag, burning ornate graffiti onto distant asteroids with tiny autonomous drones you can rent by the minute. One of them has walk-assist exoframes.

"Five minutes in a health cradle and the kid would be walking without machine assistance," I say.

Sanders scans him. "It appears his father is severely debt constrained. Preferring games of chance."

"Not the kid's fault." Halo flags me with a warning.

"That's not the way the debt system works, Crucial."

"Hover here," I say. "This is it. The Perseverance."

We exit the rocket and walk over to the bar. The door slides open, revealing a dark interior with a long counter at the back running the length of the 20-meter or so structure and stools lined up against it in a neat little row like uncharged anthropods. I sit down at one. Sanders stands beside me.

Behind the bar are some tattered pieces of machinery in a sagging display case. Part of one of the original Mars Rovers, apparently, according to a little sign.

"I don't think that sign is accurate," Sanders says. "The alloys used in the components date from almost one hundred years later than the Mars mission of 2020."

"You got a problem with history?" the bartender asks.

The bartender is basically skin and bones. The angles of his shoulder bones poke through the skin. And he's covered with long, rough scars, as if he was taken apart and then put together again. And a few pieces went missing. Not many, just enough to throw everything off a little.

My scroll grabs his vitals. Samir Volgov. Third-gen Docker, 70 kilos. Bio-father of two. Owner of this tavern. Clean enough record. A space elevator landed on him 20 years ago.

He doesn't seem thrilled that I'm eyeing him up and down. "Forget it, I'm spoken for," he says. "What can I get you?"

"I'll take a cobalt nova, with extra dry ice."

He nods. He's been expecting me. "Anything for the flesh-bot?"

"No," I say. "He's a mean drunk."

The bartender turns and begins making a very elaborate drink, and one that seems a bit out of place in this bar. He's measuring and muttering and pouring shots from six different bottles. A flame is involved for a few seconds. He tongs a couple of dry ice cubes into an oddly shaped container—bulbous on the bottom with a thick spiral neck leading up to a tulip-shaped bowl at the top.

He sets the contraption in front of me, pours the liquid into the top and it courses down the spiral, a pulsing, blue current that hits the cubes, reacts violently and begins bubbling and swirling back up.

"What the hell am I supposed to do with this?" I ask.

"Drink it," he says. "It's what you ordered. And just so you know, the biowaste closet is down the hall to the right. Second door. You'll need it with this drink."

I shrug and tip the weird glass up and take a long pull. It's cold and smoky and sweet and mysterious, tasting like stone fruit and shadows and spice. It hits me hard.

"Damn. That's good. One more?"

The bartender nods.

"Sanders, sit tight."

I walk to the hall. The first door is the head. The second one says, "Keep out, gristlebrains."

I wake up the nanites and tell them to cover me like I'm in the can, and then open the gristlebrains door. Jynks is tied to a chair in the middle of the room, her arm in a sling. She's pretty banged up. Two people are standing nearby, both pointing glitter guns at me.

"You're just in time to watch her die," one says.

32

"*You're* my rescue party?" Jynks asks. "I am definitely going to die here."

"Nobody is dying here," I say.

"I wouldn't be so sure," one of her captors says.

"Why are you working with the resistance?" Jynks asks. "I knew it, I knew there was more to you than just a loser burnout with a pity badge for not getting killed in the Consolidation Wars."

Damn, she's harsh.

"Fine, kill her," I say.

The woman raises her glitter gun. At least I think it's a woman. Her face is covered with an image-distorting mask, the low-tech kind popular on Earth a few decades ago when immersive avatainment was just starting. Halo banned them when people realized they fuzzed your identity.

I'm taken aback for a second because the mask distortion she's chosen makes her eyes look narrow and yellow, with razor-thin vertical pupils. Like a blizard.

Saurian.

"Stop, no, you can't," I say to her. "Not yet anyway."

She lowers the gun, but not far. I think they're wondering why the hell they should care what I think? Other than being the handsome brother of their second in command, who I heroically saved not that long ago.

I take a closer look at Jynks. She's electro-cuffed to an

old chair, a jammer by her feet keeping Halo at bay. It's a double effort, because the room is also shielded. Her face is a bruised, bloody mess, and one arm is pinned tight to her torso in a medi-sash. Must mean it's broken.

"Bad day?" I ask.

"Prok off," she says. "You should have killed me in the Choke."

"You're an idiot if you think I had anything to do with this," I say. "I'm here only because of Mel. And you're an even bigger idiot if you think the resistance had anything to do with it." I bend close. "This is going to be hard to hear. They saved your life."

"I don't believe it," she says.

"We can't believe it either," the man says. "After what she did at Korolev, and to Omar, we should have left her to die."

He's not wearing a mask, but he's got a scarf wrapped around his face so that only his eyes are visible. I can't make out much of his features, but I would recognize that hairless dome anywhere.

He was at the Korolev bunker, three seats down from me at the dinner where I met Lauren Valentine and stuffed my face full of sheetmeat gyros and kallards, about an hour before the entire place was nuked into antimatter by Jynks and her security crew. I think his name is Zobar or Zohar or Zo-something.

"We can't let her live now," Zo-something says. "She knows too much, including about you."

"Turn yourselves in now and I swear to you, we'll go easy on you. Labor, no terrorium," Jynks says.

"Jynks, shut up and let me tell you what's going on. Hoost isn't even dead."

Her eyes show her shock at this news.

"It was a duplex."

"Gross," the woman says.

"Exactly. Whoever set you up doesn't know that yet and thinks I'm getting too close, so they decided to take you out."

"And all of this?" she asks, nodding to the two resisters.

"This right here is the luckiest day of your tall, gorgeous life. You get to live, Mel gets to be happy, and all you need to do is keep one little secret."

She's chewing on that, but it's hard to swallow, like that tough cartilage that sometimes grows in sheetmeat around an impurity.

"I took an oath of loyalty," she says.

"Yeah, to protect the Five Families, who let you be framed for murder and almost killed in the Choke. Did you hear me? Hoost is not dead."

She shakes her head. "Even if I agreed, and I don't, how could I explain all this?"

"It's easy," I say. "I just happen to be a top-notch investigator …"

She snorts, and it hurts her broken arm so we both lose.

"… who found you here where two shifty Dockers wanted to trade you for some debt relief. I overpowered them but your captors, who you *cannot* identify, got away. You don't know what happened, but it probably had something to do with the people who framed you for the murder that *didn't really happen*."

"That's actually a pretty good plan," the woman says.

"Thank you. See, she gets it," I say to Jynks. "All you have to do is keep any completely unfounded suspicions to yourself, go back to Mel and keep your head down and her safe until I find who actually tried to kill you out in your little Choke prison. Then I can go back to Earth and sleep for a month in my little fake desert."

That thought brings me indescribable joy. My mind

jumps to the holo-desert where I once spent so much of my leisure time, such as it was, sleeping naked. And even now, even after nearly dying in the sunbelt, I want my holo-desert. Maybe *because* of the sunbelt, as it turns out. Fake desert is much better than real desert.

Essential once told me that sleeping in the desert was really a thing, that the ancient Greeks had a name for it—anachoresis. And not just hanging out naked, like I do, more like withdrawing for philosophical reflection. That was back when Essential was trying to convince me that my habit was probably a sign of grief.

She's wrong. I do it to escape. Huge difference.

Jynks is silent. She's thinking through the implications for her future. She lands right where I would have.

"Does Mel know?" she asks.

"Not a thing. I mean, she knows you're innocent. We all knew that."

I can see the light behind her eyes changing. She won't risk Mel. Nobody should ever risk Mel. She learned from my mistakes. Finally, she laughs. A harsh and dry sound, like the echo of arrogance from someone who's been knocked down low and knows she may never get all the way up again.

"We'll probably all go to a labor camp, but sure, it's worth a try," Jynks says.

The tension in the room drops by several degrees.

"Good choice," I say. "Now tell me what's going on. Let me help end this."

She takes a deep breath. "I don't know, exactly. It has something to do with the sunbelt. The evidence led to Singhroy Darlinius. I was meeting with Hoost to share my suspicions when it all went to hell in a bucky ball."

"That little shit? He doesn't have what it takes to wage war on the Five Families."

"The evidence was faint but clear," Jynks says. "He's been diverting funds, hiding flights to Earth and assembling an army of genetic mistakes."

"Mistakes?"

"There's something very weird going on with Mytikas. But the data is gone now."

"I'm a people person," I say. "I'll talk to him. Where's the young rascal hanging out these days?"

"Darlinius is part of the Younkers. They have a private dome."

"Younkers?"

She shrugs. "Inherited wealth warps brains. Like genetic inbreeding, only for emotional intelligence. The young, pretty ones hang out in their own dome."

A few days ago, I was talking to the Saurians, today I'm drinking with the Dockers. Soon I'll be shaking down some Younkers. I may need two solid months of anachoresis.

"I hate to say it," Jynks says, "but I think your plan just might work."

"Thank you," I say. "I know admitting that was painful."

The lights flicker. Blink, really. Three times. Then a pause. Then three more times.

"Mars security is here," Zo-whatever says.

Godsdamn it. It was such a good plan.

33

I use the nanites to hijack a lens in the bar. Hotsip Chundar has a whole army of muscle with him, loaded with armament. Hotsip is talking to Sanders. Sanders is pointing in my direction.

What the wobbling gyroscope is Hotsip doing here? He's supposed to be investigating the fake coordinates Essential broadcast.

I return my attention to the room. "Okay, new plan," I say, and nod toward the resisters. "Jynks, you have to go with them."

"No," Jynks says. "No way. Turn me over to Mars security."

"Not a chance," I say. "We don't know who to trust. And if word gets out that Hoost isn't dead, I can't fix this. You have to remain a fugitive."

I look at the two resistance fighters.

"No prokking way, we are not keeping her," the woman says. "She's a murdering ideologue, doing the bidding of the capitalist despots."

"Yes, she is, with capital letters, and you can yell those old, tired slogans at her the entire time she's in your care," I say. "You'll probably even convert her to your side by the end."

"That is not the plan," Zo-something says.

It's Zohar. I'm sure of it.

"Listen, it's *essential* we stick to this plan," I say.

I know Essential is tracking the fun through a hidden channel.

"You really owe me now, big brother," she says in a degrading font-speak message.

She's already told her compatriots and they are glaring at me, pulling Jynks to her to her feet and wrapping her in a detainment muffler.

"You can't leave me here with these traitors!" Jynks yells as the hood goes over her head. "Get me out of here you prokking sympathizer, I'm gonna ..."

They turn off the volume and now she's just raging inside the suit and wobbling from the strain.

"How do we get past the Mars SF?" Zohar asks.

It's a good question. We're in a small room in a small bar in a small dome next to the Button. Think, Larsen, think.

An image of Sanders pops into my head. "The history of irony is a fascinating journey through the evolution of human intelligence." No, *no*, not that. "The Dockers are notorious smugglers." That's the one.

Smugglers are smart. They internalize risk and tip the odds in their favor. There must be another way out of this room. They wouldn't risk trapping themselves in here, or anywhere.

"Look for hidden exits," I say, and we focus our attention on the walls, tapping and shuffling, looking for a way out.

Nothing doing. We can hear the rumble of bootsteps getting closer.

I slump down hard in the chair Jynks was in and feel the floor give a little. Just a microfraction.

That's odd. I kick the floor with my heels and it moves slightly.

There are old cloth rugs covering the entire floor and I

pull one back to reveal a gleaming metal surface. Frissive palladium. Just like the Button. Those sneaky little spy-bots. They built their floor over a network of tunnels perfect for moving stolen freight.

And the key to getting in is to use just enough force.

I kick one of the rugs out of the way. "Quick, hit this with your glitter gun," I say. "Max nonlethal."

There's a ruckus next door as the cops all crash into the empty bio-baller, then there's some cursing and mumbling.

The masked resister fires a volley of flechettes into the floor and the force ripples the metal back like a stone dropped into a waste pond. There's a dark tunnel below, with soft, shock-absorbing cushioning on the floors. I don't even hesitate, just push Jynks over the edge and watch her fall, twisting and yelling silently inside her muffler until she bounces softly at the bottom.

"Take care of her," I say to the fake Saurian and Zohar.

"No promises," Zohar says, and they jump in after her.

A fist pounds on the door, rattling it, but it holds. Then more shouting. I can hear an arc-lever being deployed. The flat crack of the joints locking into place is unmistakable.

The metal floor ripples and flows back into place and I spread out the rug.

Sanders is yelling at them to stand down, saying that I'm an official representative of the Five Families.

They're going to come in hot. I'll probably get glittered, unless I'm not facing them.

The arc-lever whines and with a pop the door crashes open and a dozen Mars SF officers rush in, all in full tac gear. They are caught up short by the sight of me, back turned, pissing on the wall.

"What the burning meteor?" I ask. "Can't a guy have a little privacy in the bio-baller?"

Hotsip is looking at me with disgust. "This is not the

toilet," he hisses.

"Hey, what do you know?" I shake off and look around. "You're right. Damn, those cobalt novas hit hard. You should try one."

Apparently, he's not interested in having a drink with me. After I answer a lot of questions with "Huh, really? I don't know anything about that," Hotsip and his crew leave. They are not happy.

Our scrolls are blowing up with news headlines. *Hotsip outwitted by former boss* and *Odds of catching Jynks shrink* and *Don't worry, citizens of Mars, justice will be served.*

"It's curious," Sanders says as we watch the Mars cops leave. "You have imbibed a great deal of alcohol in my presence before with only marginal impairment to your functionality. And yet you claim this particular drink limited your abilities."

"I don't know, buddy," I say. "Maybe I just hadn't eaten enough." I turn to the bartender. "Any food in this dump?"

"None worth eating," he says.

"I'll take that cobalt nova then, but regular dry ice. I have work to do."

"It's also odd that not a single person came or went during the time you were in there, as if the establishment were closed," Sanders says. "But I checked and it was not. Many people walked by, but none entered."

"I mean, look around," I say. "This place is a dump." The bartender sets my drink down. "Sorry, no offense. It's a *great* dump."

"Flattery gets you this one on the house."

I take my time. This one seems even stronger. Just as I'm draining the last few drops, I realize it's exactly the color of the gunk that passes for blood inside Sanders. The thought makes me a little nauseous.

"Sanders, why do you ooze blue goo when you die?"

"My designers thought it prudent to be abundantly clear, through the visual indication of blue liquid, that I am not human in the case of a terminal action. It causes less confusion, stress and waste of security resources."

"Do me a favor, turn it a different color. Like red, like real blood red, right now. So I can keep my drinks down."

"My charge is to assist you in this investigation. If you inform me this is needed to assist you, I will readily comply." His eyes roll back in his head in that alarming way he has and stay there for a few seconds, showing only the whites, and then re-center.

"Done," he says.

"Thanks," I say. "And speaking of adjusting your parameters, would it be possible to stop that eye thing?"

"Sorry, that's hard-coded. I've made a note for the next time I cease functioning for reconsideration of that lever."

I'm a little wobbly when I stand up. "Don't make any immediate plans," I say. "I need you to get us to Herschel dome while I take a curcumin flush and sober up."

"Take two," the bartender says. "Cobalt novas will kick you right in the rover. I've never seen anyone make it past two without medical intervention."

I want to take that challenge, but I need to go see my old friend Darlinius.

34

The first thing I notice about the Younkers is that they have their own ocean inside their dome. Sanders and I are flying in low over Herschel crater and can see down into the dome, which is relatively small—about 300 kilometers in diameter—and crystal clear.

The second thing I notice is about a hundred gun turrets tracking our approach.

So, they have their own ocean and are paranoid. Or maybe just careful. Either way, it's a little out of character for this age group—narcissistic and still convinced of their immortality.

"I'm not clear on the plan," Sanders says.

"I've told you like six times," I say. "We're going to try and rattle him and see what shakes loose. Why is that so hard to understand?"

"Perhaps because I rely on a literal definition of the word 'plan,'" Sanders says. "One that involves a thoughtful design with a definitive purpose. What you are proposing seems to more closely track the definition of wishful thinking with the potential for violence. I can't find a single word to adequately describe that."

"If you could, that would be a good word," I say.

I check my feed to confirm a hunch. There are no fewer than 4,000 separate fir-per channels streaming out of there, with at least 500 million Earthers connected in to marvel at how the young and wealthy live on Mars. The fir-pers, or first-persons in full lingo, are the current fashion that allows the newest generation of Martians to monetize the attention of Earthers.

Unlike the other domes, Herschel crater is a shared space with the bored youth from all Five Families living together chasing one thrill after another.

I blink away the list of channels and overlay the history and geography. The crater is named after father and son astronomers from back in the old days, but nobody calls it that. Not anymore. Not after they put in the fake ocean.

Seems the crater was known for some active sand dunes. So, using the credits they siphoned off Earth, someone had the bright idea early on of making a self-contained little ocean dome on Mars.

In keeping with the weird way that the Five Families worship ancient assholes, they called it Salacia. Apparently, she was the wife of some old sea god. The Younkers call it Dome Salacious.

I'm flipping through some of the fir-pers of the Younkers—seems like they got the name just about right.

We're right over the top of the apex, looking down. About half the domed space is pure, sparkling water. That much water would be a fortune six times over on Earth, and a million rehydrated lives saved. There's a crescent of beach bisecting the middle of the crater floor, maybe a kilometer wide, made from original crater sand, feathered in angles of black and red. Nestled into the thin part of the beach is a small city of twisted, impossible buildings. The design, like their lives, is supposed to shock and inspire.

We land at the reception portal next to the dome's edge.

The security area is filled with a handful of guards and a virtual chessboard of cybanisms—mostly nude and all with exaggerated breasts and penises along with guns grown right into their hands. And those are the normal-looking ones. Others are lumps of flesh and muscle with eyes for mouths and glitter gun barrels protruding from their taut stomachs.

I know why Jynks called them an army of mistakes.

"This is unconventional," Sanders says.

One of the humans motions us over. He's private muscle, not Mars SF. Built like a charging station with a crooked nose. It must be intentional; you can get a reshaping poultice for less than a credit. Probably thinks it makes him look tough.

"What's with all the irregulars?" I ask.

"Our employers have an odd sense of humor," he says, scanning my information. "Don't let their shapes fool you, they're capable of defense."

"I wasn't talking about them," I say. "Your employers have something against the Mars security forces?"

"Yeah," the guard says. "They want to keep living. We're paid twice as much with twice the enhancements." He raises his hand and flexes an exoglove bolted right into the bone. "I can pop your head like a bubble scone with this bad boy."

"You must have to be very careful when you take a stream," I say. "They have a lot of enemies, these layabouts?"

"Maybe you've heard about the resistance? And how Tarteric Hoost was recently assassinated."

"Pretty sure the resistance isn't going to target a bunch of 'tocin-addled underperformers."

"My job isn't to guess what's best for the Five Families." He's linked to the security screen and blinks it open. "They're expecting you. And only you."

Sanders looks hurt. "But I'm his companion."

"No weapons inside."

"I'm not a weapon, I'm a …"

"Cybanism, yeah, we know. Like all the rest of these forms. Your type can do some damage up close."

"I'm sure these are not my type," Sanders says, looking askance at one of the guard things that looks like a giant neck with humanish features tottering on tiny legs with rail guns for ears.

"Play nice, buddy," I say. "I'll be right back."

I walk inside and I'm standing in a dream, with hot sand stretching out in front of me and little, symmetric waves of clear water washing toward my feet. They've got the heat turned up and a salty breeze circulating. I can see people down the full length of the beach lounging in various states of undress, most of them drinking. I zoom in.

Yeah, sure, I'm a voyeur. So what?

It's Martian absinthe. I can almost taste it from here.

That's the problem with curcumin flushes—you need a drink to get over sobering up so fast.

Darlinius is expecting me in one of the awkward-looking buildings on the faux coast. I summon a drone jacket, slip it on and hop up for a better view.

Some animals are in the water, sleek as bullets, whole flocks of them. I zoom in and question. Apparently, they're based on sea life known as dolphins. Only these have fur and angular faces. Dolphelines. The millions of fir-per viewers of these Younkers love them.

The Younkers like to mess with nature. I guess it's a way of advertising just how little they care about their wealth, by spending it extravagantly.

Luxurious platforms float in the water, with people drinking and not laughing; some of them are making love, others are watching. All of them are broadcasting fir-pers.

The buildings on the shoreline come into view. Apparently, the Younkers like their architecture like their bio-forms—gaudy and exaggerated.

Darlinius is waiting on the top of the Opportunity building—a tall, narrow experience tower that looks like a bunch of glass Zs fighting over a wedge-bot. I geo-loc him on the top floor. He's sprawled out on a chesterfield bigger than my squat. The light—fake and real—reflecting off the water makes his pale skin almost translucent. Kyrinth Corolis, who I met the other day in the cafe, is again by his side. She seems more at ease here than in Jezero.

"What do you think of our little dome?" Darlinius asks, simultaneously not caring and caring too much.

The children of the wealthy are even worse than the wealthy. They delude themselves into thinking their luck is deserved so they are constantly anxious to prove their worth, which is impossible, and that makes them insecure and unstable and unpredictable. It's exhausting. And hopefully just the psycho-wedge I need to get inside his head a little.

Irritating people, I've learned, is one of my talents. I need to rattle his altimeter just enough to get him to tip his hand and then get out before I do something a rational person would regret, something that would land me in the Choke solitary cell Jynks recently vacated.

"It's not so bad, as far as domes go," I say. "Perfect pond for little fishes, I guess."

His face falls, but not Kyrinth's. She lights up at the put-down, her eyes shining with something like sadistic interest as she leans in closer. Dome Salacious is a brutal place.

He glares at me. "Why are you even here? According to the people who watch the news for me, Jynks Martine escaped. It should be obvious to even the densest of Earthers that she's guilty. It's only a matter of time before they find her. Shouldn't you be heading back to your own planet?"

"There's nothing I would like more," I say. "Except

maybe a little of that absinthe."

There's a service set on the table between them. The booze, in a crystal decanter, is glimmering like liquid rubies in sunshine.

"I do not drink with trash from a trash planet," he says.

"Don't be boring, darling," Kyrinth says. "He came all this way. And I could use a drink." She nods and a handsome young man—a lottery winner from Earth— hurries out from the shadows to pour a glass full, and hands it to me. He sets the decanter down too hard and the jarring clink makes Darlinius wince.

"Stop being so loud," he says as the man retreats. "We can have you replaced."

I take a sip and let the ruby heat spread through me, and sigh. "Oh, that's good."

"Enjoy it then," he says. "That one glass is worth more than you'll make in a year."

"I better have two then," I say, refilling my glass and setting the decanter down with an intentionally loud clink. "Here's the thing. I'm not going anywhere until Jynks receives a fair trial and the murder of Hoost is solved."

"Tarteric Hoost," he says. "Even our dead deserve the respect of familial conventions."

"I've found the dead don't care much about anything I say."

"Nor do the living. You're blocking the view," Darlinius says. "Either leave or sit down."

I pull up a chair-like object that looks like a cross between a lab-grown myco-cap and a kid's fleece ball. It's very comfortable, but I wonder if it's made from one of those furry dolphins.

"What can you tell me about your interest in the sunbelt?" I ask.

There it is.

His pulse flickers and his pupils dilate—I'm not authorized to access his feeds, but I am monitoring him on the law enforcement interrogation silhouette to track his peripherals. He's clearly nervous about something.

"I can assure you that I have no interest in some burned-over region of a failing planet," he says a little too loudly.

"Darlinius, have a drink," Kyrinth says, topping off his absinthe.

That's interesting. She didn't wait for the servant. He gulps some of it down and seems to find a little courage.

"Why are you asking me about a biological hazard area on a planet I've never even visited?"

"You've never been to Earth? Lucky Earth," I say. "I was just there a few days ago, specifically in the sunbelt."

"What about the blizards?" Kyrinth asks. "So creepy. What are they like?"

"Their booze is a little rough in comparison," I say, thinking back to the ant gin. "But they treated me pretty well. It was the humans I had a trouble with. I was attacked there, but it didn't go well for the attackers. They mostly ended up smeared along the edge of a crater. But one ship got away."

"And I strike you as some sort of interstellar pilot?" Darlinius asks.

"You strike me as a barely functioning biped," I say.

He almost chokes on what's left of the absinthe. Kyrinth laughs at his discomfort. She can't help herself. It's a high, pure sound, like a glass-etching tool. She's got a mean streak wider than the great solar flare of 2028.

"You did not just talk to me like that," he says.

"Yeah, I did," I say. "Rewind and spool it. Clear as day. You can watch it on repeat. I know I will. That's going in my top ten scorch list. The thing is, I know you didn't fly that ship. You aren't capable of doing anything except wasting credits and oxygen. But I think you're tangled up in it. In the sunbelt, in this illegal brain research at Mytikas."

His pulse spikes again.

"You and Singhroy Clystra are up to something. I don't know what, but I'll figure it out. I'm patient. The Fist is footing my bills. You and your little pod of turd waffles can't stop me."

"I think you should leave now," Kyrinth says. She's suddenly all hard and focused. I like her. She has layers. "Brash can only go so far before it becomes insolent." She nods her head and some of the private security guards suddenly appear.

I finish my absinthe. "I'm on to you, Darlinius. Your precious aunt can't save you. Won't save you. The Fist wants me to figure this out. And as for you," I say to Kyrinth, "you should stand up for Earth a little instead of turning your back on it. And pick your friends more carefully."

"We're much more than friends," she says, with that same peculiar hard-edged laugh. He has a petulant look on his face, somewhere between embarrassment and anger.

As I make my way out, two things have become abundantly clear: Darlinius is indeed up to something, and his companion is way better than he is under pressure.

I hope I haven't shaken them so much they order the goons to just glitter me and dump me in the fake ocean with the dolphelines. Luckily, they know as well as I do that Halo is observing very closely.

35

Sanders is visibly relieved to see me. The other cybanisms, hundreds of them, are standing around him, staring. At least the ones with eyes.

They're probably jealous that he's normally shaped. I mean, I know "normal" sounds judgmental, but at least he mimics a form that evolution proved to be advantageous. If not for the quirk of form, and the quirk of our brains inside those forms, humans would never have been able to dominate and ruin an entire planet, then hurl themselves into space to start the whole process over again on Mars.

These things, this army of mistakes, exist somewhere between the whim of the bored and a fevered dream of science.

"You all caught up with your new friends?" I ask.

"They are not particularly interested in a spirited conversation," he says.

"Don't be too hard on them," I say as we get into the hansom rocket. "Most of them don't have mouths."

"Where to?" he asks. "Do you have another hunch?"

"Still working on it," I say.

A priority ving comes in from Singhroy Able. "Maybe this is it," I say to Sanders.

I receive. Able looks worried.

"What have you learned?" she asks.

"Nothing useful yet," I say, "but I'm pretty sure your nephew is tangled up in something over his head."

She sighs. She's standing next to a window in some luxurious personal dome that faces Jezero.

"It wouldn't take much for him to be over his head," she says. "I don't think he's smart enough, or ruthless enough, to take advantage of this situation."

They're hiding something from me, of course. It's what they do. "What situation?" I ask. "Able, tell me what's going on."

"The spa, the data lost at Mytikas, is vital," she says. "You must find that, and you cannot let anyone outside the Fist know. If it falls into the wrong hands, the future of Mars will be changed forever."

I'm trying to decide if I care. She knows what I'm thinking.

"And that means the future of Earth will be in jeopardy."

"I need clearance to surveil Singhroy Clystra, and you need to keep Hotsip and Mars SF off my back.

"Done," she says, then breaks the connection.

Sanders is looking at me expectantly. "So, is that our destination?"

"Not yet."

Another ving comes through. From Mel.

"What is happening?" she asks.

"Hi Mel, nice to see you," I say.

"You promised me you would bring Jynks home."

"That's not a promise I should have made. But I can promise I'll keep her safe."

She lets that sink in. I hope she understands the distinction. Her jaw relaxes a little.

"The news feeds say she'll be caught any second."

"That might be true."

"Where is she?"

"I don't know," I say, which is the truth. "But I will let

you know the second I have more information."

I really need to stop moping around after her. She's in love with Jynks. I had my chance and I destroyed it, cremated it and shot the ashes into the sun.

"Now do we have a destination?" Sanders asks.

"Yes. Lauren Valentine's squat."

"Is Lauren Valentine another hunch?"

"Not really," I say. "But she's good company for the stakeout."

He enters the coordinates with a glance.

"I have a question," Sanders says.

"Stakeout is an old-fashioned term for watching a suspect," I say.

"I have a linguistic module with full access to Earth lingo," he says. "I'm familiar with the term. I'm curious why Lauren Valentine would be better company than me."

"Oh, not better. I mean in addition to."

That seems to make him feel better.

I ving Valentine. "Hey, are you up for a fun night sitting in a hansom rocket with a needy cybanism and a handsome labor cop temporarily serving as a Mars special investigator monitoring a potential suspect?"

"That sounds far too good to pass up," she says.

"We'll be there in a few minutes."

After I end the connection, Sanders looks puzzled.

"Where is this needy cybanism located?"

The hansom slides to a hover in front of Valentine's coordinates—a small building covered with a green plant, a climber, all over the red stones. Looks old, crumbling even, but that's fake. Nothing on Mars is old. They use design to manufacture meaning. The floating holo-sign says: *Singhroy University—Labor Dormitory.*

Valentine messages she'll be out in a flash.

Mel used to tell me about the era on Earth when people

gathered in physical places, some of them luxe, to learn things. But that was long before the viruses and the age of contagion changed the world into one giant, crowded, lonely digital connection.

The door pops up and Valentine is standing there smiling like she's actually happy to see me. I will never understand relationships. She should be mad at me. I guess I think that because I'd be mad at her, which probably says a lot about our respective levels of maturity. She slides in next to me. It's a pretty roomy transport, but she buckles in close enough I can smell her scent, something minty and lemony.

"What's going on?" she asks. "Do you really need a history expert, or did you just miss me?"

"A little of both," I say. "I want to talk more about your sunbelt research, and stakeouts are boring so I thought why not see if you had some time."

"I take it Mel was busy," she says.

Maybe I do understand relationships.

But then she smiles. "Just yanking your orbital tether a little. Who's the target?"

"Singhroy Clystra."

Sanders is already lifting off.

"Wow, high rank," she says. "Does the Fist know?"

"Of course," I say. "Our interests are temporarily aligned."

"A stakeout sounds exciting, but it all seems so twenty-first century," she says. "Why not tap into their feeds?"

She's right of course, but that's the tricky part of the modern world. Everyone is always on guard against digital surveillance, so sometimes you need to shake things up a little.

"I like to try unconventional approaches," I say.

"To just about everything," she says.

"That was a very good joke at your expense," Sanders says. "I would characterize that as a witty rejoinder."

I can tell he's filing that away. It's going to be a long night. I fill in Valentine on what I've been up to, including my time with the Younkers.

"Dolphelines?" she asks. "You're kidding."

"Wish I was," I say. "They have some odd creations there. Like maybe rejects from Mytikas. It's all connected."

I pull out a salt beer pouch from the coolbox, tear open the corner and squeeze out a long drink. I offer it to Valentine, but she shakes her head.

"Maybe a little later," she says. "Dolphins, the real ones, were believed to be exceptionally intelligent."

"I am sifting that data now," Sanders says. "By the close of the twenty-first century, before their extinction event, their vocabulary had been largely decoded, although investigators never accurately measured their intelligence."

"Part of the problem is they attempted to measure any intelligence using human intelligence as the baseline," Valentine says.

"Please elaborate," Sanders says.

"Are you familiar with Sparkman's paradox?" she asks, and he snares the data and absorbs it. "True understanding is always limited by the incorrect assumption that human understanding is at the pinnacle of thought. Our certainty about our cognitive abilities in fact dooms our pursuit of certainty."

"Fascinating. Perhaps artificial intelligence is the way to resolve the paradox," Sanders says.

"Perhaps, but at present, Halo acknowledges the limits of understanding based on programming constraints. Interestingly, it was the ancient research on dolphins that helped Sparkman develop her paradox because of the mirror experiment."

"Like, did they keep trying to attack the other fish in the mirror?" I ask.

"Dolphins were mammals," Valentine and Sanders say simultaneously.

I may not have thought through the evening completely.

"Historically, scientists measured animal intelligence based on whether they recognized their own image in a mirror, to assess if they had an interior world, a sense of self. Dolphins easily passed this test," Valentine says.

I can see Sanders looking at his reflection in the display console, smiling and moving his head from side to side.

"Congratulations," I say. "You're officially smarter than a fish."

"What do you see when you look in the mirror, Sanders?" Valentine asks.

"I see an image I logically recognize as my own synthetic form. But I don't see that form in a way that is measurably different than how I recognize your form, or Crucial's form. What do you think this means?"

"Something about your still-emerging sense of self," Valentine says.

"Very curious," he says. "Perhaps Melinda Hopwire could recreate the existence of dolphins at Baldet crater for further study."

Valentine looks over at me as nighttime flows past, then up at the stars and twin moons. She's not going to say anything. That's how she is, I get that now. Like, nothing seems to bother her. I wish I could be like that. I mess up everything. Like I'm about to do right now.

"Sanders, could you pretend to give us a little privacy?"

"Of course, Crucial," he says. "I will contemplate my sense of self."

His eyes do that back-in-his-head thing I hate. I guess

he doesn't really need them to see.

"Yuck," Valentine says.

"Right?" I take her hand. "I'm sorry. I'm messed up, have been most of my life, and don't see a future in which I become much less messed up. I should have been honest with you about that."

She looks up for an instant, avoiding my eyes, but she doesn't move her hand away from mine. Finally, she looks at me.

"Crucial, it's okay, really," she says. "I know you're damaged. We all are. And you can stop thinking you have to do everything perfectly or alone. We can exist next to each other, from time to time, giving each other a brief escape from the pain of the past." She squeezes my hand. "I don't need anything more from you, I don't need you to try to be better. I like that you're completely comfortable in the wreckage of your life. That predictability feels like a priceless gift right now."

And in a flash, I understand that I have been a deeply selfish man, focused only on my own past, my own grief.

"I'd like to learn more about that someday, hear your story."

"Maybe but not now," she says. "Let's just keep things where they are, two people who don't hate each other and occasionally can wrestle some moments of joy out of the darkness."

She leans across the bench and kisses me. I pull her in close. She's got my face in her hands, I've got my hands on her waist. And then higher.

The rocket slows suddenly and starts to drop. Sanders rolls his eyes back and takes the controls. "The climate sensors must be malfunctioning," he says. "The internal temperature has increased and there is excess humidity in the air." Then he pauses. "And your heart rates are elevated. Are you well?"

Valentine smiles. "Yes, very."

The rocket drops to a quick landing near the red-glass residence of Singhroy Clystra.

36

"You'd think a doctor would be able to afford a nicer place," I say.

Singhroy Clystra's place is enormous, a cluster of seven large hexagonal tubes, each about 40 meters long and four meters tall, and made of thick, cloudy, glassified Martian sand. One end faces the transpo-corridor and from our perspective, looks like a networked hive with an array of small sunlight side ports. The other side overlooks a manufactured oasis shared by neighboring palace-houses, with similar design but different colors.

"Yes, it is a veritable consolidation area for storing medical waste," Sanders says from the driver's seat. "And it's on fire." He looks at me expectantly.

His sense of humor is terrible. And seems to be getting worse.

"A joke. Another joke. That's good, Sanders," Valentine says.

"Yes, because it's so obviously untrue," he says. "I was saying an exaggerated and opposite version of the truth, which is what makes it funny."

"Really funny," I say. "Especially when you explain it. Let's change rides."

The most important part of surveillance is not necessarily seeing what others are hiding, but staying hidden from counter-surveillance. The Fist has given us a lot of latitude to conceal ourselves from most people on

Mars, and the means to do it. The unmarked zadel they've provided, a luxury conveyance with all the appurts including the most important—the ability to hide from Mars SF database—is hovering. The zadel is big and comfortable and shielded from prying feeds with a dozen levels of reaction-based camouflage. In the rare event someone wanders by, a signal from the zadel penetrates the virtual experience loop inside their OCD eye, transforming the vehicle into whatever they expect to see—a repair-bot recharging for the night or an oxygen generator.

We send the hansom rocket back to the stable and pile into the zadel. Sanders redirects the dome cameras above to give us multiple perspectives on our feeds. I zoom in on the crystal blue pool at the back of the home. It's ringed with plants. I query for foliage identification—orchids and tall red maples dripping with fuzzy moss called tillandsia usneoides. It's all very lovely and irritating.

When we left Dome Salacious, Sanders tapped into Halo and has been monitoring Clystra's outbound feed. He's sharing it with me and Valentine. I sent some fleas and microdrones up ahead to watch the house, and we've patched the feeds into one multipoint column in our scrolls. Nothing is happening.

There's no anomalous activity yet—in or out. Clystra is inside with his family, each on a different floor. He's been inside for about an hour.

I'm sipping a hot coffee foam and eating wheatine crackers with gravity cheese faster than the dashboard printer can spit them out. And sitting next to a beautiful woman who is holding my hand. All in all, it's a pretty good assignment.

I once spent most of a long night next to four other cops shivering knee-deep in waste-bilge water waiting for some disconnects to return to their squat with stolen beetle chargers. We got them, and they all got reconnected to Halo—without anesthetic—and a triple life labor sentence.

I couldn't get that smell out of my nose for a week, And I couldn't get the parasites out of my gut for a month. It was a new worm the doctors had never seen before. They still call them C-worms around the precinct. Most people just call them poopworms. Or microfecal flukes. There's a pill that flushes them right out, but it takes a few unpleasant hours.

It seems counter-intuitive but monitoring people in a surveillance society is harder than it seems. Everyone knows they are being monitored all the time and escaping detection is not really a possibility, so it's not like people are willing to risk doing anything to draw attention to themselves. To hide from Halo requires either cutting-edge nanites circulating in your blood stream—and there are only two of us in the universe riding in that rocket ship as far as I know—or unlimited resources at your disposal.

But even with the wealth of the Five Families, it's still a risky proposition to try avoiding notice. Halo feeds on anomalies and hiding from Halo is built on the risk of generating anomalies. To succeed, you need luck. Or desperation.

Turns out Clystra is somewhere in between.

I almost missed it at first.

We can't hack his personal feed—he's still a member of the Five Families—but we are watching in real time the goings-on inside that fancy house. His partner is listening to some liquid musical arrangement, numbed out on a plush slouch. The younger of the two kids is playing spin-the-feed, swapping perspectives with a half dozen friends until they get dizzy-self and fall over laughing. The older kid is in an avatainment module with their girlfriend. They're in a pocket loop though. It looks like a quest module on the outside, but it's really a union module. And they swapped genders. I bet they are really learning a lot about each other. Not a bad idea.

As for Clystra, he's doing some boring administrative work. His feed is tapped into new research data from the spa. He's collating information on a half dozen patients who received facial enhancements to shave a little off their zygomatic arches, and he's running analysis in a dozen different ways.

This is what rich people worry about—a little bit of their skull is thicker than they want. Why are they all so desperate to conform?

He's sifting through the 4D recreations of before and after photos, hundreds of them, twirling and rotating and freezing them for just a second to capture the areas of swelling in the surrounding muscles. Over and over. So boring, it's easy to ignore.

Too easy.

"Sanders, check his digital history. Does he often manipulate images like this?"

Valentine leans forward. "What is it?"

"No one can be this boring," I say.

"Apparently, he is," Sanders says. "He looks at similar data almost every night."

"When you say similar, what does that mean?"

"Most patients are usually not suffering from quite as much trauma."

"Catch the last few minutes of data, save only the color-coded areas and string it together."

He does and plays the clip into our feeds.

It's a covert message. The areas of irritation, separated from the context, are splotchy letters, easy to overlook by a system that thrives on the hard edges of data.

Nervous. Am I safe?

It's been running for almost 20 minutes.

Valentine is looking at me with something bordering on awe.

Don't say Mel, don't say Mel.

"You look surprised, Valentine."

I did it.

"I am a little impressed," she says.

"Just a little? I mean, I am a cop after all. We're supposed to be good at investigating."

"This really is remarkable," Sanders says. "You just picked up on a pattern that Halo overlooked. That I overlooked."

"Don't be embarrassed, buddy. It could have happened to any interstellar AI or priceless cybanism."

"I don't think embarrassment is in my operating protocols. Perhaps I should request that."

"Trust me," I say. "Nothing feels more human than a good dose of embarrassment."

Sounds like Clystra has been iced out. He's nervous and panicking. The only question is whether Darlinius shows up to help him or to shut him up.

Well, not Darlinius himself. He doesn't do his own work. But some of his muscle. I hope it's the humans and not those torturous-looking cybanisms. It's not that I'd mind glittering them. They're just so disturbing to look at and they probably make disgusting corpses.

Turns out I don't need to worry.

When the errand-bot shows up, it's a familiar face: Chundar Hotsip. He walks right by us in the zadel. The camouflage is working overtime. He thinks we're a storage module for dome repair tech. He looks nervous and sweaty. I don't think he's here for an extraction.

"Is that—?" Valentine starts to ask.

"—the acting head of Mars SF?" I finish for her. "Yeah.

Looks like the conspiracy runs a little deeper than we thought. Hoost, Able, I hope you and the rest of the Fist are watching this. Getting that data might be a little tricky."

"Crucial," Sanders says. "I'm scanning him. He has seeds for organic nukes. If he successfully plants them, Clystra, his family and all residents of Jezero within a four-kilometer radius are in grave danger."

"Correction, *very* tricky," I say.

37

Organic nukes are nasty pieces of work. They grow fast in almost any soil—even wet dust, as I once proved in the deserts of the Nebraska ward—and yield the fruits of destruction in minutes. Set them off when they're green and you can level a building. If they reach maturity, they can level a city. Or a dome.

And worse, since they're organic, once planted, they can't be turned off. Or uprooted.

"First things first. Valentine, you need to take the zadel and get the hell out of here."

"Okay," she says. "Good luck."

"Wait, really?" I ask. "Aren't you going to argue about how we're all in this together and you want to help?"

"There's literally nothing I could do here," she says. "I have zero familiarity with weapons of war, or fighting, or any of the things that might be helpful. I mean, I don't want you to die. But I *really* don't want me to die."

"Chancellor Valentine has unassailable logic," Sanders says. "I will be rebooted, of course. There's no reason you should both die, especially when one of you has no technical expertise or even related experience to offer."

I'm a little flustered.

"I assumed you wouldn't leave," I say. "I had this whole speech worked out."

"That's really sweet," she says. "Would it help speed things along if you said it now? I really think I should make my way to a safe distance. Also, he's planting the seeds, so we're kind of wasting time."

She points over my shoulder. Hotsip is twisting the cap off the packet.

"Halo has notified Mars security forces," Sanders says. "They're deploying a blast cup to contain it, but it's unlikely to be here in time."

"Fine, let's go."

Valentine squeezes my hand as I climb out. "Good luck."

"Thanks," I say, but she's already pulled the door shut and the zadel is powering up and rolling off.

I watch her leave in a glow of afterthrust.

"She's a remarkable human," Sanders says. "So exceptionally clear-headed."

"Most of the time," I say.

"Do you have a plan?"

"Not yet. But something will come to us, right?"

"I am not trained in inspiration," Sanders says. "As I have explained to your repeatedly, I'm better deployed for linear problem-solving."

"So, solve this problem. How do we kill an organic weapon using nothing but our bare hands?"

He nods and starts running queries. He's sharing them on my feed. Most of them end with us, and a quarter of Jezero, vaporized. We make our way toward Hotsip, who is so focused on the task at hand—shaking the seeds into the dirt by the front door—that he hasn't seen us.

"Focus on the scenarios that work," I whisper to Sanders.

The good news is I doubt Hotsip is on a suicide run, so the nukes are likely set to ignite after he's gone. That means two things: We have some time before we get vaporized and he has an escape plan. He's not blocked from Halo, so he doesn't care about official notice. You blow up part of the Five Families dome and you better be able to disappear like Voyager 5 into a black hole on the distant edge of nowhere.

Or you better be certain you threw in with the winning side.

My training kicks in. Ask questions later, neutralize the most immediate threat—a motivated and well-armed cop—first.

We're just past 50 meters away and his proximity alarms will sound any second. I can't risk getting Sanders glittered until he helps me figure out how to ungrow a nuclear vine.

I summon a drone jacket and hop up into the air. Gravity makes a great partner in a surprise attack. I center above Hotsip and drop hard and fast. I'm within about ten meters before he looks up, swears and reaches for his glitter gun.

"Chundar Hotsip, I detain you in the name of the Five …" is all I get out before I land on his face like a frozen waste cube jettisoned from a sub-hyper prison transport at the end of a long run to Earth.

I feel his zygomatic arches crumble under my heels and he's out cold with me standing on his face. I pick up his glitter gun and press it into my grip belt in case I want it later.

The nukes are growing fast. The soft little tips are sprouting, glowing pale green.

"You are very good at improvising," Sanders says, joining me.

I cuff Hotsip and lock him to an illumination column next to the street. He's bloody and rattled, but slowly regaining his senses.

"I planted nukes," he says.

"I know. Why are you trying to kill Clystra?"

Hotsip avoids my question. "You have to get us out of here."

"Nope. What I need to do is stop those nukes," I say. "Then you are going to answer my questions."

"We'll all die," he says.

I look at Sanders. "What do you have for me?"

"I have fourteen options," he says.

"How many have a greater than fifty percent chance of success?"

"Three."

"And of those three, how many involve not blowing off an extremity?"

"One."

"Let's go with that."

"We must poison it with a fast-acting toxin," Sanders says.

"Such as?"

"Herbicide, for example?"

"Did you happen to pack any herbicide before we headed over?"

Sanders shakes his head.

"We've got less than four minutes," Hotsip says.

"When will the containment cup be here?"

"Five minutes," Sanders says.

"There has to be something …" I race toward the house, Sanders running with me.

I lower my shoulder and ram the front door; it holds and bounces me back onto my ass. Sanders hacks the lock with a blink and then gives it a shove with his cybanetically enhanced strength and the door tumbles in off its guides.

Clystra is standing inside, drawn to the door by the noise. At first, his face is frozen in surprise and then it melts into fear.

I jump up and punch him in the gut so he can't run off

and then I rush into the room where his partner is listening to liquid music. Just what I was hoping for—a liquor cabinet. The man jumps up, shocked, as I grab two bottles of absinthe from the shimmering shelves. I crash the necks open against the wall, then step over Clystra as I make my way back out front.

I pour most of the absinthe onto the plant. The vine is big enough to do some real damage now, the nuclear gourds swelling up with deadly potential.

I check the bottles. I saved just enough for a big glug. If I die, it will be with a nice warm buzz.

I don't think I'm going to die. The plant is struggling, withering. It droops and curls up and expires. The nuke fruits pop with little fizzy stutters.

"You should definitely drink less of that," Sanders says. "And those little flashes delivered some high-level radiation. Appropriate mitigation would make sense."

"Later," I say, watching Mars security forces arrive with the blast cup. It's a bunch of anthrobots. They approach fearlessly because why not, they can live forever, after a fashion.

"What happened to the plant?" the lead containment bot asks.

"It had a drinking problem," I say. "Place Chundar Hotsip under arrest for the attempted murder of Singhroy Clystra."

"I will query the Hive," the bot says.

The Hive must have answered in the affirmative because the anthrobots drop the blast cup and circle around Hotsip.

"What is happening here?" Clystra asks. He looks rattled.

"I saved your life," I say.

Something is wrong. The anthrobots are reaching for

Hotsip, but they aren't undoing the cuffs I put on him. Five of the bots pull him in five different directions simultaneously. He has time for one short squeal of pain and surprise and then he's in pieces.

Shit.

"And I'm still saving your life," I say, pulling Hotsip's glitter gun from my grip belt, tapping into the override and targeting the five anthrobots simultaneously right in their power cells.

The glitter gun whispers out a barrage of flechettes that riddle the bot containment squad right in the center of their chests, chewing up the metal and punching the batteries into tatters. The only sound we can hear is the crackle of energy, then the thud of heavy bodies dropping.

Clystra looks at the servo carnage, and the withered nuke plant, then turns a sorrowful look at his partner. "I am so sorry."

"What have you done?" his partner asks, arms around the frightened children.

I get a ving from Valentine. "I'm glad you didn't die," she says when I connect.

I smile, and Clystra mistakes it as something hopeful for him.

"Time to make a little visit to the Hive," I say to him. "Your life is about to get very complicated."

38

The Hive feels smaller this time, less threatening, more irritating. Maybe because it's not new to me any longer—familiarity breeds contempt, or apathy. Or maybe it's because I'm dragging a fear-crazed, babbling research doctor alongside me so the focus is definitely not on me this time.

They were ready for us and the security forces are looking at me with slightly less disdain. I was there when Hotsip, their traitorous boss, was killed. And I prevented half of Jezero from exploding. I guess that earns me a pass.

Clystra has basically been sobbing the entire time. He's sitting between me and Sanders in the tiny chairs in front of the enormous emerald table as four of the five fingers of the Fist settle into their ass shaped-air cushions and glower down at us.

Everything these people do is to make other people feel small. It's like after four generations on Mars, that instinct has become bred in the bone. Or maybe it was that instinct that got them to Mars in the first place.

But at least this time, they're diminishing one of their own.

Clystra is whimpering, which is better than the wailing on the way here. Seeing Hotsip pulled into pieces and the desperation on his partner's face put him into full panic mode. I've ignored him up until now but he's starting to push my buttons.

A door at the back of the room slides open. Singhroy Able is standing there. "I want to meet in the inner chamber," she says.

"But I just got comfortable," Hoost says.

She motions with her hand. "Crucial, come through and bring the other two."

I knew it! She is starting to like me. I mean, why wouldn't she, I am very likable.

We stand. Clystra wipes his face with the side of his sleeve. We walk into the adjacent room. The lighting is soft, almost dark, the furnishings informal, with a large round table of polished wood in the center of the room. Able nods at three empty chairs—large and comfortable—at the far side of the table. The other Fisters—Blevin Flunt, Fehrven Modo, DuSpoles Koryx and Tarteric Hoost—take their seats.

It's just a flat table, and it's not like they're neutralizing my debt, but sitting at it puts us at the same level and it feels good. And weird and anomalous. Anomalous in my line of work almost always means something bad. There are no guards, no connection to Halo—nothing coming in or going out.

The door behind us slides shut.

Able looks tired and there's a yellowish sheen to her skin. I scan all their faces. They all look worn out, unwell. I start to say something but Koryx holds up her hand, palm facing out, stopping me.

"We don't need to hear anything from you yet," she says.

I will never do that to Mel again. Or anyone else.

"Thank you for preventing a disaster at Jezero, but we watched the recordings of Hotsip's actions and subsequent expiration," Koryx says kindlier. "We don't need additional information from you at present."

Hoost leans forward on the table. "Clystra, you've got five minutes to tell us about your research or I will have the cybanism strangle you to death in this room and send your family to Earth with your corpse."

Wild-eyed, Clystra looks over at Able, hoping to find an ally given their shared family membership. But she shakes her head. "You must tell us everything about your research. I can't help you otherwise. Everything."

He's so scared. He's twisting his hands together and his forehead starts to shine. All eyes are on him, but he keeps his own beady blues glued on his wringing hands. His lips are moving a little, as if he is working up the nerve to speak aloud. Or maybe praying.

Finally, after a full minute, he places his hands palms down on the table. He straightens up, sitting tall. He takes a deep breath and then holds his head high, scrappy little chin thrusting forward.

"I did it. I have a cure." He's a different person now. Calm. Certain. Not wailing. His words brim not just with confidence, but with pride. He is fully in control of himself.

"A cure for …?" Modo asks.

"It," Clystra says. "Neural tryphoprionia."

Clystra lifts his hands from the table, placing his fingers together, tip to tip, forming a triangle in front of his face. The wet palm prints begin to fade almost instantly.

The five members of the Fist take a simultaneous deep breath.

Hoost leans forward. "Tell us more. And I warn you, Clystra, the quality of the rest of your life, indeed, its duration, depends on what you say now."

"I have discovered a cure for neural tryphoprionia. Before proceeding, I want to lay claim to naming rights for the disease, causative bacteria and the cure, given the current phylogenic legal coda, and I want the Singhroy family associated with my discovery in perpetuity, as well as certain relegated revenue streams—"

"I don't care what you name it, and you'll get plenty of credit if you've really done this," Hoost says. "Now get to the point. Immediately."

Clystra doesn't hesitate. I'm not sure how it happened, but he has the upper hand now and he knows it.

"The fluids generated from Earth's magma beneath the sunbelt, the area formerly known as Crater Lake, with a small amount of geochemical modification, contain a form of bacteria that reverses the neurological damage caused by the wasting disease. All of it. And if used pre-emptively, in vaccine form, can prevent the damage from ever occurring."

I have no idea what Clystra is talking about but there is a collective gasp from the all five members of the Fist.

"When you say reverse ..." Blevin Flunt says.

"Complete eradication," Clystra says. "And any damage sustained is reversed to pre-infection baseline levels."

"Are you certain?" Able asks, and as she speaks, I see something resembling relief or hope or maybe joy wash across her face.

"The research was conducted with a confidence level requirement of ninety-nine, which was met in all experiments," Clystra says.

"How?" Hoost asks.

"There is a form of genetic material in our cells, hitchhikers from the earliest days of human existence, that responds negatively to the absence of gravity on Mars despite the installed offsets. The response of this genetic material to the ambient conditions causes the wasting, the neurological damage, by hijacking the cellular structures within the amygdala for their replication in defense against what is deemed a threat. While this would be damaging on

229

its own, the more significant problem is that a byproduct is released during the associated RNA transcription process. The byproduct builds outward until neural functioning is impaired, effectively creating a contiguous fibrous net within the brain."

"We know the cause," Hoost says.

"The response, in essence, creates a protective shield that trades function for security," Clystra says. "Hence the wasting and spongiform activity. The bacteria from the sunbelt disrupts the binding protein of the RNA transcription byproduct, in essence melting the fibrous stuff inhibiting the brain."

I think of all those brains in the lower level of the Mytikas spa. "Hold on," I say. "Who has this spongy brain disease?"

"Everyone on Mars has it," Hoost says. "Or will eventually."

"Even me?"

"Well, you won't be here long enough to experience any noticeable symptoms."

"And you didn't think of, you know, telling anyone about this?" I ask.

Like all those lottery workers, I'm thinking.

"And panic people? Don't be ridiculous," Koryx says. "As if we could move back to Earth."

"Clystra, this sounds very promising. We need to move your microchemistry into a manufacturing process. You will share your work," Hoost says.

"I can't," he says. "I don't have access."

"Do not overplay your hand," Hoost says.

"Whoever was funding this research, which was based on the physiology of the blizards, was careful to lock down the data. It's not accessible, and the final process for synthesis is gone."

"Who was funding your work?" Able asks.

"I don't know."

"How could you possibly not know who pays the bills?" I ask. "How did you get the samples of the brains and the fluid?"

They don't seem to be bothered by my outburst. I guess I'm asking what they're all thinking.

"I was contacted on a dark channel. Truthfully, at first, I thought it was one of you," he says to the Fist. "I started working with samples from deep under Olympus Mons where I found rudimentary chemolithotrophs. The work progressed well, there was funding for every need and eventually I was able to isolate the bacteria unique to ancient hydrothermal vents in the sunbelt."

"And you never knew who was behind it?"

"The only contact I ever had was with Chundar Hotsip."

"That's why Hotsip wanted you dead," I say.

"I don't believe that," Clystra says.

"Oh, it's quite conclusive," Sanders says. "I ran every possible data scenario and Hotsip wanted you dead and was willing to sacrifice thousands in the process."

The members of the Fist seem almost gleeful and I'm struggling to deal with the fact that they put Mel and Jynks and everyone on Mars in danger. They're smiling, and I don't think it's just because they're no longer scared of this disease.

"Someone is trying to corner the market on the cure," Koryx says. "And use the lives of every member of the Five Families on Mars as hostage for that profit accumulation."

She's in awe.

"It's absolutely brilliant," Hoost says. "But who? Is it one of us? Because, bravo."

"No," I say.

All eyes turn to me.

"It's Singhroy Darlinius."

Hoost laughs. It starts small but grows. Then Fehrven Modo joins in. His laugh is big to begin with. Able doesn't look happy about the laughing. They see the serious look on her face and tamp it down.

"My nephew would never do this," Able says.

"No offense, Able, but the operative word is could, not would," Hoost says. "It's far too complicated."

He's not wrong in this estimation. In my experience, it doesn't take the brightest floodlight in an orbital platform landing deck sensor to undertake criminal activity, but Darlinius's insecurity and fragility make it hard for me to believe he has what it takes to pull off something like this.

"Pretty sure it's him," I say. "I visited Darlinius earlier today and told him I knew what he was up to with Clystra."

"You lied?" Hoost says.

"Let's say I rattled. A distant cousin of lying. I had a hunch that if Darlinius was behind it, he'd panic and make a mistake. Hotsip was the mistake. He sent Hotsip to do away with the doctor and when that failed, hacked the Mars SF to do away with Hotsip."

There's a long moment of silence. "We've definitely underestimated Darlinius," Hoost says. "Able, you must be very proud."

She doesn't look proud. She looks unconvinced.

"Talk to him, ask him how he would like to shape this deal," Hoost says. "You'll be the principal, but we can offer him very favorable terms."

I can't help myself. "Let me get this straight. You are singing the praises of someone who is scheming behind your back to corner the market on a therapy that would keep all of you from literally losing your minds, and has done it by masquerading as resistance fighters in the sunbelt, murdering you, Hoost, or rather your duplex, trying to murder Clystra and then actually murdering Hotsip, so he can become even richer and take over the Five Families?"

"Take over is a bit much," Hoost says. "Move forward in the succession line behind Able here, certainly. But yes, that about sums it up."

"He's certainly showing exceptional promise and ambition," Modo says.

I don't know why I even bother to be shocked anymore.

"But you will need to rein him in now, Able," Hoost says. "He failed to close the deal. You'll need to take over from here. Clystra, you will remain in custody for your own safety until this is satisfactorily concluded."

"What about Larsen?" Koryx asks.

"You are free to leave Mars," Hoost says to me. "Hopefully, this will be the last time you're needed here."

"Nothing would make me happier," I say. Sanders is staring at me with a glum look on his face. "But what about Jynks Martine?"

"If she turns up, she'll be fully exonerated," he says. "I'll release the information immediately."

39

It's all over.

I just need to connect with Essential, get her people to drop off Jynks some place safe and I can go home.

Not that I'm in a huge rush at the moment.

I'm watching Mel prepare lunch. She's actually assembling most of it by hand. On Earth, no one trusts anything that machines don't make and bathe in ultraviolet light before popping out. It's the only way to keep the viruses at bay. But on Mars, with their health cradles, no one worries about getting sick. Except for a brain-wasting anti-gravity disease, apparently.

The worst part is I can't tell her about Jynks yet. Hoost won't reveal that he's still alive until the deal is closed.

Wisp is at Mel's feet, snaking around her shins and mewing, occasionally eyeing me suspiciously. Mel looks sad and beautiful. I'm never getting over her. I've resigned myself to that fact. She's saying something and I try to focus.

"Clystra is working for someone trying to extort the Five Families?"

I nod. "Looks that way. They're dying. You're all dying. Slowly. Humans aren't made for Mars. It gets worse with each generation."

She takes that information in and slices cubes of yeast cheese.

The challenge is, until recently I never thought I *needed*

to get over her. I always just assumed I'd nurse my secret, fruitless love for Mel until I drank myself into an early molecular dissolution and compost flush.

"But now there's a cure, which Singhroy Darlinius funded?"

"Yes," I say. "Built on the geochemical fluid from the sunbelt. It's ready for production, now just a matter of them now getting the recipe and how they'll be charged for it."

This situation with Valentine is complicating the sad little trajectory I had planned. She's forcing me to see a different path. One that allows me an opportunity to be ... gods, almost happy, I guess.

"I imagine the cure will only be available to the Five Families at first," Mel says.

"You could always just come back to Earth."

She turns and looks at me curiously, the glow from outside lighting up her face. There's something unreadable there, something that simultaneously gives me hope and closes a hatch.

"No, I don't think that's a possibility. I haven't finished what I set out to do."

"We need trees on Earth too, Mel," I say.

She nods, but I can tell her thoughts are still here on the red planet. What does she have against Earth? Other than it's where I tend to hang out. Maybe she wants me to be miserable, punishing me because she doesn't want me to move on. But it's not like I'm moving on if I see where things go with Valentine, not really. More like stepping back a little, I guess.

Anyway, Mel doesn't play games. Whatever her motivation, it's not to flux with my state of mind. She's not like that.

"And Jynks was caught up in it?" Mel asks.

"Yeah. She was investigating on behalf of the Five Families. Whoever tried to kill Hoost ..." I let that hang there for just a second, but I don't think she picked up on it. It would be so much easier to just let the nanites shield the room and tell her what's really going on. But I can't put her at risk. "... realized the investigation was going to drag on, thanks to yours truly. So, they targeted her."

"That means I brought this all on her," she says, using a laser cleaver to finely slice up some greens. Her hand is shaking a little.

Is it fair, though, to be with someone who isn't the person you most want to be with? Do I even need to care about that?

"No," I say. I can't stand to see her in pain. It's probably true though. Once Hoost revealed he wasn't dead, Jynks would have been sprung and probably reinstated to her old job. Now, as far as most people know, she's disappeared.

"She was going to prison for life," I say. "And at least now we know she's not guilty."

"I always knew she was innocent," Mel says. She has tears in her eyes. "But now I don't know if she's still alive."

"Listen to me, Mel. Jynks is tough. Tougher than a stabilizing fin on an asteroid wrecker. I know she is alive. Have a little faith."

My certainty seems to help. Jynks really is alive, of course, so I'm not lying.

"Faith is in short supply these days," she says. She sets the salads on the table, then returns to the food counter. "On either planet."

There are a hundred good reasons why I should cut the tether to our past, set us both free, but all I want to do right now is make her feel better.

I should talk to Essential. She's forever going on about emotional stuff, telling me how to live and making up faults in me just to have something to criticize. I could really use some of her overwrought insights to sort through all this.

What is happening to me? Since when do I need my sister to organize my love life? Maybe I have neural trycycletops or whatever the Martians have, and my brain is turning into reactor foam inside a case of muscle.

Mel returns with a tiny bowl of some creamy liquid. Wisp is meowing and hopping around, excited. Mel puts it on the table and the little cat scrambles up my leg in a flash of tiny, needle-sharp claws.

"Godsdamn it," I say, half standing, but Wisp is already up on the table lapping the nutrient cream while I'm probably bleeding to death from a thousand tiny cuts. I sit back down and take a bite of my salad. It's been a while since I had soil-grown produce. It's delicious.

"What are we going to do?" Mel asks. "Now, I mean."

What I'd like to do is put my arms around her and pull her close. Tell her everything is going to be okay. But I know it's the wrong thing for her, and for Valentine. At least until I get this all sorted out.

Great. I just found a new way to be miserable—I'm worrying about the well-being of two probably former lovers, both of whom I've hurt and underwhelmed.

People who think there's an advantage to doing the right thing are idiots. I feel miserable and lost, pulled in two different directions. Like riding on a quantum rocket into an uncertainty field.

And then I think of the Five Families. They don't even bother trying anymore. Doing what's right for them has become the default right thing for two planets. I'm starting to see some wisdom in that approach.

"Able will take care of dealing with Darlinius, and I'm going to hang around until we can find Jynks. Once that's taken care of, we can figure out what's going on between us and then I'll head back to Earth for good."

Dammit.

That last part was supposed to stay inside me head.

"There's nothing going on between us," she says, eyes narrowed.

"No, I mean, of course," I say. "I think of you like a sister now."

Mel pushes her salad away. "You locked your sister in a terrorium, so that doesn't make me feel great."

"I just meant, you know, sorting the case out before I head back to Earth. Leaving on good terms before the wedding, that sort of thing."

Wisp finishes her cream. She's purring so loudly it sounds like a mini-rocketbike is coming to life inside her. She hops down and sits by the window, full and sleepy. Mel blinks to life a warming beam of light that seeks out Wisp and hits her with its gentle rays. The little cat, overcome by heat and comfort and a full tiny belly, curls up and goes to sleep.

"I think the odds are against us getting trothed," she says. "Find Jynks, then go home. Mars has asked too much of you. I've asked too much of you."

She seems so sad. I want to reach across the table and take her hand. Instead I finish my salad while she talks about the giraffes and zebras at Baldet crater.

I've got about one bite left, and I'm already thinking about how to drag this out longer before I contact Essential, when my feed lights up. It's Sanders.

"Crucial, I'm sorry to interrupt. I know how much you value your time with Melinda Hopwire."

I've got the blankface, because Mel stops talking.

"It's Singhroy Able. Her residence was attacked. Mars security forces are on the way, but she requested you specifically. Then Halo lost track of her."

40

"I need full immunity!"

I'm patched through to Tarteric Hoost in the Hive on a secure column.

"I will instruct our Mars security to treat you as an ally," he says.

"That won't do. Mistakes happen. Earthers get killed. With Hotsip dead and Jynks on the run, there's no one in charge of security now and everyone is more than a little high-strung. I need you to flag me in Halo with full immunity. Otherwise I stop right here and leave you all to sort this out on your own."

Honestly, I would prefer that course of action. But I'll be damned if I'm going to let Mel down and leave Jynks hanging in the wind. Of course, I can't tell Hoost that.

"Very well."

"I need more than your word here."

He's not used to being challenged.

"Confirm with Sanders," he says, then breaks the connection.

"He did it," Sanders says. "You have full immunity. No one on this planet can legally harm you."

"Why don't I feel comforted? Set an alert on that and tell me the second my status changes."

He nods.

"And pull up the schematics of Able's home. I assume you have access."

It flashes into a column on my scroll. Damn. It's huge. Why are all these Mars houses so godsdamned big?

"Singhroy Able is in a private dome several kilometers west of Old Jezero," Sanders says. "We arrive in under one minute."

Of course, she has her own dome. Domes, really. A cluster of them, perched on the peak of a mountain a few kilometers west of the Grande Dome. Like a stack of bubbles—the kind that spill out of a pouch of over-carbonated celebration prosynccho—only these are giant and cling to both sides of the peak. Some are clear, others are partially shaded to obscure the interiors.

I tap into the satellites for a real-time view. Most of the bubble domes are currently on fire, with pieces falling off and rolling down the slope.

One side of the compound has a view of the Grande Dome, which must look special at night, and the other side looks over a deep, brutal canyon. That's where Able's attackers are hunkered down. There's a contingent of armored ground vehicles lobbing explosives at the compound. Rich people are paranoid though, so there's a pretty stout defense. But not stout enough.

Mars SF has positioned a big flier nearby and it's dropping a lot of heat on the attackers. The canyon is filled with smoke and dust and death.

Her bubble home is a hot zone though, and the last place I want to be is caught between rogue armor and a leaderless Mars SF armada. But Able must have a reason for wanting to see me.

Sanders brings us in low, dropping down behind a ground contingent of security forces. They are surprised to see me, and even more surprised when their feeds flash my immunity status. In theory, their guns couldn't hit me even if they pulled the trigger. I don't want to test that theory.

Able's compound is connected to the Grande Dome by a personal lev-train, but the tracks have been destroyed and the train is tipped over and smoldering in the Choke. It's cold and airless out here, so I slip on an airhoodie and thermal suit and turn on the gravity modulators in my shoes so I'm not bouncing around everywhere like an idiot.

I geo-loc the highest-ranking person on-site and make my way toward him. Glitter flechettes are zipping around and rail slugs are crashing into things. They're not used to all this heat. I crack into his feed to ask where Able was last located. He stands and starts to say something but a volley of flechettes catches him across the forehead, piercing the protective helmet. He might make it.

I find the next highest-ranking person, a woman smart enough to keep her head down in a combat zone. She listened during training—that's literally the first thing they teach you. I catch her attention with a prompt. "Where was Able last located?"

"Singhroy Able last transmitted from the health activity bubble," the woman says. "On the lower level, east side. There are attackers in the compound. Really weird attackers."

"I need a gun and a contingency vest."

The woman tosses me her shoulder-fired rail gun. I rattle the bag. There are enough slugs in the pouch to bring down a small army, which is what I may have to do. She prompts a nearby squaddie who grabs me a contingency vest from their Jane. The vest is packed with battle gear and is somewhat armored. It's at least projectile averse. That's R&D speak for barely better than nothing.

"Keep the incoming down long enough for me to find her," I say. "Come on, Sanders. And don't get hit. I don't want you oozing out blue goo in there."

"Remember, it's red now. And self-preservation seems

to be an emerging part of my consciousness," he says.

"You're making real progress," I say. "You'll be making selfish decisions soon."

"Oh, I hope so," he says. "I would value the opportunity to experience regret."

We sprint into the ruined luxury compound through the main entrance bubble, which is mostly a walkway floating over pools, now empty and lined with slowly dying ornamental fish, some flopping feebly in the thin air desperately trying to suck up oxygen.

We enter the reception dome, a cross between a meeting space and a relax-room, with desks and reclining pods and a thick, living carpet. There are dead and wounded scattered among the burning luxury. Most are lottery workers from Earth, but I scan two family members.

The walls are trying to self-repair, but there's a lot of damage and the cold, unbreathable air is pouring in. I tell security to send in the med-bots.

We take some low stairs to the next level, an indoor garden space. I see one of those godsdamned misshapen cybanisms from Dome Salacious lumbering through the remains of a sprawling green space full of tiny sculpted trees. Mel would love this; actually, she probably helped make it. By now, most of the trees are scorched stumps, with a few currently on fire. A handful are unscathed, with micro-lights flickering on their miniature branches.

The cybanism sees me, but I don't know how. It doesn't have eyes. It's basically a human-sized bicep on skinny legs with a glitter gun for a nose. I hit it with a slug and it pops like a fuel bladder, spraying the tiny flickering forest with blue slime.

"It's one of your pals from Dome Salacious," I say to Sanders. "Guess we know who sent the troops."

"I can say unequivocally that I did not form any fraternal social bonds with those beings," Sanders says.

There's an air waterfall down to the next level and it seems to be mostly working. We jump in and let the currents carry us to the next bubble. The ride is bumpy, but gets the job done.

This bubble is for eating. There's a food garden up one curving wall and kitchen space, along with what was until a few minutes ago a dining area overlooking Jezero. The edge of it is shattered, falling off and down the rocky slope. But the repair-bots are more active here and there's enough oxygen to breathe.

I double check the Priestly numbers, then take off the airhoodie and survey the wreckage. "Why would anyone do this to their aunt?"

"It's confusing," Sanders says, then turns toward the kitchen. "There's someone hurt. It's the gastronaut."

The man has taken some flechettes, a lot of them, glittered mostly across his legs. But he's still alive. I can save his life and, if his culinary skills are worth it, the Five Families can return his health. I pull a medical pouch out of the contingency vest and drop some triage first-aid-bots on him. They get to work, extracting the diamond points and lasering the damage. I crack a tracker and drop it on him for good measure so they will prioritize his evac.

I barely notice the proximity alert and I'm suddenly looking down the barrel of a big squad-sized glitter gun held in determined hands.

Doing good never pays. At least that's what I tell myself about why I was distracted.

It's the guard with the crooked nose from the entry port at Dome Salacious.

It's a good news, bad news situation. Since we have a history, he's going to want to talk to me before he kills me, to gloat a little. That's the good news—I have a few more seconds of life. The bad news is I have to listen to him gloat before I die.

"Not so tough now, are you?" he asks.

I have three standard responses to that question and I'm trying to pick the best one to be remembered by but before I can answer, there's a whoosh and blur and his chest caves in. The sudden force knocks him off his feet and slams him backward against the wall. He looks down at what appears to be a very large pepper mill—the kind that grows its own spice crystals—stuck almost through him, then he looks up at me with surprised, dimming eyes before he dies.

"Perhaps my throw was a bit enthusiastic," Sanders says. "I was worried he was going to terminate your biologic functions while you were being altruistic."

"I *was* being altruistic, wasn't I?" I say. "Thanks, buddy. And yeah, you should probably work on containing your enthusiasm just a bit. But don't beat yourself up. That guy was a jerk."

We make our way down another level into the sleeping areas. If this is where Able sleeps, her bed is bigger than my entire squat. It's also on fire and soaked with blue goo. One, or possibly a dozen, of those freaks dissolved on it. Someone is fighting back.

Vigorously.

A glitter gun whooshes out flechettes at an industrial rate not far ahead. I use the nanites to tap into the surveillance. The next level down has a pool—had a pool; it's cracked and empty, the water long since dribbled out into the Choke—and some zee-gee weight harnesses for exercising.

Able is slumped at one end of the empty pool, bloody and sheltering behind a clear shield that's stopping thousands of diamond flechettes. They're piled up a half meter deep in front of her. There are two cybanisms and one guard advancing grimly toward the pool, firing incessantly. The shield is cracking. She's holding a rail pistol, but it's out of slugs. Glitter guns grow their own flechettes and they are damn near inexhaustible, so she's been shooting it a lot.

Able is tough. They chased her all the way to the bottom before they cornered her. I'm no fan of the Five Families, but she's by far the best of them. She only lied to me a few times.

The attackers are in a half circle near the edge of the little globe, stepping over the weight training equipment. A bad formation. They're about to learn the hard way why minimizing group targeting opportunities is the second thing they teach you in combat training.

I dial up the power on the rail gun. "Stay here," I say to Sanders.

I slide down the air waterfall and punch a slug right into the middle of the weight harnesses. The force opens up the floor and the attackers are swept out into the Choke in a tangle of straps and cords that, malfunctioning in the blast, suddenly weigh tonnes.

They tumble away, weighted down in the straps and struggling for air.

I'm being pulled toward the hole as well, but grab the edge of the pool and pull myself in. The room is losing air, so I pull on my airhoodie and crawl closer to Able. She seems almost pleased to see me.

I share my hoodie with her. She's badly hurt—her gown is stained with blood and she's pale and going into shock. I'm sending details to the security forces, but she catches my arm.

"Do you still have them?"

I know what she means.

"No, of course not," I say, but use the nanites to shield the room.

Then I nod. "It's safe now."

She smiles. "I knew it. I knew you were smarter than you let on. You hide it well though."

Damn. Frosty all the way to the end.

"I don't think even a cradle can heal me," she says. "The wasting disease, it's bad. And I've lost a lot of blood."

"We have to try."

"No," she says. "I'm tired. This has all gone wrong. And I know Darlinius is not capable of this, of attacking me. He's just not that …"

I expect her to say bloodthirsty or ruthless. She surprises me. "… competent." She grabs my wrist tightly. "Promise me you will protect him. Save him from whatever all this is."

"It's just …"

Her grip tightens. "Promise me. I can make it worth your effort."

With a blink, she transfers a small fortune in credits to my account. Actually, a large fortune. "It's a ghost account," she says. "Untraceable."

"I don't want your money," I say. And I mean it.

"Then give it away. It's shielded. My transfer activity is shielded. What can I reach you with? Everyone has a price."

I think of Essential.

"Tell me where the Halo servers are located."

She smiles again. "So, you *are* part of the resistance?"

"No. Just a shitty brother who's trying to be a little better."

Able nods. I think we're running out of time.

"It's probably just as well. The servers are on Deimos. Now swear to me you will keep Darlinius safe."

"I'll try."

That seems to give her some comfort as she slips away. "That's enough," she says. And then she's gone.

My lungs are screaming so I take the hoodie back and breathe deep.

Sanders pokes his head over the edge of the pool. "Crucial, are you okay? I lost contact with you."

"I'm all right. Able didn't make it."

He looks as shocked as a cybanism can muster.

41

Repair-bots scurry around the dome's exterior closing the gashes. Oxygen is flowing inside again, and the place is mostly safe for human life. The misshapen cybanisms are dispatched with ruthless efficiency. Sanders is wired into the dome's control panel, eyes rolled back in his head, helping oversee the on-site work.

The lev-train is still overturned out in the Choke, useless. The sight of it lying lifeless on its side, isolating Able's dome from Jezero, puts a fine point on how vulnerable Mars is to a targeted offense. Not sure how long the Five Families would last if they were forced to fend for themselves in the face of adversity.

Credit to Essential and her people, I guess, for trying to change the system instead of just burning the whole thing down.

CSI balls and human investigators comb through the wreckage. But it's clear who launched the attack. Right on cue, a priority ving comes through. It's Hoost. He looks seriously mad.

"That impertinent coxcomb has gone too far this time," he says. "Larsen, we have granted you temporary authority to lead the Mars SF strike force to apprehend Singhroy Darlinius and bring him here."

"That's a hard pass from me," I say. "Find another idiot."

"You are the only idiot we can trust right now. This is

not a request. It's an order. If you hope to return to Earth, do this. We will strike ten years from your sister's term."

Great. Like I want them to crack open the terrorium early. But it's not like I can say no. Too suspicious.

"Fine. He already knows we're coming, so give us a few minutes for Sanders to finish up here, and for me to have several consecutive drinks."

He breaks the connection.

Construction-bots are rumbling toward the mini-domes from the Choke. Able's compound will be pristine in days, and ready for the next Singhroy to move in. It won't be Darlinius.

As I watch Able's body leave the compound in an elegant air coffin, decked out with the Five Families shared crest and ceremonially guarded by members of the Singhroy militia, I wonder where they keep the booze.

I head back into what was once Able's kitchen and rummage around in the storage columns. I find plenty of pots and pans and knives and even another spice mill, but nothing to drink.

I open some of the deep drawers that hiss out on servo arms revealing dishes and glassware—enough for a small army. Maybe there's something in the chillbox. There's a lottery domestic leaning deep inside it, cleaning.

"Hey, excuse me, can I take a quick look in there?"

"Sure stranger, but unless you have an external liver module, you might want to lay off the booze."

It's Essential.

I realize all the feeds are rerouting. I turn on my nanites to double the protection.

"Acting head of Mars SF?" she says. "You've come up in the world."

"What are you doing here?" I ask, overjoyed to see her.

"I knew you'd be hunting for the booze," she says.

"No, I mean, what are you doing *here?*"

"I figured wherever a dome is exploding, you're involved somehow."

I grab her into a hug, and she laughs and squeezes me tight. My proximity alarm sounds as a bedraggled soldier walks through. To his feed, she just looks like a dazed and confused gastrochef employed by the recently deceased Able Singhroy.

He passes through and she relaxes. "Here, have a synthgin." She pours a drink. It makes me think of the Saurians and their ant cocktails.

"I'll make you something to eat. We can talk that way."

She spends a few minutes poking around and opening various containers, chopping and slicing, then she puts a plate in front of me with cheese and bread, and a collection of round vegetables or fruits, I'm not sure which. She pulls a tall bottle from a rack next to the chiller box and pours dark red liquid into two glasses.

"What is all this?"

"Able Singhroy, like many others up here, has certain historical predilections. She liked old France, now in the Moscow ward. These three cheeses are made from cloned cow's milk—Camembert, Roquefort and Neufchatel. You spread them on the bread, which is also a recipe from ancient France, and if you like, add some of the vegetables to it. That's the way she liked it. And with plenty of wine."

She spreads some for me and it isn't bad, although I don't understand why anyone would want to eat something made from actual animal lactate. But the red stuff, that's damn good.

"How do you know this about Able?" I ask, but I figure out the answer before I finish the question. "She was one of your clients in the H-suite."

"Yes. A regular, in fact. She was nicer than most."

I remember the last party Essential threw at the H-suite, the one that Halo reconstructed for me when I thought she was dead. It was set in a café in ancient France, with people smoking and someone singing.

"Why didn't you tell me?" I ask.

"It didn't seem relevant."

"And when she kidnapped you to try to get the nanites?"

"That was mostly for show. She was nice to me, just not in front of the others. She liked me. She came to the H-suite often, and occasionally brought her partner along with her. They both liked me. We had fun doing French things."

"That's what Tarteric Hoost meant when he said you were a favorite there."

"He said that?" She feigns innocence as she pours me another glass of wine and hands me a fat piece of bread smothered with cheese. "Eat up. You'll never get this good stuff again."

She doesn't have to tell me twice.

"Where's Jynks?"

"Still with Jepsom and Zohar."

So it *was* Zohar.

"We need to get her back to Jezero. Mel's losing her mind."

"I bet," Essential says.

She refills my glass.

"What you're doing is really sweet. Protecting her, helping keep them together," she says.

"It doesn't feel sweet. It feels stupid and painful, like eating your own teeth."

"How's it going with Valentine?" She takes a swig straight from the bottle.

"Surprisingly well."

Essential nods. "She's great. She's had a hard life, but I'm glad she's finding a soft place to land with you even for just a little while. If we could ever find those prokking servers, she could relax a little, maybe spend some time with Seneca."

I gulp down the rest of the wine, spilling some down my chin.

I know where the servers are, but I don't want to tell her. She'll get herself killed trying to do whatever crazy thing she has planned. And she'll want me to help her. But if I don't tell her, she won't give up. I'm persistent and focused, but she's flat-out stubborn.

She leans in and wipes my chin with the side of her sleeve, and I flash back to when she was just a baby, after Mom brought her home. You're no longer the only baby in my life, Mom said to me. I want you to promise that you'll always look after your little sister. Mom carried a photo around with her, pinned to the top of her scroll, from that first day Essential came home. Essential is looking up from her crib at me, wide-eyed, and I'm hanging over the slats, grinning from ear to ear after having dropped every toy I had, which was a grand total of three, into her crib.

I suspect that was the last thing Mom was looking at when she died.

I need to do right by them both.

"I know where the servers are," I say.

Essential freezes.

"Able told me, before she died."

"Where?"

"You have to promise me you won't rush off and do something stupid."

"Where?" she asks again.

"I'm serious, this is dangerous stuff. You know they are

guarded like the Hive."

"Crucial, so help me, if you don't tell me I'm going to beat you to death with this baguette."

"They're on Deimos."

A look of surprise and wonder and hope lights up her nonsynthetic eye.

"The smallest moon of Mars," she says. "How appropriate. Do you know what its name means?"

Of course I do. I have a scroll. "Terror. That doesn't give me a good feeling."

"I have to go," she says. "Now."

"Please don't rush into this."

"We are too close to waste this opportunity. If Halo knows, if anyone suspects that Able told you, they will move the servers." She catches my arm. "Come with me."

"I will," I say. "But I have to arrest Darlinius first."

"Prok the Five Families. If we can confirm the location, and prime the empathy hack, their rule of greed is over."

"Essential, it's an order. If I don't go, they will find us both."

She nods. "You're probably right."

"You'll wait for me?"

She looks at me sorrowfully. "Would you?"

I wouldn't.

"I totally would," I say.

"You're a terrible liar," she says. "A terrible, sweet liar." She kisses me on the cheek.

"Wait, before you go …"

She stops.

"I need a hug, and your advice."

What is happening to me? I think the nanites are messing with my brain.

"I need to hear this from you," I say. "What kind of person does it make me if I accept love from someone who wants to give it even if I maybe still kind of love another person who doesn't love me back?"

"A normal person," she says. "It makes you a normal person."

She hugs me, then pushes me back to arm's length.

"Crucial, life is short, mostly painful and often ends in disaster. The most anyone can hope for is to be loved, here and now, in the present moment, before something else goes wrong." She touches my cheek and I feel like I'm the one in the crib and she's looking down at me. "It's okay to live again, even if that means abandoning the best part of the past."

"I don't know if I can let it go," I say.

"You can be happy with Valentine," Essential says. "Or as happy as someone so prokked up can ever be. But then again, you'll probably ruin her life. And re-ruin your life. So just enjoy it for now."

"You're a terrible sister, but I'm used to you. Get Jynks back to Mel before you go and be careful." She walks out of sight, passing Sanders as he walks in.

"Crucial, did you just say something rude?" he asks. "That staff member was crying, but also smiling."

42

So many news alerts are cracking my feed that it's hard to concentrate. I'm used to all the ads—on Earth, you have to pay for the privilege of only getting "premium" ads, something ninety-nine point nine Earthers can ill afford—but this is rich content so it's difficult to ignore. Every time I blink out a column, another one rolls in.

Second shocking murder of Five Families member. Traditional order under attack. All of Mars and Earth in mourning at the death of Singhroy Able. The resistance must be destroyed.

There are endless clips of Able doing things: dedicating new factories, pretending to be interested in the lives and babies of Earth laborers, debating new policy laws with the Fist at the Hive, petting giraffes at Baldet crater wearing zebra-skin shoes.

My favorite memory of her is the time she showed up on Earth at a tiny sheetmeat restaurant in my quadrant, barely big enough to legally hold two customers, to make sure I understood what I was up against on Mars. She was lying of course, or at least tilting things in her favor, but she did it with a kind of respect that makes it somehow seem honorable in retrospect. Or at least honorable-adjacent. Lying and manipulating are second nature to them.

Able was the best of the worst, and tough too. She

almost made it through the attack and took a lot of them with her. I wonder who taught her to shoot. Too bad she didn't get to blow a glitter stream at Darlinius. She was so convinced it wasn't him, but everything points his way.

Which is why I'm sitting outside Dome Salacious with a contingent of Mars security forces and Sanders, getting ready to arrest him. Hoost has already approved the action. Our feeds will soon transition to tactical, which means only one column will have sponsored content.

The last time I got caught up in the shenanigans of the Five Families, no one paid for their immoral behavior. Correction, Canadis Whitsend paid, but no one knows that except Essential and me. And Valentine. And a few others in the resistance. Okay, more than a few.

Maybe this time it will be different. Maybe this time, amitacide crosses the line. Oh, who am I kidding? The worst punishment they would ever dole out is making Darlinius a plant manager back on Earth. For a year or two, tops.

Dome Salacious is locked down, all the fliers and drone jackets inside disabled. Darlinius is isolated in the tower building where I met him last time. He knows we're coming. He looks sullener and sourer than ever.

The entry portal is barely staffed. Most of the cybanisms and humans died in the assault on Able's compound, including good old crooked-nose. Turns out, combat was just too spicy for him.

Dammit, I wish I'd thought of that when he was standing there with the pepper crystal mill sticking out of his chest. I'll never eat those again. Not that I could afford it anyway. The pepper crystals are grown on a Scoville matrix that costs more credits than my annual contract.

Except I'm rich. I check my balance again and laugh. Again. I can have pepper crystals anytime I want. And absinthe. A vat of absinthe.

Inside, the few cybanisms still functioning are aimless and their weapons have been rendered inert—those with eyes are watching curiously. The humans have dropped their weapons and have their hands up. They'll all wind up in a labor camp on Earth.

The Mars SF officers are focused despite the rotating cast of leaders they've been through. First with the disappearance of Whitsend (even though I know exactly where she is), then the imprisonment and escape of Jynks (I know more or less where she is too) and most recently the betrayal and killing of Hotsip. We all know where he is.

Tough job running Mars security. I pity the asshole they dump it on after me.

Sanders is recording everything, sending a real-time data feed to the Hive. I shouldn't even be here. I should be with Essential, making sure she doesn't get caught on her way to Deimos. But I made a promise to Able and I intend to keep it, even though on Mars only idiots and bilge pumps worry about keeping promises. But I'll never be able to convince my brain that promises don't matter. Maybe it's because the one promise I failed to keep cost me everything.

"For the love of stable gravity, can you arrest people any slower?" I shout.

Sanders starts to say something, but I cut him off. "It's a rhetorical question, Sanders. I just want to get this over with."

I push past deeper into the dome. The water is glimmering and dolphelines are cresting the surface in little pods, curious about the visitors and staring at us with their big eyes and sleek furry faces. A few of the cops look at me expectantly.

"What?"

I'm not used to being in charge.

"You are currently the head of the Mars security forces," Sanders says, joining me. "The senior representative of the Five Families."

"That's the worst thing you've ever said to me." I look at the cops milling about. "Fine. Listen up. I need six people here to hold the access point. No one in, no one out. I need six more in the air, so grab some drone jackets, clear them through Halo and give us some air cover. The rest of you, you're in the Gerri-skimmers with me."

There are two skimmers tethered to the docks. They use about a billion tiny monofilaments on their underside to "walk" on the surface tension of liquid. There's not much use for them on Earth anymore, not with what's left of the water confined mostly to storage tanks, but some biowaste reclamation centers use them to move shift workers over large fecal ponds. The filaments don't last long. Replacing them by hand is one of the worst jobs in an Earth labor camp.

But the skimmers are perfect transport—fast and smooth—if you have your own tiny, clean ocean on Mars.

We pile in and zip toward the city skyline. The dolphelines follow, streaking up and out of the water around us like joyful fuzzy rockets, then crashing back into the waves. Watching them, I want this to last longer, but in seconds we're disembarking on the ornate glass docks at the edge of town. A bunch of Younkers are standing around watching us. They're streaming fir-per of the action, which is going to cause their subscription rates to shoot up on Earth. I can't believe they earn credits just for being young and boring and apathetic.

As I walk toward the main door of the building, a man blocks the way. He has opaque hair, a subdermal shimmer and an attitude. He's a Blevin, an angry Blevin.

"Get the hell out of our dome, Earther," he says. "You have no business here."

He thinks I'm like the rest of the Mars SF, subservient to them. He didn't even bother to check my status.

I look at Sanders. "You'll let me know if anything gets revoked, right?"

"I will," Sanders says.

"You've got one chance to get out of my way," I say to the prince of privilege, hoping he won't take it.

"Or else what?" he asks.

"Time's up." I put a low-velocity slug into his gut that punches all the air and indignation out of him. He doubles over in pain, puking and screaming.

His friends, and a billion viewers on Earth, gasp in unison. It's a terminal offense to strike a protected Five Families member.

Halo has flagged this, of course, and Hoost has his pupil aimed at revoking my protection with a blink. But I know he's hoping I can bring this to an end. It must scorch him like an old tungsten electrode that they need me for anything. The last time they used me, they did it without my knowledge and I wound up filled with nanites and able to hide from Halo. This time, my eyes are wide open and I'm suddenly credit-rich. This time, I'm definitely getting the better end of this deal. One more mission and I'll own the damn planet.

The Younkers group melts away. They're annoying, but not stupid.

Darlinius is waiting for us on top of the building. He's surrounded by armed guards. He looks scared but is hiding it under a sheen of bluster. Kyrinth is sitting beside him. She looks … interested.

"Singhroy Darlinius, I'm placing you under arrest for the murder of your aunt."

"I had nothing to do with that," he says.

"You should probably not speak until you're in the Hive where your conversation will be protected," I say.

In other words, don't confess with a billion people watching. Even if he did, the Five Families could fix it, though it would take more time and credits. Say the wrong thing often enough, loud enough, and most people start to believe even the wildest lies. And the Five Families control all the channels and the volume.

"I wouldn't hurt my aunt," he says. "Yes, I wanted to surprise her, surprise them all, with a deal to put me on top. But not by attacking her dome. I'm being framed."

"By whom?" I ask. "Who could possibly set up a shrewd piece of work such as yourself?"

"Are you joking now?" Sanders asks on my feed and I nod. "I'm really getting humor."

"Stop harassing him," Kyrinth says. She got it too. "He didn't do anything."

"Yeah, well, that's for the Fist to decide. Come on, you just earned a trip to the Hive."

He shoots a panicked look at Kyrinth and she stands up. "Don't worry, I'm going too."

"I don't think so," I say.

"Earthers are not typically allowed in the inner chambers of the Hive," Sanders says, then looks at me. "Although exceptions have been made."

"She's coming with me," Darlinius says. "We're inseparable. She can vouch for my innocence."

"You know as well as I do, they don't care what she thinks. They're going to scrub through your records, figure out how to make your secret potion and take everything from you, and then send her back to Earth."

"I won't let that happen," he says, taking her hand. "We're in this together."

260

"Fine. Let's get this over with," I say. "You want a visit to the Hive, you got it."

She pulls on a stylish floor-length jacket, green and metallic, trimmed with sparkling accents that are so bright they're hard to look at. Then she drapes a scarf around his neck and knots it carefully, whispering some confidence-building thing in his ear.

They start toward the door and I smile. "You're forgetting something," I say, dangling a pair of electromagnetic cuffs. "You're a prisoner. Prisoners are restrained."

They'll be kicking me off Mars soon enough. Might as well go out big.

"You must be joking," Darlinius says.

"I never joke with prisoners."

I put the cuffs on and tighten the field until they hurt a little bit. And then tighten a little more.

43

"You're alive," Darlinius says.

We're standing in the main chamber facing the four remaining members of the Fist. There are four officers guarding the prisoners, including my old friend Serti Melthin. Mr. Sparkles. I still need to ruin his life, but that can wait.

"Your talent for stating the obvious is astounding," Hoost says. "Take those ridiculous cuffs off him this instant."

I do and drop them back in my pocket. I paid for them with my own credits.

Kyrinth is looking at Hoost closely. "I knew it," she whispers.

It's not a look of surprise, exactly. More like she's gratified to see him.

"Where's my aunt?" Darlinius asks, stretching his arms.

"She's dead," Hoost says. "I told her to use a duplex." He shakes his head. "How could you be so stupid? Attacking your aunt, the head of your family, with common soldiers like it was the early days of the Consolidation Wars. And out in the open for all to see? It's going to take us weeks to undo the damage."

"I had nothing to do with that," Darlinius says.

The kid looks angry but also rattled, like one more harsh word could provoke tears. I'm starting to believe him. He doesn't seem cut out for the rough stuff.

"I would never harm Aunt Able," he says. "She was my biggest supporter."

"She was your *only* supporter," Hoost says. "And it seems her trust was greatly misplaced. Share your research on the wasting disease with the Five Families immediately, end this charade and let us clean up your mess."

"Not unless Kyrinth and I are given a full stake in the patent," Darlinius says. He crosses his arms like a stubborn child.

"Don't be ludicrous," Hoost says. "She's an Earther. She has no economic standing."

"I love her," Darlinius says. "And I demand she be treated as my equal. We will troth and she will join the Families as a Singhroy."

"Out of the question. She can be your legal consort of course, take as many as you like, but if you troth, it can only be to someone within the families. It's the law. It's for the greater good. Anything else earns you a q-rocket ride to Earth. For good."

There's a long pause.

Darlinius looks at Kyrinth with sorrow in his eyes. "I'm sorry, darling, but I fear we have taken this as far as we can. I cannot be happy on Earth."

Pretty sure Earth couldn't be happy with him on it either.

"It's okay," she says, "I know we're not equals."

There is something about this girl. Her vitals are remarkably calm. If I were her, I'd be swinging blindly by now, lashing out and taking a sparkle stick in the back.

"But don't worry, I will take care of you," Darlinius says. He turns back to Hoost. "I still want a share. And a seat on the Fist."

"Half a share," Hoost says. "And second in line for the

vacant seat."

"Third," Blevin Flunt says.

It's all just a game to them. I'm grinding my teeth and remembering why I need to get off this damn red rock.

"Fine," Darlinius says. "I'll open a data merge." He pulls a blankface. The data is probably backed up on a secure server somewhere. He re-centers quickly and looks perplexed.

"That's impossible. The data is missing. All the research."

He looks at Kyrinth. I'm not liking the look of the smile she gives back. "Poor baby. Is the data gone?" she asks.

He nods, confused.

"I told you we're not equals," Kyrinth says. "I'm superior to you, to all of you, in every possible way."

She looks at Hoost. "I have the data. If you want to live, you'll deal with me directly. I'm sure you'll find my terms agreeable."

"Don't be ridiculous," Darlinius says.

"If you want to live, you'll stop talking," she says. "Your voice is irritating, like a punctured coolant bladder."

She's not wrong. But she's seriously outgunned. What is she thinking?

"Arrest her this instant," Hoost says. The four guards on either side of her reach for their weapons.

Two of them point their glitter guns at me; one of them is that dim diode Melthin who's life I still need to ruin, and he's grinning like the last time he shoved me around. The third aims his gun at Hoost. The fourth has a stubby little rail pistol and points it at Sanders.

I did not see that coming.

"They're with me," Kyrinth says.

Things just got interesting. But weapons don't work on members of the Five Families, or anyone who the Fist gives digital immunity, like me.

"Crucial, remember how you asked me to warn you if you lost immunity?" Sanders asks. "You just lost immunity."

I cannot catch a break.

Sanders looks around. "Curious. All immunity protocols have been temporarily erased for Five Families members as well."

The four fingers of the Fist let that sink in. They're all targets.

"That's right. I found a back door into Halo," Kyrinth says. "Courtesy of sweet, simple, easily manipulated Darlinius. Also, that's not a scarf around his skinny neck. It's a thermal ribbon." He reaches up for it, panicked. "Stop," she says, holding up her hand. "If it breaks contact with your body, or if anything happens to me, you're headless."

She's insane. The blast from that much thermal ribbon would batter us all.

"I know what you're thinking," Kyrinth says, looking right at me. "But my friends here are in tac gear and this stylish little coat is made of blast-activated concussion-warping fabric. We'll be fine. The rest of you will be charred and concussed."

She looks at Darlinius. "Except for him. He'll be gone from the shoulders up."

Darlinius looks horrified. "How can you do this? I thought we had something special."

"We did," she says. "A con. A very special con."

More like a coup, really. A revolt. I can't say that I'm opposed. Other than the fact she wants to join the Five Families instead of tear them apart. Dammit, Essential is really getting in my head.

Back to the task at hand. Staying alive. Honoring Able's

last wishes to keep Darlinius alive just became particularly challenging.

"You'll never make it out of the Hive alive," Hoost says.

"Nor will you," she says. "I recommend a negotiation."

"We don't negotiate with Earthers," Flunt says.

"You're about to start. I have all the research on neural tryphoprionia. Also important, I have a series of substantial nuclear explosives buried in the extraction site. If the deal isn't signed by sundown, the data degrades and the bombs go off. You lose the research, and any chance to sample the bacteria to recreate it."

"I don't care much about what happens to the Five Families," I say. "But I met some nice Saurians down there and I'd hate for them to get caught up in all of this."

"Then you'd better encourage these greedy pubic mites to sign the deal," Kyrinth says. "Otherwise, the blizards go extinct along with the Five Families and everyone on Mars."

"Saurians," I say.

Kyrinth looks at me curiously.

"They prefer the term 'Saurian.'"

It's tempting to just let this play out. If the Five Families are forced to move back to Earth, they'd have to fix it up at least a little. But I really don't want to share my broken-down planet with these soulless marrow beetles.

"Let's talk terms before Mars security tries to break in that door and we kill you all."

She does not mess around. She's got it planned down to the last detail.

Almost to the last detail.

If she's tapped into Halo, she's been running probabilities for months to plot this all out. Intricate plans are based on predictable outcomes. Sometimes the only good response is doing something totally unexpected.

That's kind of my specialty.

First things first. I need to make sure the Saurians are okay. I use the nanites to carve out a secure channel and connect with Fleiss.

I can't talk, and I can't pull a blankface for long. She's too smart for that.

I optically compose a message. *This is Crucial. Remember how I saved you all? I need your help now. There are some bombs in the sunbelt. Big ones. Where the mining was happening. I need you and Tooms and Dormer to get out there and turn them off. You've got less than four hours. So move your giant, muscly ass.*

I want him to know it's really me.

I blink-send and break the connection. I'm trusting they'll do the right thing. I don't usually have a lot of faith in my fellow humans. Or any faith. But I'm counting on it now. Probably stupid.

"I'm here with the four highest-ranking members of the Five Families trying to seal a deal for a cure for low-G brain," Kyrinth says.

Dammit, she's broadcasting a fir-per.

"What do you think, dearies, should I just kill them all and try to negotiate with the new Fist? Vote yes or no."

I watch her feed. Her numbers are spiking. The yes votes are winning by millions. They probably think it's some kind of avatainment crossover. Chances are good that anyone who is now voting yes will be shuffled off into labor conscription once all this is over.

There's banging and clattering outside. The still-loyal members of the security forces are trying to get into the secured room. The impenetrable, locked room. Leave it to the head of the Mars SF, a post I filled with distinction for several of the last hours, to lock their leaders in a safe room with no failsafe.

After three generations of inbreeding on Mars, seems

like they've gotten stupid. Or lazy. They have wealth and power and their gated planet, but they've lost their edge. Maybe Essential and her band of resisters have picked exactly the right time in history to take down Halo.

"What'll it be?" Kyrinth asks sweetly, present again. "A full partnership stake for an Earther, or do you all die here?"

"I do not want to die on Mars," I say. "And I definitely don't want to die sober. How about I switch sides here?"

"Sorry, I don't get a good vibe from you. I couldn't tell what side you were on to begin with."

"That's a fair assessment," Sanders says. "Crucial has odd motivations."

"They're not odd, you tangle of overpriced synthetic tubes," I say. "I'm on my own side." I look at Kyrinth again. "All I'm saying is take me with you. I can prove my loyalty to anyone with enough time and for enough credits."

I take a step toward her.

"Shoot him," she says.

Serti Melthin seems all too eager to comply.

"Wait, wait," I say, flinching. I pull out the cuffs and hold them up. "What if I cuff myself? I can't be a threat if I can't use my hands."

"No deal. Shoot him," Kyrinth says.

I'm so close, dangling the cuffs.

"Hold on, let me just ask you one thing. Can you pepper-mill Darlinius into the suspect?" I ask.

The words are so confusing, so nonsensical, that everyone freezes. Everyone except Sanders. He can process pretty fast. He gives Darlinius a good, cybernetically enhanced shove that sends him stumbling right into Kyrinth. By the time she's regained her footing, they're cuffed together and I'm backing away to stand clear.

"Nice job, buddy," I say, then look at Kyrinth. "Your little blast coat might be good, but it's not that good," I say. "Anything happens to him you pay the price. Anything happens to you he pays the price. So let's just all calm down. Everybody wins here. Nobody has to get hurt."

"Interesting response," Kyrinth says. "And an effective stall. But you're wrong. You have to get hurt. I'm not going to say it again, shoot him."

The soldiers raise their guns and the air hums with the discharge of weapons. Sanders is lunging toward me. The lights flicker and there's a wet punch and blood sprays everywhere. The walls are spattered red and I'm sticky with it. It's in my eyes and mouth, and it tastes like that marzaprine candy I used to eat as a kid—too sweet and too much like synthetic almonds.

Then the Hive goes dark. Or maybe it's only me going dark.

44

Lying in the dark covered with blood, I feel frenzied buzzing around me and since we're in the Hive, the thought makes me laugh uncontrollably. If I can laugh, I must not be dead yet. But I'm lying in a pool of blood; I can feel it soaking through my clothes. The laughter is probably from exsanguination. I'll be off into the wormhole of light soon.

The floor starts vibrating. And not in a good massaging kind of way.

It's really starting to irritate me. So is all the banging and shouting at the door.

Can't you just let me die in peace, Mars?

The lights are flickering, alternately illuminating the blood-spattered walls. Gods, did I lose a limb? And it's deadly silent except for the shouting outside from security trying to get in, and that damn buzzing.

The lights flare back on, illuminating a bloody mess. I'm drenched in blood, the walls are covered with it, and there's a huge puddle on the floor. It's really shaking now, sending ripples across the crimson. Even my teeth are rattling.

Of course. They're coming in from below.

A half dozen long, sleek drill-bots burst up through the floor, catch their bearings and then surround the four members of the Fist. One of them fires a single slug into the door mechanism.

It's tech I've never seen before. They look like mini-

Janes, only thin and tall with wicked-looking acoustic drills for heads. The tech extrudes some flickering, golden cryo-cordon and just like that, the Fist is untouchable again.

Nice of them to check on me. I partially sit up to inspect the damage. After poking and prodding and tensing and testing, I realize the blood isn't mine. It's what's left of Sanders. He took the full hit for me. I'm lying in a pool of bloody red goo and realize he changed his parameters based on my drunken rambling at the Docker bar. I hold my hand up and watch the stringy remnants of him drip down.

Across the room, Kyrinth is ringed by her security detail, weapons pointing out, and still electro-cuffed to a wailing Darlinius. Serti is pointing his gun at me again.

There's a clicking noise and the drill-bots extrude their weapons and aim them at Kyrinth and her squad.

I'm stuck in the middle without a weapon, so I slump back down in the puddle of goo. I'll just stay low and see how this works out. Then the door opens and a Mars SF squad in full tactical gear spills in, almost a dozen, and all very heavily armed.

The leader looks familiar. Tall and solid, competent. She pushes her visor back. It's Jynks. She must have made it into a health cradle because she looks fully recovered. And then some.

"Tarteric Hoost," she says. "I'm pleased to see you alive."

She's standing there like the warrior she is, like the last few weeks never happened.

"Martine. Very good," he says. "You made it. Sorry about all the duplicity. For the good of the order and all that." He looks at me. "Larsen, if you are still alive, you're relieved of command. Martine, you are reinstated with bonus credits."

"You were in charge of Mars security forces?" she asks me incredulously.

"Yeah, it wasn't that hard really," I say. "Almost anyone can do it."

"You exposed the four surviving members of the Fist to this lunatic," she says, pointing at Kyrinth. "And apparently, you got Sanders terminated again." She looks at the red goo. "I thought cybanisms were supposed to have blue blood. We'll have to scrub his parameters."

"Leave his parameters alone," I say. "He took a rail slug for me."

I see one of the security officers relax slightly.

"Does Mel know you're back?" I ask.

"Not yet," Jynks says.

I sigh. "Jynks, you got your priorities wrong."

"Everyone stop talking," Kyrinth demands. "None of that matters. I'll die before you can arrest me and take Darlinius with me. And the data. You're consigning yourselves to an early death. You'll live like brainless ghosts for a few more months or years, and then all stumble stupidly into a mass grave with spongy brains."

"We'll simply have Singhroy Clystra recreate the data," Flunt says with a sneer.

"Yeah, about that. I infected him with a double dose of purified neural tryphoprionia," Kyrinth says. "Try his feed. He's alive, but there's no one at the controls anymore."

Hoost must have checked because he looks sick to his stomach. He holds up his hand. "Stand down, everyone," he says. "We are willing to negotiate."

The other three gasp.

"What?" Hoost asks savagely. "We must have that cure."

"That's what I thought," Kyrinth says. Tugging Darlinius, she moves past the security officers.

Serti nods down at me. "Looking forward to seeing you again," he says. "Next time you won't be so lucky."

What does he know? Making friends with a cybanism is not luck. I had to listen to a *lot* of terrible jokes.

"I'll contact you in one hour with instructions," Kyrinth says.

At first, I don't think Jynks is going to let her pass. But Hoost waves dismissively. Darlinius hobbles along beside her, still trying to grasp how he's been outplayed by his Earther girlfriend.

"One hour then," Hoost says.

"Half of you follow them," Jynks says to her squad. "The other half with me. We'll escort the Fist to safety."

"What about him?" the guard I noticed before asks, pointing at me.

"Clean him up and put him in a holding cell," she says. "I have questions."

I'm sure she has a lot of questions, like how I found her when the resistance had her, and why she should keep my secret now that she's back on Mars SF. The cop, Fillow Bips, nods and moves my way. Soon we have the room to ourselves and she pushes back her face shield.

It's Essential.

"What in the name of the Vela Pulsar are you doing here?" I ask.

I rouse the nanites and see she's already deflecting the cameras on the drill-bots, which have mostly gone into sleep mode now that the action is over. I add my nanites to the effort.

"Saving you, of course," she says.

"Saving me? I had it all under control."

"That's not what it looked like when we came in and you were on the floor covered with blood," she says. "I thought I was too late."

"If those bots hadn't come up through the floor, you probably would have been too late."

"That was me," she says proudly. "I floated those into Martine's scroll as a tactical option."

She pulls some antibacterial wipes from her contingency vest and mops the cyba-muck from my eyes.

"Why aren't you on Deimos?" I ask.

She shakes her head. "I had to make sure you were okay. And it was an opportunity to get Jynks off our hands."

Essential helps me stand. I've got Sanders dripping into places he should not be. I'm going to need clean clothes, then a sanitizing shower and another set of clean clothes.

"She was pretty out of it from the broken arm. I met up with the others, used the nanites to blur her feed, and then my team put on some stolen Mars SF gear and called ourselves a strike force. When they arrived, we just mixed in and helped 'liberate' her. They have a mobile cradle, and then I spoofed some distress calls from here and suddenly, we're in the Hive."

"That's a really good plan," I say. "I've taught you well."

"Now you can help me check out Deimos."

She's got me there.

45

Turns out I don't have to come up with a good excuse for not visiting Deimos. Kyrinth wants to meet with me to close the deal. I get the call from Hoost, and of course I say no, that Jynks is the right person for the job.

Hoost assures me saying no isn't an option.

Kyrinth thinks she's smarter than I am, and that's why she wants me to deliver the deal. She probably is smarter, but I have a secret weapon. I'm taking Essential. A universe-class coder at my side may come in handy.

And Essential has the nanites working overtime to make everyone think she's the cop who drew the short straw when I requested Officer Bips accompany me. I'm going to need my sister if the plan I still haven't figured out has any chance of working.

Of course, Kyrinth set the handoff at the docks. Where else would you find so many Earthers embittered about the Five Families and willing to do anything for a little credit, combined with the constant motion of transports coming and going, space elevators plunging down and then being yanked back up into the mesosphere—it's a perfect setup for cover. And potential ambushes.

Jynks sent a Mars SF squadron to surreptitiously ring the docks before I get there. She's ready to roll her team in like a Martian sandstorm at the first sign of trouble. That's mildly confidence-building.

At the Dock zone lev-train platform, I find a welcome

surprise waiting for me: Sanders.

He looks different this time. Not his hair or facial structure. Or even his clothes. They all look the same. But there's something different about the way he … is. I can't quite put my finger on it. I like it though.

"Good to see you, Sanders," I say.

"I'm glad you're alive," Sanders says, politely nodding a greeting to Essential, who to him registers as Fillow Bips, a ten-year veteran of Mars SF with a heart irregularity and a diet too high in sucrose, now assigned as my personal security detail.

The three of us head toward the town square and to the Perseverance, the bar Kyrinth picked for the deal to go down. Home of the cobalt nova, and the place where I rescued Jynks a few short days ago. Well, more accurately, where Essential stashed Jynks after *she* rescued her.

"I reviewed the footage. That was close," Sanders says.

"I'd be dead if it weren't for you. I owe you my life. I'm thankful you still had protection protocols enabled."

"That's the interesting part. I was not obligated by programming to save you. It was an irrational act. I cannot identify the source of my motivation."

"We're friends. You didn't want me to die. That's a good source of motivation."

"This is true. I didn't want you to die. I am fond of you. But within the time it took to act, I was able to run a deep analysis of thirteen scenarios. Our friendship, as you call it, is not quantifiable. But my value to the Five Families is easily quantifiable. I am an expensive form to maintain. All the scenarios ended with you dead and me disarming the guards and preventing Kyrinth from escaping. It was the rational choice, though not optimal for our friendship."

"Then why didn't you make the rational choice?"

"I think I malfunctioned," he says. "It's possible my

programming is flawed."

"Not from where I'm standing," I say. "Although, the sweet red blood did kind of freak me out."

"It freaked all of us out," Essential as Officer Bips says from behind her visor.

"I was honoring your request," Sanders says to me.

"I wasn't really thinking that through," I say. "Go ahead and turn your blood back to blue." His eyes roll back into his head as he submits the request. "And let's hope we never spill that blood again."

"I believe I can accommodate that directive," Sanders says. "I received an upgrade. This skin is made from puncture- and blast-resistant aramidium. I'm close to invulnerable now."

"Good to know. I always wondered why they made such an expensive, you know, you, that came apart at the first sign of trouble."

"It is curious. It seems I passed some threshold test with this reboot."

"Maybe you just reached the limit. Like, there won't be any more reboots."

He stops walking and looks at me curiously. "I'm mortal?"

"As mortal as a synthetic, pre-programmed life form inside glitterproof casing can be, I guess."

We enter the town square and cover the few meters to the Perseverance on the other side quickly. The square is empty. Eerily so. The whole godsdamn Dock zone has gone silent. Kyrinth has more pull than I gave her credit for. Or Jynks has cleared everyone out. Either way, I'm good with it. Better to have clear shots, with no place to hide.

"I really do not wish to no longer exist," Sanders says, stopping outside the bar. "Perhaps I should wait outside?"

"Just don't think about it," I say. "If you worry about dying all the time, you forget to live."

"That makes zero logical sense," he says. "Worrying about ceasing to exist seems like the best way to extend existence."

"It's complicated," I say. "And there's no time to debate the nature of existence right now. You do what you want. We're going in there, the ones who *don't* have bomb-proof skin."

"The cybanism makes a good point though," Essential says.

"Don't start with me, Bips," I say.

I step inside the main entrance, expecting to take a long flechette right though the skull. I get a lot of dirty looks, but nothing terminal.

"Are either of you coming?"

Essential and Sanders both nod and follow me. He's nervous now that he might be mortal, scanning everything repeatedly, looking from side to side so quickly his head is almost a blur. It would be hilarious if it weren't so sad.

According to her last transmission, Kyrinth said she'd meet us near the bar to hand over Darlinius and sign the contract. The bartender doesn't look surprised to see me again. I don't even have to order a cobalt nova. He just nods me back to the small room.

Kyrinth is still shackled to a battered and bruised Darlinius. Serti is covering the door with a squid, a boring-looking but particularly nasty crowd-control weapon. It locks onto targets and shoots out barbed, self-guiding monofilament wires that deliver an axonic jolt that lights up every pain receptor in the body simultaneously.

I got hit with one once, along with six other labor cops. It was a training accident. The pain was the second worse thing I've ever felt. I still have nightmares. And so does the poor new trainee who hit us accidentally. After we all stopped screaming and crying and flopping, we tracked him down and gave him a dose. Actually, two doses.

I'm in no rush to take another hit. I wonder what it would do to a cybanism though.

"Don't worry," Serti says. "I've got one dialed up special for the flesh-bot there."

"I said come alone," Kyrinth says.

"I practically am alone. Sanders just learned they won't reboot him again, so he's going to duck at the first sign of trouble. And as for Officer Bips here, I mean, look at her, she's practically useless."

"Hey," Essential says. "Rude much?"

"Stop talking," Kyrinth says. "I know you've been authorized to finalize the deal. I get a share, my own dome, and the legal protection and status of a member of the Five Families. I don't care which one. And Dar-loser here is exiled to Earth forever."

He looks distraught.

I've got an idea, a nugget of a plan.

Darlinius is not going to like it.

I'm standing close to him and put my arm around his shoulder. "Sorry kid, your uncle and the Fist have made their ruling. She wins, and you get nothing except a trip to Earth."

His face contorts with revulsion. I honestly think the thought of living on Earth is torturing him more than the possibility of having his head fused off by the thermal ribbon around his neck.

"You win, Kyrinth," I say. "He's on the next rocket."

"No!" he wails. "Anything but Earth."

"You know, it's not that bad," I say. "You get used to the brown clouds and acid rain and beetlers and rats. I mean, the marrow beetles suck, I'm not gonna lie. Let me just get these cuffs off."

"The thermal ribbon stays on until he's on the rocket," Kyrinth says.

"No problem," I say, fiddling with the cuffs. "Dammit, I can't get the blasted things to release. Sanders, give me a hand."

He steps close.

"It's like the catch won't release," I say, using his body to block my move.

The trick with thermal ribbon is if you break contact with the target, it ignites. If I do it wrong, he loses his head and I lose my hands. While Sanders blocks us, I lift one end of the scarf over Darlinius's head and quickly loop it under his arm, tighten it and slide it down toward the cuff.

So far so good.

"Let's test that new skin of yours," I whisper to Sanders so low only his receptors can pick it up.

He doesn't look happy, but he gets it and keeps the loop of scarf moving. Essential is in tac gear and five meters behind me, so she should be fine. Pissed, but fine.

Kyrinth figures it out too late and gets the first half of "no" out before the thermal ribbon clears Darlinius's hand and ignites with a blinding flash and sizzle. I'm down behind Sanders, but the heat and force split the room. I can smell fat burning. It's Darlinius's hand. And probably hers too if she didn't get it inside the blast cloak in time.

Even though I closed my eyes, my vision is messed up—popping with starbursts and twisting loops of light. When I can finally almost make sense of things, I see she's gone. Sanders didn't turn to blue goo, so his new skin works.

"I guess I am not mortal," he says happily, turning around. His face is scorched and his eye sockets are bubbling strings of flaming jelly.

"Oh, shit," I say. "I forgot about the eyes."

"They are mostly decorative," Sanders says through blistered lips. "I can see quite well without them. I have digital receptors over approximately twenty percent of my body."

"You're going to need to get them fixed though," I say. "Like, soon. It's disgusting."

He touches the sockets with his fingertips. "Oh, yes, I can see how that would not be aesthetically pleasing."

"Nor is that," I say, pointing at Darlinius. The kid is looking at the scorched stump of his wrist, just one raw nub of burned gristle. It happened so fast the pain hasn't even got to his brain yet.

He starts to scream. Now he's got the pain.

Serti is down and blinded, but still reaching for the squid, patting the ground desperately. Gotta respect his tenacity. We're already programed into the weapon as targets so if he pulls the trigger, things are going to get complicated.

I lunge toward him just as he gets his hands on the gun and pulls the trigger. I kick it up under his chin. The three wires he had dialed in for us shoot out into the fleshy part of his throat and dump a double dose, plus whatever special little toxin he had juiced up for Sanders.

He's screaming and moaning and voiding his bladder and bowels, and Darlinius is screaming and sobbing and looking at his blistered arm knob and Sanders is standing there patiently with burning jelly dripping out of his roasted eye sockets. This is a weird way to spend a day on Mars.

Kyrinth is gone. Damn, she's good.

Essential punches me on the arm. "You could have warned me."

"Things were moving too quickly," I say. "And also,

you have full tactical gear on."

"Still, you don't have to be such a turdle all the time."

"Have you worked with Crucial before?" Sanders asks.

"I read his folder," she says. "We all read his folder. It's good for a laugh."

"Sanders, can you get stumpy out of here for some medical attention? He's going to need a new hand," I say. "And see what you can do about those eyes of yours, would you buddy?"

"I will never forgive you for this," Darlinius says.

"Could be worse," I say. "You could be heading for Earth."

That seems to bring him some comfort.

"Come on, Officer Bips," I say to Essential. "We need to track down Kyrinth and I need your help. Where is she?"

Essential rolls her eyes and then does what I assume is pretend cop work, but then her face looks unexpectedly concerned. "Get on the security channel," she says. "Jynks, I mean Commander Martine, just said Kyrinth is headed to the Button."

46

On a planet filled with so many ways to kill you, the Button might be the surest bet. It has the lack of breathable air and freezing cold of the Choke and then adds the possibility of a space elevator suddenly dropping out of the Martian sky to deliver people or freight from the orbiting entry platforms up in the exosphere crushing you flat in an instant.

The Button is a big flat disk of frissive palladium alloy almost 1,500 meters in diameter and ten meters deep. When the elevators hit, the force opens the palladium in a small area, giving temporary access to the honeycomb of gravity-controlled travellators below. The people or goods come off, the elevator is yanked back up and the palladium heals, stoically waiting for the next fall.

If you happen to be under one of the space elevators when it hits, you're gone—flattened and vaporized. That's why an almost infinite number of alarms are sounding in my feed. Humans are not supposed to be on the Button.

And it's certainly not a great place to try and talk sense to your revolutionary sister.

We're using the nanites to make sure Halo doesn't catch our conversation and she's also wearing a tac helmet, so her lips are hidden. I'm using my scroll to lookspeak, which is distracting.

"Thanks for helping with this," I say.

"I wasn't sure you could get through this on your own."

"So, a lack of confidence motivated you? That's nice."

"It sounds ugly when you say it that way, but also right."

"The chance to make me feel bad is worth more than the fate of everyone on Earth?"

"When have you ever known me to not have a backup plan?" Essential asks. "Plus, now that I know where the servers are, we've basically won. I need to confirm their location on Deimos, and then we flip the switch for our deep-cover operative to deploy the empathy hack. The whole thing is on autopilot, as the old folks say. I'm barely needed."

"That's no reason to get careless," I say.

"You're worth it," she says.

We make our way around a space elevator sunk into the palladium, a 300-kilometer tube of flexible hair-width-thin metal stretching all the way up to the platform above. This elevator is on the small side, only 20 meters or so across, which means the "freight" is humans being lowered on descent disks. My scroll tells me there's a shuttle headed to Earth soon. I envy them.

We run past it and right into the path of a bristle ark, one in a fleet of giant, self-guided polishing units that keeps the palladium buffed and free of productivity-depleting contaminants. The elevators are supposed to miss the cleaners, but it doesn't always work out that way, which is why they're made to be disposable.

"Who is the deep operative with the empathy hack?" I ask, waiting for the bristle ark to brush its way past.

"Nobody knows," Essential says. "Well, that's not completely right. Coverly knew, the genius behind the nanites—"

"The man with the rope beard living in the Fields, an image forever burned into my retinas," I say.

"Yeah, him. And it should come as no surprise he kept

everything partitioned. All I know is the operative is on Mars and the empathy hack is ready to be deployed. Whoever it is might not even know themselves," she says. "Maybe it's you."

I laugh. "Yeah, maybe. Wait, hold on. The nanites aren't going to make me do anything heroic, are they?"

"Gods forbid," Essential says. "Nothing is *that* powerful. And don't worry. I was just yanking your motherboard. The plan, and the empathy hack, were in place long before you got tangled up in this."

"Try *forced* into this," I say. "Remember, I was happy on Earth, back when I didn't have to think my sister was dead, or see your eyeball, or save my ex's fiancée from a glitter squad."

She puts her arms around my neck. "Thank you," she says. "Whatever else happens, I love you and appreciate all you've done. For me and everyone else. You've been a good brother and, despite everything, including your best efforts, you're a good person. I mean it. I am grateful and lucky to have a good brother like you."

The emotion catches me off guard.

"Essential, I ..." I need to change the conversation before I start blurting out stupid stuff. "I'm a *great* brother."

She laughs. "There he is, the real Crucial. Come on, let's wrap this up. I have a planet to save."

Halo has prioritized Kyrinth. She's making for the far side of the Button. Probably has some escape flier stashed. Even without me requesting it, Halo optimizes my optics. I see her now and she is making surprisingly good time. Mostly because she's headed in a straight line and counting on a clear path from dropping space elevators.

You can't always count on that. They're programmed to avoid human casualty but that doesn't always work out. It's a one-in-a-million kind of thing, but it happens. Especially when a master coder like Essential is involved.

"There's a big one dropping," Essential says.

She's tapped into the control grid and shares the stats. It's full freight.

The tube, a good 140 meters across, drops like a hammer from the sky and hits the Button with shocking force. The bristle arks weigh more than a tiny planet, so they are mostly unaffected. But the three humans are not—the force sends us all tumbling.

Especially Kyrinth. She was closest to the elevator plunge and it missed her by only a few dozen meters. The concussion sweeps her off her feet and sends her spiraling in the thin atmosphere right toward us. Her long blast coat took most of the blow, but she's still rattled.

Essential and I are farther back but it still knocks us over and rips off my airhoodie. I feel the cold attack my face as the lack of air attacks my lungs. My nose is bleeding. Essential is on her hands and knees. The tac gear edged some of the force, but she's coughing and sputtering too.

I get my hoodie back on and help her up.

Kyrinth is tough, I'll give her that. Even bloody and damaged, choking for air and missing most of her hand, she's up and trying to keep the deal alive.

"I want to talk to Tarteric Hoost!" she screams. "He's not stupid. They want to live. All they have to do is negotiate with me."

"You asked for me, Kyrinth. That was your one stupid play," I say. "Do I look like a negotiator? It's over."

"I will blow the whole sunbelt," she says.

I hope my faith in Fleiss and the rest of the Jane crew wasn't misplaced.

"Go ahead," I say. "Who'll miss a few blizards?"

"Fine!" she screams and pulls a blankface to trigger her bombs.

I hope this isn't one more terrible mistake to add to the long list of mistakes that is my life. I'm monitoring satellite data and zoom in on the sunbelt. Nothing happens. Fleiss coming through in the wormhole! She realizes it's not going to blow and her shoulders slump. Kyrinth has run out of plays. There's a sorrowful look in her eyes.

"I just wanted something better," she says. "Is that so bad?"

"No," Essential says. "We should all want something better. We deserve something better. The problem is how you go after it. You hurt people. Innocent people. In the end, you are no different than them."

"You don't sound much like a cop," Kyrinth says.

"You sure don't," I say, hoping Halo isn't interested. "Let's stay focused, Officer Bips."

"It doesn't matter," Kyrinth says. "Take another step and I wipe the data. All of it. Lives will be lost and that's on you."

I catch Essential's eye and she nods. I take a step.

"I don't care anymore! The data is wiped, lost in the digital abyss. You can all burn in a mantle of lava, you Martian-flesh craters!" Kyrinth screams in frustration.

I know the data is not gone. When Kyrinth opened the connection, Essential slipped in a digital snare and pulled the data out.

I take another step toward her.

"What the prok is wrong with you," Kyrinth asks. "I hope you're pleased with yourself. You consigned the Five Families and everyone on Mars to a certain excruciating death. They won't be able to replicate the research until it's too late. They'll all die sucking their thumbs and asking for their nursery-bots."

She laughs, and I almost want to laugh with her, because that's not a bad outcome for the Five Families. But there are other factors in play. And Essential wouldn't think much of me if I didn't take the high road here.

"Come on," I say. "It's time to end this. You had a good run, but you're an idiot if you think you can go up against the Five Families. They always win in the end."

I hope Essential knows that was for her, not Kyrinth.

"That's a dumb way to look at it," Essential says, still playing the Officer Bips role but aiming her words at me. "We're all going to die someday, much sooner for you than me, statistically speaking, but that doesn't mean we should just give up."

"It also doesn't mean you should try to blow up everything at once. There's a smart way to get what you want."

"Like drinking yourself numb, sitting in a puddle of regrets and waiting for the end? That's not getting what you want, that's just wanting less."

"It feels like you two are having an entirely different conversation," Kyrinth says.

She has a rail gun in her undamaged hand pointed at us. Godsdamn it, I shouldn't let Essential distract me.

"As much as I want to let you two stay here and work this out, I plan on using the credits I drained from Dumblinius to create a new identity. And I can't have any witnesses," Kyrinth says.

"How are you shielding us from Halo?" I ask, now aware Halo is no longer my trusted assistant in this pursuit.

"I'm full of surprises," she says. "It can see us, but only from a distance. And I can't let any of this unspool once you're both reconnected."

She points the rail gun at me. I start to say something stupid like, "Essential, save yourself," but Kyrinth pulls the trigger.

The slug whistles over my head.

"I can't believe you missed," I say.

"I don't think she missed," Essential says, pointing behind me.

There's a terrible ripping, sucking noise and the alarms in my feed go ballistic.

I turn. The slug tore through the space elevator. The big one. The ruptured end is flopping around like a sparking cable, dropping freight pods the size of city blocks around us, shaking the Button and jarring open the palladium. It's utter chaos.

"Sorry, but you both have to die," she says. "Nothing personal."

She's backing up toward the elevator tube for humans. I'm getting readings. They're about to yank it back up to the orbiting platform, giving her a clear shot at escape. Kyrinth levels the rail gun. I don't think she'll miss this time.

One of the containers lands close to us and crashes open, spilling brand new fliers and drone jackets out. The force rattles the palladium, causing Kyrinth to wobble unsteadily and stumble back against the flexible metal fabric of the elevator, the tails of her blast-resistant coat flapping in the wind.

I've got one chance. I get my glitter gun out and squeeze off a long volley of flechettes.

And I miss.

Dammit.

She's still standing. She points her rail gun at me.

She says, "I guess I wi ..."

I think she was probably going to say "win."

Sometimes luck is better than skill. Apparently, the missed volley of flechettes accidentally stitched the tails of her fancy blast coat to the side of the space elevator. She just got pulled up into space in the blink of an eye.

One second, she's about to kill us, and the next she's gone, along with the space elevator. Her gun and airhoodie are still there, both dangling, and then the airhoodie drifts off and the gun clatters down onto one of her gravity boots. There's a sound like a thin leak on a high-pressure hose. I think it was her screaming. It didn't last long.

"What the prok just happened?" Essential asks.

"Kyrinth decided to head back to Earth," I say. "She just forgot to get inside the space elevator first."

"Oh, that's terrible."

"No, it's quick. Flash-frozen before she suffocates. Getting crushed by cargo is terrible."

Another freight container lands near us.

"Let's get inside before we test that theory."

"Good plan," Essential says. "We should be on our way to Deimos. Should be a piece of moon cake compared to hanging out with you on your missions."

"Not so fast for me," I say.

Jynks is crossing the palladium and I'm pretty sure that look on her face means I'm not going anywhere.

47

"Tarteric Hoost will see you in the study."

Sanders and I are waiting outside Hoost's building. Jynks is a few meters in front of us. Her back is ramrod straight. She's proud to be delivering me to the Fist. I should be angry, I suppose, but it's hard to keep a grudge. I'm just glad she came out of all this in one piece.

We're surrounded by an armed contingent, and Jynks has vowed that Mars SF won't let me out of their sight until the Fist can make sense of what happened. And it's a real security detail this time, not the nanite-induced version featuring the solo performance of Essential. Turns out, Officer Bips upped and disappeared. They think she was killed—and all traces of her vaporized—by the falling space elevator.

In theory, Essential should be close to Deimos by now. I hope she's all right. I should be with my kid sister, but as she said herself, there's nothing to it. Besides, as I keep telling her, it's not my fight, although I'll admit I'm having a harder time convincing myself of that lately.

An Earth lottery winner performing butler duties beckons us inside. He must be a recent arrival, with his pocked face and chapped lips. Nothing a trip to a Mars derm-portal won't fix up. We walk through a long corridor, shadowy and ominous. Armed guards, shoulder to shoulder, line both sides.

The floors are soft. I think we are walking on dead

animal skins, maybe even giraffes. I don't understand why anyone still celebrates death in this fashion. The Interspecies Consciousness Accord of 2081 decoupled self-awareness and sentience from human language. That's when the sheetmeat industry exploded and animal skins as adornment came to a screeching halt. Not among the Five Families it seems. And after all my time on Mars, I know why—wealth begets boredom, which begets fetishism. The H-suite, where this entire fiasco started, is proof of that. Along with dolphelines.

At the end of the muscle-packed corridor, the acned lottery winner throws open two sculpted doors revealing a spacious room.

"I'll wait out here," Jynks says. "Thanks for everything, Crucial Larsen." She says it awkwardly, like she means it. I guess she thinks I'm about to be killed, or worse. After a nice, sincere goodbye like that, she's going to be seriously irked by what happens next.

Hoost is behind a desk. Behind him in the shadows is an enormous animal, nearly three meters tall, easily 300 kilograms, frozen in mid-snarl. It has fangs for teeth and knives for hands. The expression on Hoost's face looks even deadlier.

I sit down in a chair facing him. Sanders stands behind me.

Hoost focuses his rage on me. "You've ruined everything. Your carelessness put the entire Mars project in jeopardy and doomed everyone you love. You'll be serving out the rest of your life in prison on Mars as a test subject for research on neural tryphoprionia."

I don't answer. I'm still looking at the stuffed creature looming behind him.

"The sunbelt was saved but the research is gone and Clystra is a gibbering idiot. It will take us years to recreate his work. Years we don't have!" he shouts.

The glassy eyes of the creature gleam in the half-light. Hoost follows my gaze.

"Oh, for the love of the Hadron Collider," Hoost says. "It's a grizzly bear. The last wild one on Earth. My great-grandfather slayed the beast in Earth's far north in an area once called Alaska. It has been in the family ever since. The bear was old, the last of his kind. Now pay attention to what I am saying!"

I am so tired of these monsters. I should just let them all die. If I go to prison, keep my mouth shut, they're all doomed. Or at the very least, they'll have to return to Earth. I guess that's close enough to doomed from their perspective.

But I can't keep my mouth shut. I can't let innocent people die just to rattle these assholes. Mel. And Valentine. And Seneca. They have the disease now too.

"What if I told you that I have the data? All of it. What would you say to that?"

A deep, cruel, triumphant smile bends his mouth and reveals his perfect teeth. "Go on."

"How about something to drink first? It was a long ride over here."

He snaps his fingers and the lottery laborer brings a tray with a decanter of sparkling brown liquid and matching glasses half full of the same, and long brown tubes of dried plants.

"It's whiskey," Hoost says. "I detest absinthe. Too cloying." He picks up one of the tubes. "And these are cigars. Made of tobacco. Have one. They're self-lighting."

"I'll pass on the cigar," I say. "Don't see the attraction of intentionally inhaling noxious smoke. That's why I never open the window in my squat on Earth." With my whiskey, I sink back into the comfortable chair.

An unfamiliar feeling washes over me as I realize that possibly for the first time in my life, I hold all the cards. Literally every one of them. I've got the encrypted research. The bombs in the sunbelt were neutralized so the Saurians are safe. Essential is on her way to Deimos and hopefully will soon find out her little scheme to neutralize Halo is doomed to fail. She'll come back to Earth. Mel is reunited with Jynks, who has her job back, and I have the secret ironic pleasure of knowing Jynks owes it all to me and the resistance. Valentine is safe and with all the credits Able Singhroy transferred to me, I can help her bring Seneca back from the shadows to live a normal life. Or whatever passes as normal these days.

And best of all, I get to go back to Earth.

This is what winning feels like. I drain the whiskey. Apparently, winning tastes great too.

A sweet-smelling cloud of smoke brings me back into the moment. Hoost exhales a thick stream of the stuff into the air above his head. "In the old days of Earth, long, long ago, deals were made behind closed doors in smoke-filled rooms by a few men, so it was said," he says. "The kind of deals that decided the fate of millions. The kind of deal we will make now."

"Not sure those deals turned out very well," I say. "If some of those folks in smoke-filled rooms spent a little more time thinking about the well-being of others instead of their own advancement, maybe we wouldn't be where we are."

"They called them robber barons in those days, which was meant to be derogatory. But without their focus, we would never have had the industrial, technological and surveillance advances—and the concentrated wealth—to make the leap to Mars. I am grateful for their vision and tenacity. They were rewarded for it, as you shall be."

Sanders coughs loudly. He is experimenting with one of the cigars. Puffs of smoke burp out with each cough and his new eyes are generating additional lubricant. He puts the cigar out on the inside of his palm and hands it back to the lottery Earther. "I've learned enough," he says.

"You are more like us than you realize," Hoost says to me, leaning back into his chair and putting his feet up on a stool. The soles of his shoes face me. I know it's an insult, and signals that the negotiation is underway.

"I'm not a godsdamn thing like you," I say.

"You value certain things, and you'll do whatever is needed to protect those things," he says.

"I value people and their safety. You value credits and power."

"The only difference between us, then, is what we choose to value and how far we will go to protect it. How much will this cost?"

He thinks this is about the credits. He doesn't know Able made me rich in one blink. It's not lost on me that without that secret stash of wealth, I might be tempted to make a little extra right now.

"I don't want your credits," I say.

That seems to surprise him, but only for a few seconds. "Name your terms then."

I've been practicing this in my head ever since we left the Dock zone.

"One. The Saurians get full control of the sunbelt and can sell the bacteria at market price until you can synthesize it, and they receive a five percent stake in the product."

He looks at me curiously.

"Three percent."

"Fine."

I was aiming for two.

"They get an addendum to their original resettlement

contract so that it stays in force in perpetuity."

"You have a soft spot for the blizards," he says. "Fine."

"Two. Upgraded health portals, and more of them, in all wards on Earth," I say.

He hesitates.

"They are very expensive to maintain," he says. "And healthier people use more resources overall."

I thought of that.

"Three. Upgraded beetlers for anyone who wants one. With better food pouches."

"You're rewarding failure."

"Four. A Martian absinthe distillery in the Multnomah Ward," I say. "And I get unlimited access."

He laughs at that. That's good. I want him to think he understands me.

"Is that it?"

"Yes."   ·

"Counteroffer," he says. "I fire Jynks Martine for ties to the resistance."

"Jynks had nothing to do with them," I say.

"There are large timing gaps in her story. We can fill those in as we see fit."

The feeling of winning didn't last long.

"Fine, I retract the absinthe distillery."

"Counteroffer number two," Hoost says. "I send Melinda Hopwire back to Earth on the next Dart with no hope for future employment."

"In the past minute, an uptick in drone activity in the vicinity of Melinda Hopwire's building has occurred," Sanders says.

"New terms," I say, a little panicked and hoping I don't show it. "No harm ever comes to Melinda Hopwire," I say. "And one upgraded health portal for each ward."

"Done," he says.

"And beetlers get an upgrade."

He smiles. It makes me think of that grizzly bear.

"You can knock a point off the Saurians," I say. "But the sunbelt is theirs until they say otherwise."

"Deal."

"What happens to Darlinius?" I feel a sense of loyalty to Singhroy Able, misplaced of course, but there it is.

"His initiative will be rewarded, but clearly he needs some, how shall I put it, mentoring. The Fist will split the revenues five and a half ways. He gets the half-share and will take over Mytikas."

"Sounds like he will have his hand full," I say.

Hoost doesn't even bother to acknowledge my joke. "Do we have a deal?"

"Sure," I say. "Sanders, have you been tracking all this?"

"Yes, Crucial." Sanders transfers the contract to both our feeds and Hoost affirms it. I decrypt the research and pass it over to his scroll. Just like that, I save the Five Families.

I finish my whiskey and reach for more. Hoost is blankfacing, verifying the accuracy of the data Essential snared for me. At last he nods. The directives are shared. Earth will be getting more health care. I stand to leave. I'm ready to get off this planet, once and for godsdamn all.

"I don't understand why you didn't ask for anything for yourself," Hoost says.

"I've got everything I need," I say. "The system makes sure of that."

48

"This is really goodbye?" Mel asks.

"I think so," I say.

"Things have a way of falling apart around you," she says.

"I always seem to be in the wrong place at the right time."

She laughs, but it's only on the surface. "I think the wrong place follows you around."

"Sort of like Wisp follows you?"

She stoops to pet the tiny cat and it arches its back against Mel's ankle.

"Despite everything, you managed to save the Five Families and make sure they have the cure they need."

"I'm basically one of them now," I say.

It's not too far from the truth. She doesn't know how many credits Able gave me. I wish I could tell her. I imagine buying a place across the boulevard from her so I can watch her wake up every morning and make kelp porridge, and wave through the window. That thought feels creepier than intended.

"Thanks for all you did with Jynks," she says.

She seems off. Upset. Wisp is picking it up, never straying farther than a few centimeters from her feet.

"Where is Jynks? I figured she'd want to say goodbye too, maybe even say thanks, you know, for saving her life and getting her job back."

"She ... we ... we're taking some time apart," Mel says.

"Wait, what?"

I see a flash of irritation cross her face triggered by the flash of hopefulness crossing my face.

"Don't," she says.

"Don't what?"

"This is about Jynks and me, not us and our ancient history," she says.

"I mean, 'ancient' might be a little strong. And anyway, I'm not doing anything."

"You are," Mel says. "You're hoping. All along, you thought if you just waited around long enough, I'd fall right back into my old habits, our old routine."

"Would that be so bad?" I need to at least say the words.

She sighs and rubs her temples. It's been a while since I last triggered that response. I'm making real progress.

"You should go," she says.

I'm sitting at the kitchen table looking out over Jezero, and I can see the edge of a device mostly covered by a cloth napkin.

I recognize the base of the unit. It's a jammer. I quickly close my OCD eye and reach down and pull the edge of fabric over the tech. "This is a nice-looking napkin," I say. "I haven't seen one like this in a long time. Very costly."

She knows I know there's illegal contraband in her apartment. Their apartment. If Halo saw the same thing, there'll be an official flag. Or worse.

"I find it worth the price," she says. "Sometimes it's comforting to have things out on the table. Out in the open where everyone can see and understand."

This is taking a very weird turn.

An ad crashes my scroll.

It's for some avatainment series. *Space travelers have found clues to an alien artifact that can harness the power of dark matter.*

Would you like to join their quest? The team is assembling on Deimos.

It's Essential.

This will be awkward. I can't talk to her because Halo can't know. And that means Mel can't know. And that means I share my feed so Essential can do all the talking and I can lookspeak.

"Hey, big brother," she says. "Oh, you're with Mel. Wow, she looks great."

"I don't understand at all," I say to Mel. "But then again, I've never been great at, you know, napkins."

"Why in the name of Orion's belt are you talking about napkins?" Essential asks. "I want you to know I made it. I'm on Deimos. And so are the servers."

"How did you get to this point?" I say to both Mel and Essential.

Mel pours us two thin, tall glasses of Martian absinthe, then sweeps the cloth off the table, removing the jammer and dropping it into a drawer that seals with a hiss.

"Valentine would be jealous, if she were the jealous type," Essential says. "I launched from an O-plat on dark mode and then hitched on a satellite and then made the last push under the cover of space junk until I could grapple onto a regularly scheduled service shuttle."

Essential is fearless. Any one of those maneuvers could have been terminal. Or discoverable. The same outcome, I guess.

"Let's just say you're not the only one who can destroy a relationship," Mel says.

She raises her glass and I pick up mine as well.

"I'm sure I'm not the perfect blueprint to follow for long-lasting happiness," I say.

"Amen to that," Essential says.

"Amen to that," Mel says. "I'm not following your path

though. The opposite, really."

"You really prokked up when you let her go," Essential says. "It's weird up here. There's no security, just some old ramshackle domes. And inside them, just under the surface, the most powerful servers you can imagine. Hectares of tech. The nanites are working overtime—lots of cameras, but no guards, no weapons, nothing."

"To destroying relationships and other things," I say, "however they may fall."

Mel clinks my glass, her mouth twisted by a bitter smile.

"She's not doing well," Essential says. "Where's Jynks?"

"I don't know," I lookspeak to just Essential. "Just finish up and come home, okay?"

"Yes," Essential says. "I'm signaling the empathy hack in three, two, one. Crucial, we did it! I mean, mostly I did it. My role is done. Thank you for everything. The Five Families are about to get a big shock, when empathy overwrites self-interest and greed. I'll hitch back to Mars, and maybe on to Earth if things go well."

"Be careful."

"Be nice to Mel," Essential says. "She's really hurting."

She breaks the connection.

Mel is looking at me closely.

I drain my glass and Mel tops it off, then sits down and pats her lap. Wisp jumps up, curls into a fluffy little ball and starts purring. Really purring. Like, loud enough I can hear it halfway across the room.

"Do you think you'll stay here then?" I ask. "I mean, even if you and Jynks don't ... aren't, you know, if things don't ... can you turn the volume down on your cat?"

"Maybe its power core is overheating," she says. "I should get it to the lab."

Now the thing's eyes are flashing.

"What is going on with your cat?"

Its eyes glow dazzling blue in two short bursts. Then the flashing stops. Mel looks flustered.

"That is weird," I say.

She looks at the kitten, then at me, then back at the kitten. "You should go. Now." She stands, scooping Wisp onto the table. The cat is purring so loudly now, she's basically vibrating in place.

I drain my glass. "I'll miss you. And I'll miss Martian absinthe," I say. "If you're ever on Earth, you know where I'll be."

"Take care of yourself," she says. Mel puts her arms around my neck and hugs me tight. So tight, it almost hurts. "I won't be back, Crucial. And no matter what happens, I will always treasure what we had."

Her words surprise me, and I manage to hold back one last attempt to get her to come back to Earth with me. Instead I say, "Me too, Mel. And I'll always be there if you need me."

My last view of Mel is her standing at the big window with her back to me, looking out over the city and to the edge of the dome and the Choke beyond. She's lit up by the soft light. Wisp is draped over her shoulder, purring like a rocket and glaring suspiciously in my direction.

49

"I like your new eyes," I say.

Sanders is walking me into Port Zunil to say goodbye.

"They're blast-resistant now. Thank you for exposing that vulnerability."

"What are friends for, if not to accidentally melt your eyes while using you as a living shield?"

"That is a very specific definition of friendship," he says.

"Did you just make a joke?"

"I believe so."

"That was actually funny. Well done, buddy. But how blast-resistant are they? Like, would they stop a glitter gun?"

"Theoretically," Sanders says. "But I would rather not test that specification. Ocular replacement is a time-consuming and expensive process."

"I don't have a gun anyway. You can't take weapons on the Dart," I say. "It's weird that you are invulnerable now. I mean, I've watched you ooze out so many times."

"Those days appear to be over," Sanders says.

There's time to kill before the space elevator drops to load up the Dart back to Earth.

I intentionally check my scroll and filter for news. The Five Families are already marketing their new miracle cure. It's not cheap. Luckily, credits are irrelevant on Mars. Getting more, or giving more, is all part of some long-term ego game and only they understand the rules. And rewards.

Speaking of rewards, I've got three bottles of absinthe, one each for Fleiss, Dormer and Tooms, for saving the Saurians. It really should be ant gin.

A location-specific announcement pops in about the Dart. The crews here have been doing a lot of work to clean up the Button after the fiasco with Kyrinth. And Officer Bips. New protocols and better security. All humans strictly prohibited on the landing pad, according to the scroll alert.

Then the really big news shows up. *The labor lottery will be ended, effective immediately. All humans on Mars will be transitioned back to Earth, with some exceptions to fulfill essential positions.*

I'm not surprised. Kyrinth exposed the risk of letting random Earthers up here. Between her and the resistance, too many people are nursing secret grudges against the Five Families.

A new system of direct recruitment to work in the Mars service sector will be initiated. Applications will not be accepted. Recruitment will be by nomination only.

Not surprisingly, the news is not being received well on Earth. The story is swimming in thumbs down.

No matter how bad things got on Earth, which is usually pretty bad, you always had a sense, this belief— almost a certainty—that your luck could change, was *going* to change. Even though everybody else had a terrible life, you would win the lottery and rise above it all, some cosmic force would anoint you as worthy of a better fate than all the rest, and you'd get a chance to live the good life on Mars.

Without the lottery, without that false hope, I'm not sure how they can keep the system propped up. Maybe nominations could work, but I'm hard-pressed to see how that doesn't just become a favorites game, leaving out all the people really down on their luck. What happens when 99 percent of Earthers realize they don't have a chance?

The Five Families haven't thought this through.

Humans need to believe, despite a mound of evidence to the contrary, that they're special, that their lives are going to be different. A person can put up with almost anything if there's even a sliver of hope that they can beat the odds, that disasters can be dodged or turned into blessings.

At some point, it becomes clear that you're not any different, that you're not special and your life is going to turn out just like everyone else's. That's when the optimism starts to evaporate—for me, it was about 20 years ago—and you're left with nothing but bitter regret. Unless you can rewrite the past and tell yourself that all those years you spent hoping, you were happy all along and you're glad that things didn't turn out differently. Because who likes different?

"How about a drink?" I ask. "For old times' sake."

"I did not enjoy the consumption of alcohol," Sanders says. "Purposeful hindrance of cognitive functions is a pleasure unique to humans."

"And birds. Birds like to drink too," I say. I can tell he is doing the research on that now—his eyes go back into his head—but I'm not interested in debating the drinking habits of birds. "No bird talk. Bring your eyeballs back to normal. I'll drink for both us."

We walk into a Button bar and there, over in the corner, I see a familiar figure. Jynks. She's sitting at a table by herself, a couple of empties crumpled in front of her. We walk over.

"Surprised to see you here. Want some company?"

She looks at me for a long time. Like a solid minute. It's

uncomfortable.

"And if I say no?" she finally asks.

"We'll sit close by and talk about you."

She nods and we pull up two chairs. I access the menu and order two synthgins—time to reset my drinking to Earth-standard booze—and another chiller pack of wine syrup for Jynks.

It's getting dark, the blue sunset is stretching indigo fingers across the Choke. The dome is starting to clear so you can see up into the night sky and the stars beyond.

The table whirs open and pushes the drinks up. Jynks pulls the tab to chill the syrup and then sucks the carton so hard it crumples up from the vacuum of her attention.

"Pace yourself, Jynks," I say. "You're going to be wobbling home after I leave."

She looks at me, half laughs, and then drains the carton. "I'm not here to see you off. I'm going back. I'm heading to Earth. I've requested a transfer."

"What?"

"Yeah, we'll be working together. Well, I'll be your boss, so technically you'll be working for me."

"On Earth?"

"Yep." She orders another carton.

"Listen, I know we haven't always seen eye to eye," I say. "But you're making a big mistake. Whatever's going on between you and Mel, don't let it end like this. Don't walk away, don't ruin things."

"You think I ruined things?" The wine syrup is hitting her hard. "I didn't ruin things."

"What the hell happened?"

Jynks just shakes her head. "So many secrets. I can't talk about it."

Secrets are hard to keep in this world.

I get a ving. It's from Valentine.

I let Sanders and Jynks know I'm taking a call by making a ring with my finger and thumb and holding it over my eye, then push away from the table and stand against the window looking out across the Choke.

"Valentine."

"Sorry I couldn't make it to Port Zunil to see you off. The Singhroys had some last-minute work on the sunbelt deed. I think I should be thanking you for that."

"My pleasure," I say. "Come and see me on Earth?"

"I might. I enjoy our time together. Well, except for the almost getting killed."

"That's never fun."

"Until then, try being happier. It's not that hard. There's a lot of good in the world, in the small moments. Let some of it in."

She's right. I should let the good in. I've got more credits than I know what to do with, secret nanites that let me hide from Halo and a beautiful woman who seems to like me and doesn't expect that much of me. It's more than any person needs. Or deserves.

"That's good advice."

"I'll be on Earth in a couple of weeks," she says. "Let's have dinner. I'll bring the thistle."

"Sounds like a good plan," I say. "I'm going to send you a funny video clip I saw of one of the Younkers. Promise me you'll watch it."

"Okay," she says, her voice registering curiosity.

It's not really a clip. I used the nanites to make a shielded credit bubble with some of Able's wealth that will pop into her account along with a receipt for a grief transference cybanism modeled on Seneca, her niece. She can just bring Seneca home from the orbital dump and Halo will never know the difference.

Turns out doing good feels a lot like winning.

And whatever drama Jynks and Mel have going on, it's their problem.

I return to the table. "What did I miss?"

"A great deal of contradictory inputs on Melinda Hopwire," Sanders says. "Jynks Martine seems to be pairing almost diametrically opposed characterizations of her."

"She's a hell of a person," Jynks says. "I'll never forgive her, but above all else, she's a hell of a person."

"To Mel," I say, and raise my glass. "And to new beginnings."

"I'll drink to that," Jynks says, raising her carton and then sucking the syrup out of it.

There's a thud that shakes the whole compound.

"The space elevator has connected," Sanders says. "Loading will begin soon. I find myself curiously affected by the thought of your departure, Crucial."

"Sanders, we'll see each other again."

"The odds are astronomically against that."

"I know. That's just something friends say."

"I think I understand," he says. "They will begin retraction in eighteen minutes. You should make your way to the elevator soon."

"Let's just sit here for a minute and let me enjoy my last look at this blasted red death of a planet," I say.

I lean back in my chair and look up at the deepening dark of space. The stars are really shining tonight. And there seem to be more of them than usual. Even Sanders appears taken with the view. He's looking up at the sky with a curious, enigmatic expression. Resting cybanism face, I guess.

I'll be glad when I'm back on Earth. I want my feet on a planet that has mostly breathable air, and gravity that doesn't bulge my brain into my skull or turn it spongy. I'll be even gladder when Essential returns.

A meteor streaks across the night sky. That's odd. First one I've seen since I've been here.

I read somewhere that in the old days, meteors were thought to be proof of the gods fighting. Another meteor flares by. I hope this doesn't mean the trip back to Earth will be rough. I hate quantum flight, especially through meteor showers. It's weird that this one wasn't predicted though.

I hope it isn't making it rough for Essential to get off terror-moon.

I keep expecting some terrible ad to crash my feed, something about laxatives or micro-rat infestations, so she can tell me she's safe. So far, it's just the normal ads that cause normal people to buy too many abnormal things to prop up the system of debt that makes the world go 'round.

But that may change soon, if Essential gets her way and the empathy hack works. Although how it will change, I'm not so sure. I suppose she's right. I'm not capable of imagining a different future.

"Come on, boss," I say to a clearly inebriated Jynks. "Let's get you on the Dart and on the way back to your home. You're gonna fall in love with Earth all over again."

THE END

ABOUT THE AUTHORS

Scorched Earth is the ninth book from authors Clark Hays and Kathleen McFall. They live and work in the Pacific Northwest region of the United Sates.

Made in the USA
Middletown, DE
04 November 2022

14072028R00189